A Fatal Feast

A *Murder, She Wrote* Mystery

OTHER BOOKS IN THE *MURDER, SHE WROTE* SERIES

Manhattans & Murder
Rum & Razors
Brandy & Bullets
Martinis & Mayhem
A Deadly Judgment
A Palette for Murder
The Highland Fling Murders
Murder on the QE2
Murder in Moscow
A Little Yuletide Murder
Murder at the Powderhorn Ranch
Knock 'Em Dead
Gin & Daggers
Trick or Treachery
Blood on the Vine
Murder in a Minor Key
Provence—To Die For
You Bet Your Life
Majoring in Murder
Destination Murder
Dying to Retire
A Vote for Murder
The Maine Mutiny
Margaritas & Murder
A Question of Murder
Coffee, Tea, or Murder?
Three Strikes and You're Dead
Panning for Murder
Murder on Parade
A Slaying in Savannah
Madison Avenue Shoot

A Fatal Feast

A *Murder, She Wrote* Mystery

A NOVEL BY

JESSICA FLETCHER & DONALD BAIN

Based on the Universal television series created by
Peter S. Fischer, Richard Levinson & William Link

AN OBSIDIAN MYSTERY

Obsidian
Published by New American Library, a division of
Penguin Group (USA) Inc., 375 Hudson Street,
New York, New York 10014, USA
Penguin Group (Canada), 90 Eglinton Avenue East, Suite 700, Toronto,
Ontario M4P 2Y3, Canada (a division of Pearson Penguin Canada Inc.)
Penguin Books Ltd., 80 Strand, London WC2R 0RL, England
Penguin Ireland, 25 St. Stephen's Green, Dublin 2,
Ireland (a division of Penguin Books Ltd.)
Penguin Group (Australia), 250 Camberwell Road, Camberwell, Victoria 3124,
Australia (a division of Pearson Australia Group Pty. Ltd.)
Penguin Books India Pvt. Ltd., 11 Community Centre, Panchsheel Park,
New Delhi - 110 017, India
Penguin Group (NZ), 67 Apollo Drive, Rosedale, North Shore 0632,
New Zealand (a division of Pearson New Zealand Ltd.)
Penguin Books (South Africa) (Pty.) Ltd., 24 Sturdee Avenue,
Rosebank, Johannesburg 2196, South Africa

Penguin Books Ltd., Registered Offices:
80 Strand, London WC2R 0RL, England

First published by Obsidian, an imprint of New American Library,
a division of Penguin Group (USA) Inc.

First Printing, October 2009
1 3 5 7 9 10 8 6 4 2

LIBRARY OF CONGRESS CATALOGING-IN-PUBLICATION DATA:

Bain, Donald, 1935–
A fatal feast: a murder, she wrote mystery: a novel/by Jessica Fletcher & Donald Bain.
p. cm.
"An Obsidian mystery."
"Based on the Universal television series created by Peter S. Fischer,
Richard Levinson & William Link."
ISBN 978-0-451-22796-6
1. Fletcher, Jessica (Fictitious character)—Fiction. 2. Women novelists—Fiction. 3. Thanksgiving Day—Fiction. 4. Maine—Fiction. I. Bain, Donald. II. Murder, she wrote (Television program)
III. Title.
PS3552.A376F28 2009
813'54—dc22 2009017373

Set in Minion
Designed by Ginger Legato

Printed in the United States of America

PUBLISHER'S NOTE
This is a work of fiction. Names, characters, places, and incidents either are the product of the author's imagination or are used fictitiously, and any resemblance to actual persons, living or dead, business establishments, events, or locales is entirely coincidental.

The publisher does not have any control over and does not assume any responsibility for author or third-party Web sites or their content.

With gratitude to Angela Lansbury
for having given life to the wonderful character
of Jessica Fletcher.

A Fatal Feast

A ***Murder, She Wrote*** Mystery

Chapter One

"Mornin', Mrs. Fletcher."

"Good morning, Newt. Lovely day."

"That it is. Pleasure to be out on a day like this."

He pulled a sheaf of mail from his bag and handed it to me. "Seems like you got quite a lot today."

"I'm not certain that's a good thing," I said, sifting through the envelopes. "Depends on what's in them."

"S'pose that's true. Mebbe somethin's there can help uncatch that there typewriter of yours."

My face reflected my surprise. "You know about that, Newt?"

He looked contrite. "Didn't know it was a secret," he said, "the way folks are talkin' in town. Well, better keep to m'rounds. You have yourself a good day, Mrs. Fletcher, and good luck finishin' that book."

As he turned to walk away, we both looked across the street to where a man stood.

"Do you know him, Newt?" I asked.

"No, I wouldn't say I know him, but I know who he is. Name's Billups. Hubert Billups."

"He must be new in town," I said. "I'd never seen him before last week."

Hubert Billups had a long, scraggly red beard. He was like a statue, arms crossed over his chest, eyes focused down the road, although I'd caught him staring at me several times. It was an unseasonably warm day for mid-November, yet he was dressed in a red-and-black wool mackinaw, scarf, black wool cap, and heavy boots, the same outfit I'd seen him in on most days the past week as he stationed himself on the side of the road across from my house.

"You okay, Mrs. Fletcher?" Newt asked, taking note of my concerned expression.

"What? Oh, yes, Newt, I'm fine."

"He's from away, come up heah about a month ago, or so I'm told," my mailman said. "He's livin' in that rooming house over behind the industrial plant. Somebody said he was a cook once, only you can't prove it by me. Strange-lookin' fella, doncha think? I see him around town now and then, just sittin' on a bench or inside one of the buildings when it rains. Just sits and stares. Probably tetched or mebbe a rumdum, if you ask me. Well, you take care, Mrs. Fletcher. I hear that friend o' yours from overseas is comin' for Thanksgiving. That must give you somethin' t'look forward to."

The Cabot Cove rumor mill was operating in high gear.

I sighed. "Yes. I am looking forward to it. Thanks for the mail, Newt. Best to your family."

I returned to the house, where I settled in my study and plopped the letters, catalogues, and other mail on my desk. I swiveled in my chair and looked at the words on my computer screen. Those same words had been there for two days; seeing them caused a knot in my stomach.

Newt had been right. I'd recently suffered a rare case of writer's block on my latest mystery novel, whose deadline was coming up fast, December 15 to be precise. I've always prided myself on meeting publishing deadlines. I know other writers who consider deadlines set by their publishers to be arbitrary, at best. I've never felt that way. For me, meeting deadlines is a sign of professionalism in any line of work, and above all I like to consider myself exactly that, a professional.

But unless I broke through this bout of inertia, my track record of always delivering on time was about to be broken. While I readily took responsibility for having lagged behind in my writing, other external forces had also played a part.

It was a little more than a week until Thanksgiving, which naturally meant a flurry of activity having nothing to do with mystery novels or any other form of professional writing. I'd agreed to host Thanksgiving dinner at my house this year, although Sheriff Mort Metzger's wife, Maureen, an enthusiastic if unseasoned cook, offered to help me with meal preparation. There would be nine of us at the dinner table, including—as the town obviously knew, based upon Newt's comment—my dear Scottish friend from London, Scotland Yard inspector George Sutherland. I didn't harbor any illusions that the number of guests would remain at nine. In past years, there were always a few last-minute additions to the dinner table, which was fine with me. With a few extra leaves, my table can squeeze in fourteen.

George and I hadn't seen each other in many months and I was delighted when he accepted, albeit at the last minute, my invitation to experience a traditional American Thanksgiving holiday in Cabot Cove. I wanted it to be special for him and intended to go all out in serving up a splendid meal, along with the requisite warm feelings that always accompany it.

I looked at the computer screen again and winced.

When will I find time to finish the book?

There were other distractions that kept me from my writing.

Each year, the town held a Thanksgiving pageant to re-create the holiday's earliest celebrations in America. I'd written much of this year's script, and had devoted far too much time to collaborating with my pageant cowriters, not to mention attending rehearsals and watching our joint effort blossom into a full-fledged production. In addition, I was also doing what I did every year at this time, helping out at the local senior center, where we serve a Thanksgiving spread for the town's less fortunate.

No wonder I was blocked. I've often been accused of biting off more than I can chew, no pun intended, and this year gave validity to that charge.

I went to my front window and parted the curtains. Mr. Billups was still there, his pose never changing. When he spotted me, he turned his head, gazing off in the distance down the road. I had the same unsettled feeling I'd suffered for the past week, ever since he'd begun loitering there, not every day but often enough to make it obvious that it wasn't by chance that he'd chosen that spot. I'd waved to him a few times when leaving the house but received nothing in return, just a hard stare.

My guess was that he suffered from some form of dementia rather than drinking, as Newt had suggested—I'd never seen him stumble—but I assumed he was harmless enough, and was glad that he was at least able to afford a room. My heart goes out to those who've fallen out of life's mainstream, often through no fault of their own. Of course, some end up in that situation through their use of drugs or alcohol, and Cabot Cove has a few individuals like that, the natural consequence of the town's growth. Fortunately, our mayor, Jim Shevlin, and the town council have instituted programs to help them abandon the street as a place to live.

I took a final glance at the computer screen and decided to open mail instead of continuing my struggle with the novel. One envelope, a classic number-ten size, caught my eye. My address had been meticulously hand printed. There was no indication of the sender's identity. Strange, I thought as I opened it. Inside was a single sheet of eight-and-a-half-by-eleven white paper folded in thirds. I unfolded it. A large red letter *G* that had obviously been cut from a magazine was pasted in the center of the page. I stared at it for a long time. What could it possibly mean? Who'd sent it? *Why* had someone sent it?

I pulled a magnifying glass from my desk drawer and closely examined the paper and envelope. There was nothing I could see to provide a clue to the person behind this strange piece of mail. There was, however, the canceled stamp, which was smudged and almost impossible to read. I squinted through the glass in an attempt to decipher the post office of origin. The best I could make out was that it had been mailed from Ohio.

Ohio?

The doorbell rang. I laid the envelope and paper on the pile of other mail and went to the door, where a driver from the local cab company I use regularly stood. "I beeped a few times, Mrs. Fletcher," he said.

"Oh goodness, Nick," I said. "I didn't hear you. I'm sorry. Just give me a minute."

"That's what I figured. Take your time. No rush."

I'd forgotten that I'd called for a taxi to take me to a meeting of the Thanksgiving pageant committee. I grabbed my purse and a folder containing the script, cast a final, fleeting glance at my mysterious piece of mail, and joined the driver outside. Before climbing into his car, I looked across the street. Hubert Billups was gone.

"Everything good with you, Mrs. Fletcher?" Nick asked as he pulled out of my driveway.

"Yes, everything is fine. Thank you for asking."

Had I been honest, I would have said, *"I'm not sure."*

Chapter Two

Following the meeting, I strolled over to Mara's dockside luncheonette for a cup of tea and to catch up on the latest gossip. Obviously, I'd been the subject of some of it, and I thought I might learn something about my writing struggles that even I didn't know.

Although the busy tourist season was over, there was still a crowd filling the seats. I craned my neck trying to spot an empty table, or at least one where the occupants looked as if they were waiting for a check. I'd resigned myself to a seat at the counter when Beth Wappinger waved at me. "Come sit here, Jessica," she said, indicating the second chair at her table.

"Love to."

"I have to get back to work in a minute," she said, "but this way you don't have to wait for a table to open up."

I'd met Beth three years ago when she and her husband, Josh, moved to Cabot Cove from Portland, Maine. Soon after arriving, she opened a successful clothing shop in the middle of town that featured designer clothing at discount prices. She often kidded that without the shop, she'd go mad from boredom. Josh, a manufacturer's representative, was on the road for most of every month, traveling the country in search of customers for the various firms he represented.

"All set for Thanksgiving?" she asked after a recently hired young waitress took my order.

"I wish," I said, blowing a stream of air to emphasize my frustration. "It all comes on so fast, and with everything else going on, there aren't enough hours in the day."

"You must really be feeling the pressure," Beth said, "with your book deadline and all."

I laughed. "It seems the whole town knows about that," I said.

"The price of fame, Jessica. You're Cabot Cove's first citizen."

I started to deny that characterization, but Beth excused herself. "Have to run. I don't like leaving my new teenage clerk alone for too long. Finish that book. Can't wait to read it."

As she left, Seth Hazlitt came through the door. I looked beyond him and saw Hubert Billups on the dock, leaning against a railing, arms crossed over his chest.

"Mind company, Jessica?" Cabot Cove's beloved physician and my dear friend asked, sitting without waiting for an answer.

"You look chipper this morning," I said.

"Feeling tip-top. Just came from the hospital, where I checked in on Mrs. Watson. She came through the surgery just fine. Lucky thing I had my suspicions about what was ailing her and sent her to the specialists."

"You've always been a superb diagnostician, Seth."

"I try." He motioned for the waitress and ordered a short stack of Mara's signature blueberry pancakes, with a side of bacon. Seth may be a wonderful diagnostician, but he sometimes comes up short as a nutritionist, particularly when it involves his own diet.

We talked about a variety of things, including my plans for Thanksgiving dinner. Eventually, he brought up George Sutherland joining us this year. "So I hear Scotland Yard will be making an appearance at your groaning board. You've been after him to come here for Thanksgiving for years now."

"I know, and I'm so pleased he's decided to do it. Thanksgiving is my favorite American holiday, warm and welcoming to everyone, a reminder of everything good about our country."

"No running yourself crazy buying gifts, you mean."

"That, too. Just sitting down together for a good meal and giving thanks for all we have. I'm happy to show him another side of our country than he gets from the media."

"Where's he staying?" Seth asked.

"I don't know. His decision to come was so last-minute. I meant to call around this morning to find him a hotel or motel, but time got away from me. I'll do it when I get home."

"Make any progress on your novel?"

I sighed. "No, I haven't."

I sat back as the waitress set Seth's plate in front of him.

"Not like you to get behind in your work, Jessica," he said, concentrating on pouring syrup over the pancakes. He'd first cut them into pieces. "Makes for nice edges to catch the syrup," he explains when someone questions his practice.

" 'My work,' " I said with an exasperated sigh. "I know I'm behind." I leaned closer. "Seth, did you happen to notice the fellow on the deck wearing the red-and-black jacket when you arrived?"

"Ayuh, I did. Why do you ask?"

"This may sound silly, Seth, but he's been spending a lot of time lately outside my house."

"Is that so? What's he do there?"

"Just stands and stares."

"No harm in that. Probably hoping for a handout, like a moose bird."

"Perhaps, but his constant presence is a little unnerving."

"Constant?"

"Well, often enough."

Seth twisted in his chair to see Billups through the window. "Seems peaceful enough," he said as the waitress topped off his coffee cup.

"I'm sure you're right," I said.

I considered mentioning the strange letter I'd received, but decided I didn't want to come off more paranoid than

I already had. "I'd better get moving," I said, "if I'm to find George a hotel room."

"Soon as I finish my pancakes I'll drive you home," he said.

His attack on his breakfast was interrupted a number of times by people saying hello and stopping to chat with Cabot Cove's favorite physician. Fran Winstead asked if she could get a renewal on her husband Wally's blood pressure medicine.

"Ayuh. Call me at the office in an hour," Seth told her.

I recognized one couple who'd waved at him, although I didn't know their names. They'd moved into a house at the end of the road on which I lived. I asked Seth who they were.

"Name's Carson, Mr. and Mrs. Haven't met him yet, but his wife's a new patient."

I mentioned that they'd bought the old Butterfield house, which had been on the market for some time. "I haven't had time to stop by to say hello."

"Seem like nice folks," Seth commented, enjoying his last mouthful of pancakes and bacon and wiping his mouth with a napkin. "Should be good neighbors."

When we left Mara's, I noticed that Hubert Billups was no longer on the dock. *Good*, I thought. As irrational as it might be, his presence generated discomfort for me.

Back home, I started calling hotels in the area, beginning with what I considered the nicest ones. No luck. Every one was booked solid over the holiday weekend. The better motels were full, too, as were the few bed-and-breakfasts in which I felt George would be comfortable. "Sorry, Jessica," I was told by innkeeper Craig Thomas, who, with his wife, Jill, owned Blueberry Hill. "We've been sold out for months. If we'd known you needed a reservation we would have—"

"That's okay, Craig," I said. "I know how late I am in looking for space. Please keep me in mind if you get a cancellation. Love to Jill."

The lack of accommodations should not have come as a surprise, but it did. I hadn't considered that the Thanksgiving holiday would bring scores of visitors to Cabot Cove. Had George announced months ago that he was coming, finding him suitable lodging would not have been so difficult. But he'd made his decision only a few days ago.

Initially, I'd considered having him stay at my house, but thought better of it. The Cabot Cove grapevine was spending far too much time speculating on my activities as it was. Furthermore, my friends had been linking George and me romantically ever since we first met in London years ago, and I didn't want to feed their well-meaning fantasies. Of course, there was some truth to their conjecture. George Sutherland and I had immediately "connected," and romantic sparks had developed. But we'd been content to express our feelings verbally and to leave it at that. Both widowed, we'd forged busy, independent lives for ourselves, separated by the vast Atlantic Ocean, and had decided to honor that, unless . . . unless we had a change of heart. That hadn't happened yet, and I didn't know if it ever would.

While I was trying to come up with an alternate housing solution for George—and looking longingly at my inactive computer screen—Seth called.

"Any luck finding a hotel for your friend?" he asked

"No." I recounted my attempts.

"Seems like you've got a problem on your hands."

"More than one," I said. "Seth?"

"Ayuh?"

"Is anyone visiting *you* over Thanksgiving?"

"No. Why do you ask?"

"Well, you have that wing on your house that your live-in housekeeper used to use. It's a lovely apartment, with a nice view of the garden, and—"

"And?"

"And I was just wondering—I wouldn't ask if I wasn't in this bind—and I thought that maybe George could, um—"

"Spit it out, woman!"

"George would be the perfect houseguest—he's extremely considerate of others—and it's only for four days—well, maybe five—and he'd be spending most of his time with me at my house and at events around town—and I know how much he would appreciate it, to say nothing of how much I would appreciate it. Would you mind terribly if he stayed with you?"

There was silence on the other end.

"Seth?"

"I'm here, Jessica. I don't suppose I have much of a choice."

"Of course you do," I said, "and if it's too much of an inconvenience, I perfectly understand."

I also understood that Seth's ambivalence was not based solely on a reluctance to have someone share his house for five days.

While he and George had gotten along on those few times they'd been together, there was little doubt that my friend of many years harbored a certain distrust of George, not personally, but because George's interest in me was evident. Seth could be extremely paternalistic where I was concerned, like a father protecting his teenage daughter, and I admit that now and then I'd resented his intrusion into my personal life. But those feelings never lasted very long. I have no greater friend than Seth Hazlitt, and his quirks and idiosyncrasies—and they were legion—were easily and quickly excused. I knew he always meant well and had my best interests at heart, at least as he perceived them.

There was also the supposition on the part of some of my friends that Seth's interest in me was more than paternalistic, and that he considered George a competitor for my affections. It was all silly, of course, but that was the reality of the situation.

"It won't be an inconvenience at all, Jessica," Seth said, sounding very much as though he meant it. "Of course, I'll be seeing patients in my office wing."

"And I can promise that George will go out of his way not to disturb you. Thank you, Seth. You're a doll."

He grunted something in response and we ended the call.

I spent a few hours trying to get back into the manuscript but wasn't successful. My eyes kept going to the sheet of paper with the large *G* on it. What could it possibly mean? I asked myself over and over. Could it have something to do with George?

At five that afternoon, I dressed for a dinner engagement at a downtown restaurant. As hard as I tried to dismiss the mysterious letter, it was entrenched in my thinking, and by the time the taxi pulled into my driveway, I realized how frazzled I'd become—the letter, the stranger named Hubert Billups, Thanksgiving right around the corner, George's arrival, the pageant, and my manuscript that seemed to be going nowhere.

"Pull yourself together, Jessica," I told myself. "Stop making mountains out of molehills."

Good advice, I knew.

But as with all good advice, the difficult part would be in following it.

Chapter Three

I awoke the next morning feeling surprisingly rested and refreshed. I thought I might have trouble sleeping with so many thoughts rattling around in my brain, but that hadn't happened.

The first thing I did upon getting out of bed was to e-mail George Sutherland in London to let him know that he'd be staying with Seth. I wasn't certain how George would react. While he and Seth got along, people don't always feel comfortable being a houseguest, particularly when the house belongs to someone you barely know.

After a breakfast of fruit, one of Charlene Sassi's divine raspberry scones, and tea, I showered, dressed, and pledged to spend the morning working on my novel. Having so-called writer's block at this stage of my career was unacceptable. It's always been my contention that such "blocks" in the writing process occur only when the writer doesn't know where to go next in the story. Some ideas came to me over breakfast, and I was confident that I'd be productive that morning.

I'd just settled at my computer and was about to input my first sentence of the day when the doorbell rang.

"Mornin', Mrs. Fletcher," Newt said as he held out a fairly large package for me. "Too big for the box," he said, "and I didn't want to leave it just standin' there. Looks like it's fixin' to rain."

I looked up into a pewter sky. He was right. Rain wasn't far off. You could smell it in the air.

"Thank you," I said.

"And here's the rest of your mail," he said, piling it on top of the package. "Have a good one." He touched the peak of his hat with his index finger.

I looked up and down the street in search of Hubert Billups. No sign of him. The day was off to a good start.

I carried the mail and the package into the kitchen and set them on the table. I knew what the package contained: a pretty rose-colored sweater I'd bought while on a trip to New York City to meet with my publisher, Vaughan Buckley. I set it aside and attacked the rest of the mail. One piece jumped out at me. It was a bright yellow envelope with no return address, but the writing looked familiar. With a start, I realized it was addressed in the same block printing as the previous day's mysterious mailing containing the letter *G*. I turned the envelope over and stared at the flap. A shiver went through me. It's not as if I've never been threatened before. Anyone who inserts herself into murder investigations, as I have a few times in my life—well, perhaps more than a *few* times—anyone who's rattled a cage or two—or so—in her day can hardly expect to escape unscathed. There had been the occasional warnings of retribution, although they had never come to anything.

I racked my brain. Had I heard of anyone being released from prison who might harbor a grudge against me? The police often notify victims when the offender has been paroled. I was not a victim, however. My involvement in crimes was limited to helping the authorities. If a murderer I'd helped to put away was paroled or released after serving his or her sentence, I doubted it would occur to the warden or parole board to drop me a note.

I opened the envelope with trepidation and withdrew the single sheet of white letter-sized paper. This time, the letter *G* was shiny yellow, cut from a glossy magazine page, and had been pasted so that it was upended, its curved side down. What did *that* mean? Following it was a much larger orange *L*. That was it. Nothing else.

I did what I'd done the previous day, examined the page with a magnifying glass, to no avail. Again the postmark was from Ohio.

What is going on?

I returned to my study and flipped through my address book in search of people I knew from Ohio. There were quite a few, but none who I thought would engage in such behavior. Could it be a skewed reader who'd gotten hold of my address and decided to play tricks on me? I'd dealt with a few such people over the course of my writing career. Most proved inoffensive enough, except for one gentleman who attended a book signing I'd done at the Seattle Mystery Bookshop while on my way to an Alaskan cruise. This fellow claimed I'd stolen his plot for my novel, and punctuated his accusation with a wicked-looking knife. It all ended peaceably when he was taken into custody, but the incident provided for some tense moments.

I decided it would be prudent to show the letters to our sheriff, Mort Metzger, to elicit what advice he might have, and put them in my purse in anticipation of heading downtown later that morning for a rehearsal of the pageant. In the meantime, I reminded myself, it was time to do what I'd intended, sit down and get some serious writing done.

An hour later, the words on the screen had changed, but not by much. I'd managed to add one additional page, hardly a productive hour. Worse, I read what I'd written and was dissatisfied. The page represented, as Vaughan Buckley is fond of putting it, "pushing words around on paper" rather than writing something substantial that moves the story along.

"Give it up, Jess," I told myself aloud. "You're forcing it."

Which was true, although I was painfully aware why I was forcing things. Time was running out.

I went back to my e-mails and saw that George had answered my message.

Good morning, Jessica, although it's late afternoon here in London. Are you convinced I won't be inconveniencing the good Dr. Hazlitt?

I realize that there isn't much choice in where to stay considering the lateness of the situation, but I wouldn't want to be a burden. You're aware, of course, that Dr. Hazlitt and I have not had what you might call an easy relationship. Never anything overtly unpleasant, but our encounters have been a bit strained nonetheless. Do I see your fine hand here, eager to smooth away the rough fabric between a pair of your ardent admirers? At any rate, I'm most appreciative and I hope you'll extend my sincerest gratitude to him for opening his home to me. I can't wait to see you again and to share your uniquely American holiday. I'm the envy of the chaps in my office. Warmly, George.

I wrote him back immediately.

I know we'll have a wonderful time together. As for Seth, he was delighted, absolutely delighted, to welcome you into his home. I know he'll be the perfect host when he isn't seeing patients in his office wing. We'll get together and make this a truly splendid and memorable Thanksgiving. Fondly, Jessica.

All right, so I overstated Seth's reaction to having George in his home a little. Just a little.

After responding to some other e-mails, I packed up and headed downtown, deciding for this trip to ride my bicycle. Some energetic pedaling might get the blood flowing and clear my blocked brain. Hopefully, the rain would hold off.

The rehearsal for our Thanksgiving pageant was in the gymnasium of the regional high school. We'd decided to focus on the role played by various presidents of the United States in establishing Thanksgiving as an official American holiday, with members of the Cabot Cove amateur theater group playing the roles of our nation's leaders.

There was some controversy over including President Franklin Roosevelt. Until his presidency, Thanksgiving had been held each year on the last Thursday in November, the date established by President Abraham Lincoln in his 1863 proclamation. But FDR moved it up a week in order to prolong the Christmas shopping season. The public uproar caused him to reconsider and to shift Thanksgiving back to its original date. In 1941, Congress finally sanctioned Thanksgiving as a legal holiday to be celebrated on the fourth Thursday in November.

"I still say that we shouldn't even mention what FDR did," one of the thespians proclaimed loudly, and often. "It was disgraceful that he put commerce first."

"But he did," the pageant's director, Robin Stockdale, said. "We want the pageant to be historically accurate."

"We're including President Jefferson," someone else chimed in, "and he didn't even like having a day of thanksgiving. He said that the hardships of a couple of Pilgrims didn't deserve a special celebration."

The actress playing the role of Sarah Josepha Hale, the magazine editor whose forty-year campaign of articles, as well as letters to various presidents, was instrumental in persuading Lincoln to proclaim the day, said, "Frankly, I don't like this script. I liked last year's better, when we portrayed the first Thanksgiving back in 1621."

"Regardless of what you prefer, Margaret, we're using this new script," Robin said. "It's a very good script. Jessica and her committee worked hard on it and—"

Margaret walked away.

"Let's take a fifteen-minute break," Robin wisely suggested. I accompanied her outside.

"I hope you weren't offended, Jessica. Margaret has a tendency to speak her mind without considering others' feelings."

"Not at all. I'm used to getting reviews, not all of them glowing. You can't please everyone, no matter how hard you try."

"And Margaret is impossible to please. Sometimes I want to throw up my hands and forget there ever was a Thanksgiving," she said.

I laughed. "But I know you'd never do that, Robin. Just artistic temperament coming to the fore."

"You should have heard them arguing about the music selections. Elsie Frickert wants to play 'Turkey in the Straw.' Audrey Williams nearly had a fit. She wants more somber pieces for the occasion." Robin rolled her eyes.

"And you'll find a way to make them both happy. And Margaret, too. Mind if I leave? There's not much for me to do now that the script has been written, and I have a few stops to make."

"Of course not, Jessica. You run along. I'll take a few more deep breaths and go back inside."

I rode my bike to police headquarters, where I hoped to find Sheriff Metzger. I was in luck. He'd just returned from mediating a dispute between an angry customer and the owner of a hardware store, something to do with a lawn mower that didn't work but had apparently seen heavy duty over the summer.

"Morning, Mrs. F," he said brightly as he welcomed me into his office. "What brings you here?"

"These."

I pulled the two letters and envelopes from my purse and slid them across the desk. He scrutinized them, brow furrowed, chewing his cheek. Finally, he looked at me and asked, "Who sent them?"

I didn't allow my exasperation to show. "I don't know," I said. "I just thought you might have some idea of what they mean."

He looked at them again. "Haven't the foggiest, Mrs. F. What do *you* figure they mean?"

"I don't have an answer to that either, Mort. The question is, should I be concerned?"

He cocked his head. "Probably just some nut having fun, but you never can tell."

"They were mailed in Ohio."

"Oh? Were they? Know anybody out there who might be up to something like this?"

I retrieved them from his desk and put them back in my purse. I love Mort Metzger dearly, but there are times when he can be frustrating.

"Why not leave them with me?" he suggested. "I can run them over to the state crime lab and see if they can pick up any prints."

"I don't think that's necessary, Mort, but thanks for the offer. Probably just some nut, as you suggest. How's Maureen?"

"She's fine. She's poring over her recipe books for a different way to cook the turkey."

"That's . . . that's wonderful," I said, standing and thanking him again for his time. "Can't wait to hear what she comes up with."

Once outside, I allowed my true feelings to surface. Maureen, as wonderful a person as she is, and as dedicated a cook as she can be, tends to come up with *unusual* approaches to standard dishes, and they're not always successful. Hopefully, she wouldn't be offended if I cooked the bird this year using my time-tested old-fashioned way of doing it.

I was pedaling through the center of town when Tobé Wilson called my name. Tobé's husband, Jack, is one of Cabot Cove's most popular veterinarians. I got off the bike and joined her on a bench in a small park with a view of the bay. Tobé had always been a popular sight with tourists when she took her pet pig, Kiwi, for a walk. Many visitors to Cabot Cove had shots of Kiwi and Tobé among their vacation photos. Kiwi had recently succumbed to old age. I offered my condolences.

"It was always fun seeing people's reactions," she said. "And Kiwi enjoyed the attention. I miss her."

"Of course you do," I said.

"And how are you, Jessica? I hear by the grapevine that you're having problems with your next book."

"It's true, and if I knew what was good for me, I would be home pecking away at the computer right now."

"You'll get it done," she said, smiling. "And it will be wonderful, as always."

I wished I shared her confidence.

"Have you met the new folks on your road?" she asked.

"No, I haven't. Have you?"

"Yes. The wife was in this morning with their cat, Emerson. Hair balls. She's very sweet, very shy. Her owner, I mean. Her name's Linda."

"They were at Mara's yesterday when I was having breakfast with Seth. She's become his patient. I've seen them coming and going from their house, but haven't met them in person. Where are they from?"

"She didn't say, but she doesn't know anyone here. I asked. Mara said Amanda thought they might be from out West, since he's the strong, silent type."

The Carson home had been previously owned by Amanda Butterfield, widow of Sgt. Ira Butterfield, who was wounded by a grenade in World War II, and who died decades later. Mrs. Butterfield, in her nineties, had moved into an assisted-living facility some months back. The house was at the far end of my road, beyond a curve that shielded it from the view of other houses, including my own. The Carsons had arrived about two months ago, and though I'd seen them from a distance, we had yet to meet. From what I observed, they stayed pretty much to themselves. Linda was a small, demure brunette woman who seemed to move with purpose wherever she went. Her husband was much larger than his wife in every way.

"I've been meaning to stroll by their house and introduce myself," I said, "but just haven't gotten around to it."

"You should. It's always so hard moving into a new neighborhood," Tobé said.

"I'm glad you mentioned them," I said. "I'll make a point of paying a visit. Love to Jack."

I rode my bicycle home and took care of household chores, taking a break for a light lunch. At two, without even looking at my computer screen, I packed up some freshly baked blueberry muffins, put them in a shopping bag, and walked up the road to the house now occupied by our newcomers to Cabot Cove. It was one of the smaller homes in the area, set back from the road, a clapboard ranch house with mature, well-tended shrubs and pretty pink curtains in the windows. I hesitated to intrude on them without prior notice, but since I didn't know their telephone number, I decided that it was probably all right.

I knocked and waited. I heard movement inside the house, and a gruff male voice said, "Who could that be?"

The door was opened by the woman I now knew was Linda.

"Sorry to just stop by like this," I said, "but I've been very delinquent in welcoming you to the neighborhood. I'm Jessica Fletcher. I live down the road, just beyond the bend."

She seemed momentarily surprised but quickly smiled and said, "It's very, um, sweet of you to think of us."

"I baked these this morning," I said, handing her the muffins. "They're never as good as the ones from Charlene Sassi's bakery in town, but they come close. At least that's what I've been told."

"Thank you. I know we'll love them. I'm Linda, um, Carson," she said, pinching her nose. "It's nice to meet you."

A black-and-white cat wound itself around her ankle and settled between her feet.

"And this must be Emerson," I said, leaning down and extending my arm so the cat could sniff my hand.

"How did you know?"

"My friend Tobé Wilson said you brought your cat in this morning for treatment."

A brief frown appeared. Then she gave a nervous giggle. "Silly cat," she said. "It was just hair balls."

"Is Emerson named for the poet?"

"No. The college."

"Oh. Did you go there?"

"Where?"

"Emerson College. In Boston."

"No!" Linda wiped her lips with her fingers. "I mean, a friend of mine did and this was her cat. She couldn't take it home. Her mother was allergic. So she gave it to me. I couldn't very well change the cat's name, now, could I? So it's still Emerson."

"I see," I said. "But I detect a slight Boston accent there. Am I right? Is that where you're from?"

Linda scratched the side of her nose. "Boston is a nice city, so I'm told. We'll have to take a trip there soon."

"Well, I'm glad we've gotten to meet. Welcome to the neighborhood, and to Cabot Cove."

A large man wearing black sweatpants and sweatshirt, and sandals, suddenly appeared behind her, and eyed me suspiciously. His heavy beard line testified to not having shaved for a few days. "This is Jessica Fletcher," Linda told him. "She stopped by to say hello and brought us these muffins."

"Yeah? That's nice," he said, taking the bag and peering inside.

"This is my husband, Victor."

"Hello, Victor," I said, offering my hand, which disappeared inside his like a ball in a catcher's mitt.

"I won't keep you," I said.

"We'd invite you in," Linda said, glancing behind her, "but the house is such a mess. We're still getting settled."

"I know what a chore that can be," I said. "We'll probably see each other again at the Thanksgiving pageant. I hope you'll be there."

"I read about it in the local paper," she said without committing herself.

I wondered whether they had children but thought it would be too nosy to ask. Children especially enjoy the annual pageant. "We also serve a Thanksgiving dinner at the senior center for those who have nowhere else to go or can't afford to buy a turkey. We can always use extra help."

Then it occurred to me that because they were new to

the community, they might not have plans for the holiday. "Do you have family in the area?" I asked.

"No," Linda answered as her husband stepped out of view.

"I'm hosting Thanksgiving dinner at my house this year. There's always room for more—that is, if you don't have other plans."

"Oh, I don't know. I mean, um, that's so generous of you—we don't have plans, but—that's so nice of you. I'll ask Victor and call you. Is that all right?"

"Of course. My number is in the book. Fletcher. Jessica Fletcher," I said, sounding a little like James Bond. "You'll enjoy the other guests, I'm sure, and we'll tell you all about our local attractions. Well, it was good meeting you. I'll look forward to your call."

I don't know what the correlation might be, but my goodwill visit to my new neighbors seemed to free up my mind, and I had my first productive session at the computer in days. *Better start doing more good deeds*, I told myself as the words finally came.

Chapter Four

The third letter arrived in the next day's mail.

Like the previous two, my address was neatly printed on the standard letter-sized envelope. There was no return address. This time, I inspected the postmark before opening it. Cabot Cove!

The sheet of plain, white letter-sized paper provided the background for three letters cut from magazines. *G-L-O.* The *G* had been righted, the three letters aligned in a row spelling GLO.

GLO? What words begin with GLO? Glory? Glove? Globe? Glossary?

Or do the letters together stand for something?

I tried assigning possible words to them—Give Love something? Grand Lake—? I'd fly-fished for salmon on Grand Lake Stream in northern Maine a few times. Gallant Lads Overcome? Gentlemen Like Oceans? Guns, Loss, Ominous? *Ooh, I don't like that one.*

It was an impossible exercise, but I kept at it until the ringing phone brought it to a halt.

"Hi, Jessica. It's Maureen."

"Good morning," I said to our sheriff's wife. Maureen had married Mort after he and his first wife, Adele, had parted ways. Maureen, a softhearted redhead with a cheerful outlook had rescued Mort from despair and brought interest and enjoyment back into his life. She attacked every activity with enthusiasm, if not always aptitude, and cooking was an abiding passion of hers.

"Got a minute to talk about the feast?" she asked.

"Thanksgiving dinner? All right."

"I was watching the Food Network and Paula Deen was on and came up with an absolutely dynamite idea for a different way to cook the turkey this year—except that it's not a turkey."

For some reason, I thought of former Yankee great Yogi Berra and his twisted sayings. When is a turkey not a turkey?

"You use a turducken."

"Of course."

"It's a turkey except that you put a duck inside a chicken and put the chicken inside the turkey. You cook it just like you would a plain old turkey. It sounds fabulous. Paula says—there I go sounding as though we're pals—she says it gives three different flavors at the same time. What do you think?"

"I, ah—it's fascinating, Maureen. Actually, I was served it once at a dinner in Memphis. It was quite good."

"I knew you'd appreciate it. What say we try it this year?"

"It's an interesting recipe, Maureen, but I was thinking more along the lines of a traditional roast turkey because of George coming to celebrate with us. You know, show our Scottish guest what an old-fashioned New England Thanksgiving meal is like."

"I see your point," she said, her tone mirroring her disappointment. Then she brightened. "Maybe I can come up with something unusual to go with the turkey, some side dish, like a special stuffing."

"I like that idea," I said, relieved.

"What do you think of jalapeño peppers?"

"I don't think they quite fit the definition of traditional, but would you mind if we discussed this another time? I have to run."

"I bet I interrupted an important creative burst you're having this morning, and I apologize, knowing the trouble you've been having with your book."

"No apologies needed. You didn't interrupt anything important," I said, thinking of my efforts to make sense out of GLO. "We'll talk again later."

I got back to work on the novel but didn't get very far. My mind kept drifting to words with those three letters. When eleven o'clock rolled around, I put the computer on STANDBY, grateful that Wilimena Copeland had invited me to join her for lunch downtown. Perhaps the distraction would help me focus better later on. Our reservation was for twelve, but I wanted time to stop at the post office before I met her.

Midday is not the best time to visit the Cabot Cove Post Office. The window closes at noon while the three postal workers in the back take their lunch break together, and doesn't reopen until an hour later. Why they couldn't alternate and have two take lunch while the third kept the service open during that time was one mystery I'd never been able to solve. Even knowing this, I wasn't prepared for the line of customers trying to squeeze in their business before the lunchtime hiatus. I checked my watch, trying to calculate if I had enough time to talk to the postmistress before I was to meet Willie. I might make it.

If Mara's holds first place in the gossip wars, the post office runs a close second. The two ladies and one gentleman behind the desk are the repositories of all news in town, gleaned from customers as they pick up their packages or buy stamps. As a consequence, each transaction takes a bit more time than it might if there was no juicy information being exchanged. So I was not surprised when I finally reached the front of the line and Lee, the postmistress, asked, "How's that book going, Jessica? Beth Wappinger said you were stalled."

"She did? Well, I have been more productive in my life," I replied, "but it will get done. It always does."

"And how can I help you today?"

"I'm not sure you can, Lee, but I thought you should be aware of these three letters I received." I pulled the papers from my purse and spread them out on the counter in front of her.

"Oh, doing a little arts and crafts, are we?" she said, smiling.

"Lee, you don't understand. Someone is using the postal service to send me anonymous letters."

"When did you get them?"

"The *G* was the first one. I got the *L* yesterday and this one today."

"Someone is sending you a message."

"Yes, I can see that, Lee. But what kind of message?"

"I don't know, Jessica. The post office only delivers the mail. We aren't responsible for what's in it."

"Isn't there some policy that outlaws the use of the U.S. Postal Service to send threats through the mail?"

"I don't see any threats here. It's just cutout letters." She put her finger on the *O* of the letter that had arrived that morning. "What a pretty color. I used to have a dress in that pink."

"You don't see this as threatening?"

"Frankly, Jessica, I don't. It's probably just a fan who wants to get your attention."

"Well, if that's the case, he or she has accomplished the goal." I refolded the letters and tucked them in my purse.

"Is there anything else I can do for you today?" she asked.

"I guess not. Sorry to have wasted your time."

"No problem. Good luck on the completion of your book."

"Thank you."

I left the post office and arrived at the restaurant with five minutes to spare before I was due to meet my friend.

Wilimena, better known as Willie to her friends and to her sister, Kathy, had decided to settle in Cabot Cove after a harrowing experience during an Alaskan cruise. She'd disappeared during that trip, and Kathy and I had set out to find out what had happened to her. As it turned out, she'd come into possession of a stash of gold that had been panned by a close friend of a distant relative, Dolly Arthur, whose brothel was Alaska's most famous sporting house. Willie had ended up trapped in a remote cabin and would have died had Kathy and I not come to her rescue. In a lovely gesture, she had donated a sizable portion of her treasure to renovate our senior citizen center.

Wilimena had been an inveterate flirt who had gone through a succession of husbands before arriving in town. For a while, it seemed that she was content to leave the adventurous portion of her colorful life in the past. That lasted until a wealthy gentleman, Archer Franklin, decided that Cabot Cove was the perfect place in which to enjoy his retirement.

Bingo!

Willie was introduced to the new retiree, applied her famous magnetism, and they'd soon become an item, according to Cabot Cove's informal news channel—the rumor mill. I hadn't met Mr. Franklin yet, although gossip had already started circulating that characterized him as opinionated and, shall we say, less than modest about his achievements. That didn't mean, of course, that he was those things, and I would reserve judgment until I'd encountered the man myself.

I joined Wilimena, who'd already secured a table, her

cane hooked over the back of her chair. She'd suffered a mangled leg during her Alaskan adventure and went through months of grueling rehabilitation. Despite walking with a pronounced limp, she'd remained an extremely attractive woman who assiduously worked on her looks and figure. She greeted me warmly.

"How's the book coming?" she asked.

"Oh, it's coming along all right."

"I hear you're having some trouble finishing it."

"I can't imagine where you heard that," I said, laughing.

"Wasn't it on the billboard out by the highway?" she asked, tongue firmly in cheek, and joined in the laughter.

"So," I said, "what's new in your life?"

"Lots," she replied, then became conspiratorial. "I have a new beau."

"So I've heard," I said.

"How did you know already? Did Kathy tell you?"

"No. Must have been on that same billboard. Tell me about him."

"He's quite a guy, maybe a little old for me but in good shape. He exercises regularly and—"

"And?"

"And he's loaded. He said he made his fortune in the commodities market. Not that I know anything about how that works, but he obviously does. He's thinking of buying a house in Clamshell Cove. He keeps his houseboat in a slip there. He's living on it until he decides which house to buy."

Clamshell Cove was a relatively new and expensive

gated community overlooking the water on the northern edge of town.

"He says he has a house in Florida, too, and just sold a villa in Monte Carlo."

"Marital status?" I asked.

Her eyes saddened. "Widowed, poor thing. Cancer. She died more than a dozen years ago. Can you imagine that he's decided to spend his summer retirement years here in Cabot Cove?"

"I don't know what entertainments we have to compare with Monte Carlo," I said, "but I'll have to remember to ask when I meet him."

As it turned out, I didn't have to wait long for that to happen. A nattily attired gray-haired man came through the door with a flourish, surveyed the restaurant, spotted us, and made his way to our table. In contrast to the less colorful garb of the other customers, he was dressed in a double-breasted blue blazer, sported a red ascot and matching pocket square, and wore his tasseled loafers sans socks.

"Hello there," he said in a deep voice, leaning to kiss Wilimena on the cheek. "How's my favorite lady?"

"Your favorite lady is fine," she said. "You haven't met my friend Jessica Fletcher."

"No, I haven't, but I've been looking forward to the pleasure of meeting this bestselling author for some time now."

I took his extended hand, taking note of a large diamond-and-gold pinkie ring and his lacquered nails.

"Well," he said through a satisfied smile as he pulled

up a chair, "you don't mind if I join you for a moment, do you?" He tugged on the razor crease of his gray slacks, and sat heavily, his knees grazing mine.

I moved my chair to give him more room.

He leaned forward, eyes on mine, and said in a voice that was easily heard several tables away, "Willie has told me how you came to her rescue in Alaska, like the cavalry."

"Kathy and I had been searching for Willie. We were fortunate it turned out the way it did," I said.

"Ah yes, you were with Willie's lovely sister, Kathy. Didn't mean to omit proper credit."

"I'm the one who's fortunate," Willie said. "I'd be dead now if it wasn't for Jess and Kathy."

"We couldn't have that, now, could we?" he said, laying his hand on hers.

He turned his attention back to me. "I'd love to discuss writing with you, Mrs. Fletcher," he said with a smile. "I've done quite a bit of writing myself."

"Really? What sort of writing?"

He leaned back in his chair and crossed his legs, resting a tasseled loafer on his knee. "A lot of it's technical—I was involved in the commodities market for many years—but I also write poetry and short stories, and I'm thinking about starting a novel."

"That's terrific," I said.

"You'll enjoy reading some of my works. They're quite good, if I say so myself, and I'm my severest critic."

"I—ah—I would enjoy that at some point when things are a little less hectic."

"Jessica is trying to finish her latest novel, Archer, but she's got writer's block."

"I don't know if calling it writer's block is accurate," I said, irritated at my need to defend myself. "I think it's more a case of distrac—"

"I've given a considerable amount of thought to writer's block, now that I'm a writer. Not that it's been much of a problem for me," Archer said, "but I have some definite theories about its cause." He launched into his "theories" for the next five minutes, little of which was comprehensible to me, but I didn't want to appear rude by challenging him. "You know, you and I should get together," he said in conclusion. "We can be just two fellow writers talking shop, swapping trade secrets. Yes, I would enjoy that."

I assured him that I'd enjoy that, too, but stressed again that it would have to be sometime in the future.

The conversation shifted to what he called "a nasty encounter" he'd encountered on his way to the restaurant. "There's this homeless guy out on the street looking for handouts. He didn't get a handout from me, and never will. But he did get an earful. I told this bum that if he'd do the honorable thing and get a job, we'd all be better off."

"What did he look like?" Wilimena asked.

"Like a bum," Archer said. "Filthy red beard, dressed like it was the middle of winter."

Wilimena looked at me to see whether I recognized the man's description.

My only response was a noncommittal shrug.

"If I ran this city," Wilimena's new beau said, "you

wouldn't see any homeless on the streets of this lovely village. I'd get rid of them, just like that mayor in New York did back some years ago. Now you see 'em, now you don't."

"How did he do that?" Willie asked.

"Doesn't matter. That's what I'd do here, if I were mayor. Maybe it's time for Cabot Cove to elect a new mayor. I've been thinking about that."

A waitress came to our table and Archer waved her away.

"Can't you stay for lunch?" Willie asked him.

"Afraid not," he said, pushing back his chair. He checked his Rolex. "I have a conference call with my financial advisers in a half hour, but I'll take a rain check." He kissed Willie's cheek, grabbed my hand and kissed it. "This has been a rare and unexpected pleasure, Mrs. Fletcher—Jessica."

"It's so nice to meet you," I said, extracting my hand.

"We'll have to have that literary confab soon," he said. "You two lovely ladies enjoy your girl talk."

We watched him saunter through the restaurant, heads turning as he passed by tables on his way to the door.

"Well, Jessica, what do you think?" Willie asked. "Isn't he handsome? He can be a little overbearing, but I like confidence in a man."

"He's certainly self-confident," I said, grateful when the waitress reappeared by my side.

It wasn't until the end of the meal that Willie told me why she'd suggested we get together for lunch. "How many people are you having for Thanksgiving?" she asked.

"Right now, it's nine, although I've invited my new neighbors to join us. If they do, that'll make eleven."

"Just don't make it thirteen," Willie said. "That's an unlucky number."

I laughed. "Only if you're superstitious," I said, "which I'm not."

"But it would be better to have an even number," she said.

"If you say so."

"I was wondering if I could bring Archer with me to dinner."

"Well, I—"

"He's done nothing but talk about you since I told him we're friends. I know how much he'd love being there and meeting everyone. They'll enjoy meeting him, too."

"I suppose it would be all right," I said.

"Great! You're the best, Jessica, the absolute best. I can't wait to tell him. He'll be so pleased. He thought you would give my request more weight if you had a chance to meet him in person. And you see? He was right."

We parted outside the restaurant. Before we went our separate ways, Wilimena said, "You know, Jessica, Archer isn't kidding about Cabot Cove maybe needing a new mayor. He's thinking seriously of running next time around."

"Is he? That's a year off, Willie."

"It'll give him plenty of time to meet everyone in Cabot Cove and impress them."

I thanked Willie for lunch and sent my love to Kathy.

Thanksgiving dinner was shaping up to be more interesting with every passing minute. I wasn't convinced our current mayor and my friend, Jim Shevlin, would find sharing the holiday with Archer Franklin agreeable. I made a mental note to seat them at opposite ends of the table. *Maybe it's time you learned to say no, Jessica*, I told myself as I headed back home for another stab at my novel.

Chapter Five

Until this point, I'd been fairly sanguine about the three letters that had arrived with the letters *G*, *L*, and *O* pasted on them, aside from wondering who'd sent them and whether they had some nefarious meaning. But when the fourth arrived the next morning, I decided that it was time to stop sitting back, and to take some action.

Number four's plain sheet of paper had added a new letter, a large purple *T*, to accompany the original three. As with the others, it had been snipped from the pages of a magazine. Together, they now spelled *GLOT*.

The dictionary yielded only three words beginning with those letters, all having to do with the glottis, an opening of the vocal cords. Somehow, I didn't think that information was relevant to the messages being sent to me. My temptation was, of course, to try again to assign words to the letters, but I'd had enough of that wasteful exercise. I placed the letters in my purse and called Mort Metzger at police headquarters.

"Hello there, Mrs. F," Mort said. "Maureen said she talked to you about the Thanksgiving menu. Got everything settled?"

"That's right. We did talk," I said, "but I'm not calling about that."

"Oh?"

"I received another letter this morning, Mort. Like the ones I showed you. That makes four."

"Same thing, just letters pasted on a piece of paper?"

"Exactly. Today's letter was a T. That makes it *G*, *L*, *O*, and T."

"Crazy, huh, Mrs. F? Wait a minute. You say there've been four. You only showed me two, sent from someplace in Ohio."

"I received the third yesterday. That one was postmarked right here in Cabot Cove. Today's was also mailed from Maine, but not Cabot Cove. It looks like Kittery."

"Where all the discount stores are. Maybe whoever's sending them is on a shopping spree." He chuckled.

I didn't respond.

"Sorry, Mrs. F. Didn't mean to make light of this."

"Mort, I'd like to take you up on your offer to have the state crime lab check for prints."

"Sure thing. Drop 'em off here anytime."

"I'll be in town later this morning."

"See you then."

My intention was to settle in to get some serious writing done, but as my dear, deceased husband, Frank, was fond of saying, there's a road somewhere paved with good intentions—and it isn't the road to heaven. Actually, it wasn't entirely my fault that the morning got away from me. The incessantly ringing telephone played a role, too.

I'd no sooner settled at my computer when Jed Richardson called. Jed had been a pilot for a major airline until deciding he didn't like the airline's bureaucracy. He took an early retirement and settled back in Cabot Cove to establish Jed's Flying Service, ferrying townspeople to larger cities in his "fleet" of three planes, two of them single-engine, and one twin-engine craft. Besides transporting passengers, he gave flying lessons, his students including yours truly a few years ago.

That I earned my private pilot's license was the source of much amusement on the part of my friends. I don't have a driver's license and have never had any interest in getting one. But there was something alluring about piloting my own plane, and I threw myself into Jed's lessons and all the book learning that went with it. I don't fly often, usually just enough to stay current by paying Jed for an hour of dual instruction. But there have been a few instances when my flying knowledge, as minimal as it may be, came in handy when in a tight spot. That trip to Alaska with Kathy Copeland in search of her capricious sister was one such occasion.

The call from Jed this morning wasn't to set up a refresher flight for me, although it would end up being that. George Sutherland was flying from London to Boston the next day, and I'd arranged for Jed to meet him there and bring him to Cabot Cove. I'd toyed with the idea of joining them, but the mounting stress of finishing my book kept me from coming to a final decision. Jed wanted to know what that decision was.

I looked at the computer screen and realized that unless my muse suddenly made an appearance, it was unlikely that I'd get much done over the next few days.

"I'll come with you," I said.

"Great, Jess. You can get in some logged time on the trip and we'll bring your buddy back, kill two birds with one stone."

"You'll have to use one of the Cessnas," I said, referring to one of Jed's two single-engine planes. I'm not licensed to fly multiengine.

"That's okay. Be out here at the airport by eleven?"

"Count on it," I said.

I'd no sooner hung up when my new neighbor, Linda Carson, called.

"I hope I'm not disturbing anything," she said.

"Not at all."

"Is that invitation to your Thanksgiving dinner still open?" she asked.

"Of course."

"Then we'd love to come."

"That's wonderful."

"Victor's not much for social gatherings, but he knows how much I'd like to be there. He can be so, um, stubborn at times. Anyway, I had to do some convincing, but he eventually agreed."

She couldn't see the expression on my face, which mirrored my visceral reaction to what she'd said. It didn't sound as though Victor, who obviously was coming under duress, would enjoy himself, let alone provide much enjoyment for others at the table. For a moment I weighed whether or not to suggest that they might want to reconsider, but thought better of it. I did give Linda an out, however. "If Victor changes his mind, I'll understand," I offered. "Just give me a few days' notice."

"Oh, he won't change his mind," she said. "If he does, I'll kill him." She giggled; then her voice grew serious. "It's my first Thanksgiving away from family and friends back home and I'd hate to spend it alone."

"Where is home?" I asked.

She didn't answer. Instead, she said, her voice discernibly cracking, "It's so nice of you to think of us at a time like this. Thanksgiving is so special and—"

"Looking forward to having you and Victor," I said, "and I can't wait for you to meet the other guests. They're very warm and welcoming. I know you'll enjoy them."

More composed now, she asked if she could contribute to the menu. "I make a good pumpkin pie," she said.

"That would be wonderful," I said. "Are you coming to the pageant?"

"Victor doesn't want to, but I'll work on him."

We ended the conversation and I took another stab at the computer before deciding to pack it in and head downtown. I wanted to get my nonwriting errands out of the way. I would stop in at the sheriff's office to give Mort the letters, but not until after attending a meeting of a commission that had been formed to oversee the care of a small natural lake not too far from my house. It was a lovely body of freshwater, a popular spot with our local Audubon Club members who could be seen, binoculars raised or bird book in hand, strolling its shores, and there had been many times I'd visited the lake myself, to take in its beauty and tranquillity.

Mayor Shevlin had recently asked me to join the commission, and I'd readily agreed. Of course, that was before I realized that the crush of activities in November would interfere with finishing my manuscript. Still, I'm hard put to turn down requests to aid a good cause in Cabot Cove. And this was one of them. An unhealthy amount of weeds had begun to dominate portions of the lake, and we were debating how best to attack the problem. I was anxious to ensure that whatever means were employed to curb the invasive growth not upset the ecological balance. It was an important assignment, but yet another commitment that pulled me away from my work.

I thought about my conversation with Linda Carson. I was pleased that she'd taken me up on my invitation—but also somewhat disconcerted. Her husband sounded like a difficult man, and I hoped his disposition wouldn't cast a pall on the festivities. Maybe he and Willie Copeland's new friend, Archer Franklin, would find things in common to talk about. I knew I couldn't seat Archer next to our current mayor—nothing can ruin a festive Thanksgiving dinner faster than a political squabble—but I worried that the table was filling up with alpha males, men with strong opinions and few compunctions about expressing them. I hoped the women would be able to keep the Thanksgiving atmosphere as it should be: warm—and civil.

The meeting of the lake committee, chaired by Mayor Shevlin, went smoothly and quickly and I was free sooner than I'd expected. I went directly to police headquarters but was told that Sheriff Metzger had been called out on an emergency and wouldn't be back for an hour.

It was close to lunchtime and I decided to stop in at Mara's for a quick bite. As I approached the dock, I had the feeling that I was being watched. I looked around and saw Hubert Billups perched on a low brick wall that defined one of the town's parks, the same one where I'd sat with Tobé Wilson two days ago. He was dressed in his usual cold-weather garb, arms folded across his chest, eyes staring straight ahead. For a moment, I was tempted to cross the street and introduce myself in the hope of gaining some clue as to why he always seemed to be where I was. But I decided not to. I didn't know how he would react and didn't want to initiate a confrontation.

I reached the dock and stopped to chat with Richard Koser, one of Cabot Cove's top photographers and a superb amateur chef.

"Got your menu set for next Thursday?" he asked.

"I think so, nothing exotic, just a traditional Thanksgiving dinner. You?"

"I've been experimenting. I thought I might try making a turducken this year."

"You've been watching Paula Deen," I said lightly.

"Haven't seen her in ages. Why do you say that?"

"Maureen Metzger suggested I have turducken this

year. She got the idea from Paula Deen's show on the Food Network."

"Go for it."

"Not with my friend George coming from London for the holiday. I want a menu as close to traditional as I can muster."

"Can't argue with that. How many are you having?"

"Looks like twelve at this point, a few last-minute additions."

"Always fun to have strays at Thanksgiving. Livens things up."

I thought of the reluctant Victor Carson, and the overbearing Archer Franklin, and wondered whether "livening things up" accurately described how dinner would turn out.

"Well," I said, "let me know how you like the turducken."

"I'll send you a picture," he said with a chuckle.

Richard walked away. I turned before entering Mara's and saw that Hubert Billups had moved to a vantage point from which he could see the luncheonette. I stifled another urge to approach him and quickly slipped through the door.

I'd beaten the usual lunch crush and had my pick of tables. I was about to choose one by the window when I heard, "Hi."

Linda Carson stood at the counter.

"Hello," I said.

"I'm taking something out. Victor likes to eat lunch at home."

Her large brown eyes said many things to me at that moment, although I couldn't decide which of my reactions was valid. Sad? Dreamy? Looking for understanding?

"Home is always best," I said. "I'm so pleased you and your husband will be joining us for Thanksgiving dinner."

"I'm looking forward to it," she said, and I was aware that she referred only to herself.

Mara came from the kitchen and handed Linda her takeout.

"Thanks," Linda said. To me: "Well, I'd better get home before this gets cold."

"Enjoy," I said, and watched her leave.

"Nice lady," Mara said, plopping down on a stool and blowing away a wisp of hair that had fallen over her brow.

"Yes, she is. She and her husband are coming to the house for Thanksgiving."

"Oh? That's good of you to share it with newcomers."

"Have you met her husband, Victor?" I asked.

"He was in here, but we were never formally introduced," she said, then cocked her head at me. "I understand another new face will be at your table this Thanksgiving."

"Who's that?"

"Mr. Moneybags."

She can't mean George.

Mara must have seen my confusion. "The other new arrival?" she coached. "Mr. Franklin?"

"Oh, right. Willie Copeland is bringing him."

"You'd think he owns Cabot Cove from the way he talks," Mara said in a voice just above a whisper.

"He does seem a little—well, a little sure of himself."

"He was in here this morning bragging that you and he were going to get together for some writer talk."

"Did he?"

"Bet you'll enjoy that, huh?"

I glanced at my watch. "Oh, my! It's getting late. I'd better grab something to eat and go."

Mara laughed. "And I'd better get back in the kitchen. The lunch crowd will be descending on me any minute."

When I left, there was no sign of Billups. I returned to police headquarters, where Mort had just arrived. "Had an attempted robbery," he said as he tossed his tan Stetson on the desk and loosened his tie.

"How did it end up?" I asked.

"Damn fool put on a ski mask, walked into the auto parts place out east, and poked his hand in his pocket like he had a gun there. The two guys behind the counter didn't fall for it and jumped him, held him until we could get there. He's not from around here."

"That's always good to hear," I said.

"Let me see what you got."

I handed Mort the four letters.

He flipped through them. "I'll send them over to the lab right away."

"Thanks, Mort. By the way, do you know anything about a recent arrival in town, a Mr. Hubert Billups?"

Mort rolled his eyes and shook his head. "Everyone's asking the same question. I know who he is, but haven't found out much about him yet. When the weather's bad, we've had to roust him a few times from inside buildings. People in offices complained that he'd wander in, sit in the lobby dressed the way he is, and say nothing. And Wally Winstead went after him one day not long ago."

"Why?"

"You know Wally, always thinking somebody's flirting with his wife, Fran. Anyway, Wally sees Billups staring at his wife the way he does and accuses him of trying to seduce her." Mort shook his head. "As though a scruffy character like Billups would appeal to her. Wally grabs Billups and throws him to the ground and screams like a banshee that he'll kill him if he ever sees him eyeing his wife again."

"Was Wally arrested?"

"No. One of my deputies saw it happen and warned Wally to get his temper under control."

"Was Mr. Billups hurt?"

"Didn't seem to be. He's a troublemaker, no doubt about that. We've had a couple of calls from the rooming house where he lives. Some guy who also lives there keeps accusing Billups of stealing stuff from him." Mort laughed. "I don't imagine he's got a lot to steal anyway." He twirled an index finger at his temple. "Billups has got a screw loose, Mrs. F. Used to see a lot of his type in Manhattan. You know, they emptied out the mental wards and these people got nowhere to go, nothing to do. Other than that, I suppose he's all right. I just wish he'd find someplace else to hang out when it rains. Why do you ask?"

"Oh, just that he seems to be spending a lot of time on the road across from my house."

"You think he's stalking you?"

"I wouldn't go that far."

"Want me to warn him to stay away?"

"No, that's not necessary. I just thought I'd like to know more about him."

"He bothers you, just call and I'll have one of my men talk sense to him."

I got up to leave and thanked Mort for taking care of the letters.

"No problem." He looked as if he wanted to say more.

"Was there something else, Mort?"

"Say, Mrs. F, just thought you'd want to know, Maureen has come up with a couple of new recipes for sweet potato casserole she's been testing out on me. I've eaten sweet potatoes for dinner for two nights running while she experiments with ingredients. The kitchen looks like a bomb hit it. I'm not complaining—I like sweet potatoes as much as the next guy—but maybe if you two settled on what exactly it is she's going to make—"

"I'll give her a call."

"Would appreciate it. You know how excited she gets when it comes to cooking."

I sighed. I knew only too well what he meant.

Hubert Billups was not standing in front of my house when I returned home, thank goodness, but my relief was short-lived. When I tried to insert the house key in the lock, my front door slowly swung inward. I was certain I'd locked the door when I left. *Hadn't I?*

Slowly, I pressed the door open and peered into the hall and up the stairs before I entered the house.

"Hello!" I called out, thinking perhaps a neighbor

with the key had come in for some reason. "Anyone here?" There was no answer.

With a shiver, I closed the door behind me and listened carefully to hear anything out of the ordinary. The house was silent. Shaking my head, I went straight to the kitchen. Perhaps Seth, who considered my carving knife a useless relic, had stopped by to drop off his special carving knife that he'd insisted I use for the holiday. Or maybe Maureen put one of her sweet potato dishes in the refrigerator, or possibly my neighbor Tina Treyz came in to borrow a Bundt pan for her poppy-seed lemon cake. But the kitchen appeared undisturbed.

You're being foolish, Jessica, I told myself. *Hubert Billups has you spooked and now you're imagining things. You've been so distracted, you must have forgotten to lock the door.*

Even though I was convinced I was alone, I tiptoed to the study and stood in the doorway observing the layout of the room. The face of the monitor was black. I walked to the computer and nudged the mouse. The screen sprang to life and the page I'd been working on before I left lit up. There was no new copy. The sentence I'd been struggling with was still there in all its stilted glory. Why had I thought there might have been something else on the page? Had I imagined that someone—Hubert Billups—had broken into the house to leave me a message?

Everything seemed to be as I'd left it. I stared at the pile of mail, then gasped. Where were those anonymous messages with the cutout letters? They weren't on top of the other correspondence. I rushed across the room, my heart pounding, and flung open the drawers on my desk, frantically riffling through the papers in search of them. Not in the drawers, not under the manuscript box, not in the wastebasket, not at the bottom of the pile of mail. Then I sank into my chair. Of course they weren't here. I'd left them with Mort. I'd completely forgotten a visit I'd just returned from not ten minutes ago. I ran a hand through my hair, my fingers trembling.

This whole business is playing havoc with your brain, I told myself. *The next time Hubert Billups stations himself across the street from my house, I will find out exactly why he's there and what he wants.*

With the mystery of the missing letters solved, I should have been able to pick up my day where I'd left off and get back to work. But when I sat down at the computer, my hands were still shaky. *Tea,* I told myself, *a cup of red bush tea will settle me down.*

I jumped up and went to the kitchen, filled the kettle, set it on the stove, and returned to the computer, blindly rereading the awkward sentence as I strained to hear the sound of the kettle's whistle. Instead, I heard the floor above my head creak. My eyes flew to the ceiling, and the feeling of panic washed over me again. Was Billups upstairs? Was he poised behind a door, waiting for me to walk unawares into my bedroom?

Angry now, I strode to the base of the stairs, grabbed an umbrella from the coat tree, and stomped up the stairs, making as much noise as my shoes would allow. I gave the second floor a thorough search, whipping the shower curtain back—shades of a scene from the Hitchcock movie

Psycho—kneeling to inspect under the beds, poking the umbrella into the recesses of my closets. What did my search yield? Nothing! Except perhaps a determination to get out the vacuum cleaner at the nearest opportunity.

The keening wail of the teakettle brought me back to my senses, and I returned to the kitchen, grateful no one else had been at home with me to witness my mad hunt for a nonexistent intruder. Thinking about my reaction to a sound I'd heard frequently over the years—old houses often creak—I felt my cheeks color with embarrassment. *What could I have been thinking?*

I carried the tea into my study, sat in front of the computer, and contemplated the recent events of my life. Why would the presence of a harmless, maybe even pathetic drifter set off alarm bells? Why was I giving credence to some crank getting a kick out of sending me silly, nonsensical letters? So what if Maureen came up with a strange and possibly unpalatable dish for the holiday? So what if my guests were not all compatible? I would still make my book deadline if I had to stay up twenty-four hours a day to do it, I promised myself.

So what was causing all this consternation?

If I looked into my heart, I could see the truth. And the truth was that of all the events conspiring to create pressure in my life, the one I was most apprehensive about was the one I most eagerly looked forward to—George's visit.

Chapter Six

I was glad that Jed and I wouldn't be departing to pick up George until eleven the following day. I wanted to see what that morning's mail brought before leaving, whether there would be another delivery with a new pasted-on letter.

There was.

I opened it carefully and extracted the single sheet of white paper. Sure enough, a fifth letter had been added to the previous four—an orange *C*. The other letters on the page, *G*, *L*, *O*, and *T* were tiny compared to the *C*. Did that have special meaning? Was there a pointed message in highlighting it?

Like the third piece of mail, the one containing the letter *O*, this one had also been mailed from Cabot Cove.

Try as I might not to, my thoughts went straight to Hubert Billups. I know that wasn't fair. After all, I had no evidence that he had anything to do with the letters. And despite my paranoia of the previous day, he probably had nothing to do with my unlocked front door either. But the confluence of his strange behavior, and the arrival of the letters, made for a reasonable question as to whether they might be linked. Or so I told myself.

Jed was standing by the Cessna Skyhawk SP when my cabdriver, Nick, dropped me off at Cabot Cove Airport. It wasn't much of an airport compared to those in larger cities, but it had grown along with the town. There was talk of one of the airlines starting regular service there, but it hadn't happened yet.

I knew that if a commercial airline did begin offering flights, it would hurt Jed's business. He's always been philosophical about that possibility and laughs it off, but he had to be concerned about it at some level. He'd recently purchased the plane that we were flying that day, and although he'd bought it used, I knew that it stretched his finances. It's a lovely four-seat single-engine airplane, and Jed had added state-of-the-art electronic gear and avionics to bring it up-to-date. Of course, what was most important was his piloting skill honed by thousands of hours in large commercial jet aircraft, preceded by five years as a military pilot. He's a capable, meticulous professional, and I've never had a moment's apprehension flying with him.

"All gassed up and ready to go?" I asked as Nick drove away.

"Yes, ma'am," Jed replied.

If a film director were to contact Central Casting for

the quintessential pilot, Jed would fit the bill. His face is square, his jaw strong. He's stocky and keeps himself fit. The multitude of lines around his eyes and on his forehead testifies to all his hours in a cockpit squinting into the sun. He hadn't lost a single strand of his salt-and-pepper hair despite being in his midfifties. He wore what he usually did when ferrying people in one of his aircraft: jeans, a blue button-down shirt, and a tan vest of the type worn by photographers, which as he proudly pointed out had twenty-six pockets: "My answer to a woman's purse. I can live for a week on what I carry in these pockets."

After a preflight walk around, we climbed into the plane. Jed had me take the left-hand seat because I'd be doing the actual flying, at least until we entered the crowded sky around Boston. That's when things get busy and complicated with all the necessary communications with air-traffic control. But on a recent flight to Boston, Jed had insisted that I pilot the plane all the way, with him handling the radio chatter: "Might as well get used to it," he explained. At the time, I'd been as nervous as a cat up a tree when we entered the city's airspace, but managed to land with only one or two hops, and Jed had flashed me the okay sign when we drew to a stop in the airport's designated area for small craft. Today, if Jed gave me the same freedom, I hoped to pull off a no-hop landing.

We took off. I looked down as my beloved Cabot Cove slipped away, becoming smaller and smaller the higher we climbed. Jed dialed in the receiver for the global-positioning satellite; we'd fly on autopilot right up until approaching Boston's Logan Airport. It was a lovely day to fly, crisp and cool, the sky a cobalt blue with only a rare wispy white cloud far above us. Once we reached our desired cruising altitude, we sat back and allowed the autopilot to guide us to our destination.

"Understand you're havin' a desperate time with that book of yours," he commented. "Can't make any headway, the way I hear it."

"And where did you pick up that piece of news, Jed?"

"Somewhere in town."

"Well," I said, "the rumor is true, but I'll figure out a way to finish it. It's too important not to."

"You're probably just excited about seeing your Scottish beau."

I laughed. "I am excited to see him, but I wouldn't call George 'my beau.' We're close friends, that's all."

He nodded that he agreed, although the wry smile on his rugged face said something else.

"He staying with you?" he asked.

I shook my head. "No. Seth Hazlitt has agreed to put him up."

"How'd you wrangle that?"

"George coming for Thanksgiving was a last-minute decision. All the hotels and B-and-Bs were booked. I asked Seth, and he said yes."

"Doc's a good man, but you already know that. He give you that package he picked up yet?"

"What package is that?"

"Aw, now, mebbe I shouldn't have said anything."

"But you already have," I said.

"Well, I flew Doc up to Portland last week. I was going

up there anyway to pick up some parts and he hitched a ride with me. He said flying with me would save on having it shipped." Jed chuckled. "You know Doc. He's a frugal sort of man. The way he put it, I thought you asked him to do it."

"No, I didn't ask him to get anything for me."

"Well, now I think of it, mebbe he said 'pick *out* something for you.' Hope I didn't spoil the surprise."

"What sort of package are we talking about?"

"Don't know really. It was pretty big and wrapped real neat in brown paper. He didn't hold me up much, just an hour. Of course, he had to grab a taxi, which must have cost more than any shipping charges. He was back to the airport lickety-split and I flew him home to Cabot Cove."

"Did he go to a store?"

"Haven't the foggiest, Jessica. I'm just the pilot. He didn't say anything to you?"

"No. He usually tells me if he's going to Portland for something, but he never said a word. I wonder why."

"It was sort of last-minute. I was in seeing him for a backache—it's been acting up lately—and mentioned I was heading for Portland that afternoon. Just sort of happened that he came with me. I was happy to do it. Doc's done me plenty of favors over the years."

Jed shook his head and busied himself adjusting our trim tabs to keep the plane in perfect balance. I didn't bring the subject up again even though it floated in and out of my mind for the duration of the flight. Had Seth bought me a gift? If so, why? It wasn't near my birthday, and besides, we didn't exchange birthday gifts. It was a little early for Christmas. I hadn't even starting thinking about *that* holiday. Please, let me get Thanksgiving under my belt before hearing jingle bells ring. Of course, that plea falls on deaf ears these days with merchants launching their holiday advertising right after back-to-school sales.

The clear skies over Cabot Cove had been replaced by a lower ceiling over Boston, gray clouds moving in from the southwest. I piloted the Cessna on approach to the airport, and listened on my headphones. Jed maintained communication with the various FAA controllers, and I followed their instructions. I admit that my palms became damp as I aligned the plane with the active runway at Logan and guided it down—to a picture-perfect landing. We taxied to an area of the field where private planes were directed and parked near the operations building.

"He's coming in on Virgin Atlantic?" Jed asked as he shut down the engine.

"Right." I checked my watch. George's plane wasn't due in for another forty-five minutes. Of course, a scheduled arrival time depended upon the sort of headwinds the flight encountered on its way across the Atlantic. Westbound flights were sometimes delayed because of prevailing winds that generally blew from west to east; eastbound flights often arrived early because they have that same wind at their backs. Because of that, virtually every speed record is set by aircraft flying from west to east.

Signature Flight Support at the general aviation facility on the north end of the airport provided us with a shuttle to Terminal E from which Virgin Atlantic operates. A glance at the arrivals board indicated that George's flight was right on schedule, which still gave us enough time to grab a quick lunch and coffee at Bruegger's. I paid the check and we strolled down to the arrivals area outside security.

The secrecy surrounding Seth's shopping expedition lingered in my mind during lunch, but faded from my consciousness as I anxiously scanned the incoming passengers in search of George. Eventually he emerged, looking as handsome and debonair as ever in his classic heather tweed jacket with leather patches on the elbows, pressed gray slacks, tan button-down shirt and maroon paisley tie, and ankle-high leather boots shined to a dazzling glow. He spotted me, waved, and picked up his pace.

"My goodness, what a sight for these sore eyes," he said, placing his hands on my arms and looking into my eyes. He pulled me to him, gave me a quick buss on the cheek, then turned to Jed. "Aha," he said, "the man who delivered Jessica safely, and will do the same for us on the way home."

"Inspector," Jed said, shaking hands. "Good to see you again."

"Good flight?" I asked.

"Splendid, as usual. Mr. Branson certainly knows how to run a top-notch airline."

"Let's head back," Jed said. "There's some nasty weather in the forecast."

The flight back to Cabot Cove was as smooth as it had been to Boston. I would have preferred that George sit up front with Jed, but Jed insisted that I take advantage of the trip to build up more piloting time. George sat in one of two rear seats and peppered Jed with questions about flying and the dials in the cockpit. George had flown once before with me at the controls, a leisurely sightseeing flight that showed him Cabot Cove and its environs from the air. I made another smooth landing, which elicited applause from the rear seat. Jed instructed a young man, who helped him out in return for free flying lessons, to call a cab for us, and a half hour later we walked through the door of my house. George dropped his suitcase in the foyer and followed me into the kitchen.

"I feel very much at home here," he said.

"I want you to feel that way. Cold drink? Lemonade? Coke? Something stronger?"

"I wouldn't mind a wee dram of whiskey, if you have it."

"Coming right up."

We settled in my den with his drink—I opted for lemonade—and caught up on our respective lives. I've always been fascinated at his tales of the crimes and criminals he's encountered, and even more so now that he was a ranking member of Scotland Yard's elite antiterrorism unit. We talked for an hour, easy conversation that testified to the comfortable relationship we'd developed. I had been waiting for an opportunity to mention the series of strange letters I'd been receiving, and when he inquired about what was new in my life, I showed him the latest one, which had arrived that morning. He studied it carefully. The gravity with which he addressed it, and his concern over the fact that there were others, was written all over his face. I recounted what the previous ones had contained. I told him that I'd given the others to Mort Metzger, which George thought was a prudent decision.

He handed the letter back to me and said, "I know it's easy to dismiss these as nothing more than some silly prank, Jessica, but I believe they deserve serious consideration."

"You really think so?"

"I think you know me well enough to realize that I wouldn't say such a thing if I didn't mean it. I don't know what these pasted letters represent, but someone is sending you a message, and that in itself should be heeded."

"Maybe the crime lab will come up with someone's prints."

"A possibility," George said. He repeated aloud the letters that had arrived to date—"*G*, *L*, an *O*, a *T*, and now a *C*. Do you think, Jessica, that this is the end of the letters?"

"I hadn't thought about that," I said. "It could be. Tomorrow is Sunday, so we have no mail delivery. We'll have to wait until Monday to see if there are any more."

"We have people at the Yard who specialize in deciphering obscure codes. Of course, your FBI is good at that, too. Have you contacted them?"

"No. I didn't think it warranted getting the FBI involved. There haven't been any direct threats."

"Well, no need to create a kerfuffle just yet. Let's keep it in your pocket for the future." George yawned.

I smiled. "You must be exhausted with the time change and all. I think it's time I delivered you to Seth's house."

Mentioning his name reminded me of Seth's errand in Portland. That he hadn't said anything was curious, but of course he was allowed his own secrets. We all were, hard as that was to accomplish in Cabot Cove.

"I must look like I came home with the milk," George said, rising. "I'm knackered. I hate to end this conversation. We see so little of each other as it is, and I relish every moment."

"I do too, George, but I want you to get settled in for a good night's sleep. I'll call Seth to tell him we're on our way, and then I'll call a cab."

To my surprise, Seth said he would swing by to pick George up. He arrived fifteen minutes later. The men greeted each other warmly, and we walked together to Seth's car, where George deposited his suitcase in the trunk.

"What's the schedule tomorrow?" George asked. "Will I have time to hire a car? I don't want to keep badgering my generous host here."

"Not really a problem," Seth said gallantly. But I thought renting a car would be a good idea. I didn't have an extra bicycle. I didn't even know if George knew how to ride one, although I assumed he did. A car would allow us to get around easily without inconveniencing a friend or relying on local cab service. I hoped George would be okay driving on the "wrong" side of the road for him.

"We should have plenty of time," I said. "I thought it would be nice to just hang out, as the teenagers like to say. A pancake breakfast at church, and then a walk around town. There's a rental agency near the docks."

"Sounds good to me," George said.

"I brought in some dinner for George and me," Seth

said. "Nothing special, already cooked. Just needs to be heated up. Join us, Jessica? I bought plenty."

"I'm tempted," I said, "but I'll pass. I'll let you gentlemen become reacquainted over your dinner, and George, I'm sure, will want to head to bed early."

Although it was somewhat awkward in front of Seth, George and I embraced before he climbed into the front passenger seat, and Seth got behind the wheel.

"I'll drop Inspector Sutherland here at eight, Jessica. That too early for you?"

"Not if it isn't for you and George. See you then."

I watched them drive away and a sadness descended upon me. I hadn't wanted the evening to end, and briefly regretted not taking up Seth's invitation. But it was best for Seth and George to have time together alone. George was going to be a houseguest for a week, and I wanted them to establish a good relationship. They were both intelligent, thoughtful men who would have much to discuss. My presence would only interfere with their "man talk."

I returned to the house and sat in my study reading through chapters I'd already written in the hope that it would spur some creativity. It didn't. I contented myself with leftovers for dinner, changed into my nightclothes, and went back to reading a novel I'd started earlier that week. Maybe good writing by another author would get my own literary juices flowing. I enjoyed the novel and finished it a little before ten when I got up sleepily from my recliner, brushed my teeth, and climbed into bed.

It promised to be a wonderful Thanksgiving week

with George here to be part of it. That reality brought a smile to my lips as all other thoughts—letters from some crazy person, Hubert Billups's odd behavior, and my stalled novel—floated into the ether and sleep descended upon me.

Chapter Seven

When I'd gone to bed, the sky put the lie to Jed Richardson's forecast of nasty weather. It was overcast, but breaks in the clouds allowed stars to twinkle through. As it turned out, however, he was right. It just took longer for the storm to arrive than he'd anticipated. It erupted at three o'clock Sunday morning. Winds rattled the house, and torrents of rain poured down. It passed quickly, but lingered long enough to awaken me. I tried to get back to sleep but finally gave up at five.

I made a pot of tea, and read the morning papers, which had been left at my door until the sun came up over the eastern horizon, painting the clouds a vibrant orange. I usually enjoy early mornings, although I would have preferred to sleep a little longer this day. If sunrise was any indication of what the weather would be like, we were in store for what Seth would term "a fat day," plenty of sunshine in which to enjoy my walk with George.

Showered and dressed long before Seth pulled up in front of the house, I was anxious to ascertain the sort of evening they'd spent together. Had it been pleasant and easygoing? I hoped so. I looked for signs in Seth's expression. From what I could see, he seemed in good humor. I intended to ask him about his secretive trip to Portland, but that would have to wait until we enjoyed some private time together.

"What did you two do in my absence?" I asked when George got out of the car and held the door for me.

"Seth gave me a tour of his surgery," he said. He climbed into the backseat and added, "or rather 'doctor's offices' I believe is the correct term here."

"For a while there, I wasn't certain we were speaking the same language," Seth said with a chuckle as he backed from the driveway. "Served him one of Charlene Sassi's pies for dessert and he thanked me for the 'pudding.' And later he wondered if I played 'draughts.' "

"Drafts?"

"That's checkers."

Language differences aside, judging from the demeanor of both men, their time in each other's company had been positive. Spirits were high, and they took turns recounting what they'd discussed during their meal.

"Of course," George said, "I didn't last long after dinner."

"I didn't know whether he was tired from the trip, or was bored with the conversation," Seth said.

"I assure you it wasn't boredom," George said quickly

through a chuckle. "I slept like a baby. It's a lovely flat, Seth, and I hope you know how much I appreciate you taking in this weary traveler."

"My pleasure," Seth said, sounding as though he meant it. "George was telling me about the psychological training Scotland Yard offers. They're teaching their staff how to judge whether or not someone is lying."

"How interesting," I said. "Is it usually accurate?"

"Spot on," George said. "It requires careful observation, but I'd say it's close to infallible, although there are always exceptions. If the criminal element know the same signals we do, they can always find ways to outsmart the system."

"Still, the information could come in handy in my practice. Patients are not always straightforward with their doctors."

"Did he teach you?" I asked Seth.

"A few tips."

"I'd love it if you'd teach me, too," I told George. "I can use it in one of my novels."

"Happy to."

Seth dropped us at the church, where after the service we enjoyed a pancake breakfast served up by members of the congregation.

"I'm ready for that walk," George said as we stepped outside, "and let's make it a brisk one. I never should have had that last pancake."

We set off for downtown, saying little and enjoying the bracing fresh air touched with the briny aroma of the waters that define much of Cabot Cove. As usually happens when I walk through town, I ran into friends who want to stop and chat. I was delighted to introduce George to those who hadn't met him during his previous visit to Cabot Cove. Of course, I knew that our appearance together was going to spur on the gossips, who most likely would conjure up a closer relationship between us than was the case, but I really didn't care. Rumors have a way of developing legs, as they say, and there's nothing you can do to dissuade people once they've bought into them.

We stopped at the car rental agency downtown, and George arranged to pick up a vehicle later that morning. We wandered to the docks and watched the boats come and go, commercial fishermen hoping for a plentiful catch, and some die-hard recreational boaters who wouldn't put their crafts up in dry dock until the first snow.

"What a charming place this is, Jessica," George said after lighting his pipe. The aroma reached me and caused me to smile. My late husband, Frank, smoked a pipe on occasion and I've always enjoyed the aroma of pipe tobacco.

"Living here as I do, it's easy to forget how wonderful it is," I said. "I'm afraid I sometimes take it for granted. It takes a visitor from out of town to remind me of its charm."

"It's so—it's so quintessentially American," he said.

"Just a slice of America," I said, "but a precious one."

As we looked out over the water, I turned to allow the sun to play on my face. As I did, I saw Hubert Billups standing at the far end of the dock. George had rested his hand on my arm and felt me tense. "Something wrong?" he asked.

"No, it's just that—"

George glanced in the direction I'd been looking. "Is it that bloke?" he asked. "The one who looks like a tramp?"

"Yes. Well, no. He's not a tramp. He lives in a rooming house near one of our industrial parks. He's new in town. His name is Billups. Hubert Billups. He seems to spend a great deal of time watching me."

"Watching you?" George scowled in Billups's direction. "Has he threatened you?"

"No. Never. I haven't even spoken with him," I said, "but he has been spending a lot of time on the road across from my house."

"That's a bit sticky."

"Probably not," I said. "He's harmless enough."

"How do you know that?"

"I don't know. I—"

"Is your Sheriff Metzger aware of this?"

"Yes. I mentioned it to him."

"And?"

"He said he'll send one of his officers to speak with him if he causes me any trouble."

"I'm not persuaded we want to wait until he causes trouble."

"I don't want to create problems for someone unnecessarily," I said. "I know when to call for help." I smiled up at him. "I've been taking care of myself for a long time."

"So you have," George replied, looping an arm around my shoulder. He focused his attention on the water and boats again, taking contemplative puffs on his pipe.

"Let's continue our walk," I suggested.

We were leaving the dock when we bumped into my new neighbor.

"Hello, Linda," I said.

She seemed in a rush but stopped to return my greeting.

"I'd like you to meet my friend, George Sutherland," I said. "He's with Scotland Yard. He's visiting Cabot Cove for the holiday."

"Oh. That's nice," Linda said, but she didn't smile.

"A pleasure meeting another of Jessica's friends," George said.

"We're not. I mean we just moved here recently," Linda said. "I'd better get home. Victor is waiting for me."

She scurried off, causing George to laugh and ask, "Is she always in such a rush?"

"It seems that way. I don't know her that well. She and her husband bought a house down the road from me a few months ago. I invited them to join us for the holiday dinner on Thursday."

"How large a gathering will it be?"

"Twelve."

"And you're doing all the cooking?"

"Not all of it. Linda is going to bring a pie, and Sheriff Metzger's wife, Maureen, is helping."

"Nice lady. I remember her from when you and your friends visited my family homestead in Wick."

"And a wonderful visit it was, I might add."

"A shame that a murder took place while you were there. You seem to have a penchant for being where murders occur."

"Don't remind me," I said, laughing. "Come on, let's go pick up your car. I think we've walked off those pancakes."

"I'm so glad you and Seth had a nice evening together," I commented as we settled at my kitchen table with steaming mugs of black coffee in front of us.

"He's a fine gentleman, Jessica. He's certainly fond of you."

"And I of him."

"He seems quite concerned about you."

"Oh? What's he concerned about?"

"Me, I suspect."

It took a second for me to fathom what was behind the statement. "You mean he's afraid that you and I might run off together?"

"He never said that in so many words, but it's obvious that it's behind his concerns."

"Oh, dear," I said, sitting back and shaking my head. "Did you say anything to him on that subject?"

He took a moment before saying, "I was tempted to but decided it was not my place to reassure him."

"If you had said something, what would it have been?" I asked.

He paused again before saying, "A good question, Jessica. Had I been honest, I would have said that the vision of us running off and marrying is, indeed, a pleasant one to contemplate." He smiled. "But you already knew what my answer would be."

I nodded.

"Of course," he added, "that doesn't necessarily reflect

what your answer would be—should you be asked, of course."

"The truth is, George, it's a pleasant contemplation for me, too. But we've had this conversation before."

He held up a hand. "I'm not trying to raise it again, Jessica. But you asked."

"And you answered honestly."

"I've accepted the conclusion we've come to, that we are both busy, independent people, who while we obviously have feelings for each other have decided to leave things the way they are in our respective lives, at least for the near future." A warm smile crossed his lips. "But—you did ask."

"I know." I placed my hand on his on the table. "Maybe one day, George, I'll see things differently, but for now I just want to enjoy your company in the time you have here."

"In other words, as your old adage sums it up, 'If it isn't broken, don't change a thing.' "

"Actually, the saying is: 'If it *ain't* broke, don't fix it.' "

"I know, but Brits always like to correct American English."

We both laughed, and the subject changed.

"Seth said you taught him a few tricks about how to tell when someone is lying," I said after I'd set out sandwiches for our lunch. We'd decided not to schedule any activities for the afternoon to allow George's system to catch up to Cabot Cove time.

"Yes, it's been quite an education delving into a liar's psyche."

"Tell me one of the rules. Are we talking about body language, or the way someone says something?"

"Bits of both, actually. I'll give you an easy one. Be suspicious when someone prefaces what he is saying with an assurance that he's about to tell the truth. People who lie often begin with statements like, 'The truth is,' or, 'I'll be honest with you.' When you hear that, your antennae should go up. He's either colored the truth already, or is preparing to. Or he may not answer your question directly; he changes the subject altogether."

"What else?"

"Well, body language can be very revealing. One's eyes may wander to the left when one is making up a story."

"Do you think that happens to me when I'm writing?"

"It very well may."

"I'll try to be aware of that when I work on my book. Tell me more."

"It all has to do with the discomfort most people feel telling an untruth. Liars may speak quickly, chatter as it were, touch their face, scratch behind an ear, cover their mouth when they're not telling the truth. And they often hide their hands."

"It all sounds reasonable," I said, "but that can't be foolproof."

"No, of course not, but when combined with other signs, a faithful picture emerges. Of course, a professional criminal or a pathological liar, one aware of these indicators, can control his movements and defeat the system. For example—"

The ringing phone ended my lesson. It was Seth reminding me that he'd made dinner reservations for us at a restaurant downtown. Joining us would be Mort and Maureen Metzger.

I noticed that George had become sleepy, his circadian rhythms out of whack after his long flight from London. I put on the TV for him, where a soccer game was under way—"football" in England—and left him to relax while I took another stab at my novel. It went well, and I breathed a sigh of relief as a scene that had proved to be particularly nettlesome began to take shape. I peeked in on George a few times and saw that he'd dozed off in the recliner. I smiled. It was so good to have him there. I wanted it to be a special week for him, to show off Cabot Cove and our annual Thanksgiving holiday to their best advantage, and made a mental pledge to avoid further discussions of our relationship.

He awoke long after the soccer match had ended and apologized for rudely falling asleep.

"Not at all," I said. "When you're tired, you should sleep. Now you'll have to excuse me for a little while. I have to get ready for dinner. I won't be long."

"Take your time. I'll be fine. I'm a dab hand at waiting."

When I returned from my bedroom, George was standing at the window. He turned and smiled. "You are very nicely togged up, if I may say so," he said.

"You may," I said, joining him at the window and peering outside to see what he'd been looking at—Hubert Billups.

"Has he been there long?" I asked.

"I don't know. I just started watching him."

Perhaps he became aware that we were observing him, because Billups shrugged and walked away in the direction of town, looking over his shoulder once or twice.

"I should go out and have a word with the chap," George said.

"Please don't," I said.

"You may be taking him too lightly," George said as Billups disappeared from view.

"We can discuss that later," I said. "You're about to get another chance to drive on the right side of the road."

"I didn't fare too badly this morning."

"Well, you didn't run anyone down," I said, straightening his collar.

George's hand settled over mine. "I like when you look after me, lass. Is the tie all right?"

"Perfect." I smiled up at him. "Let's go. We don't want to be late for dinner."

We caught sight of Billups on the road, and as we drove past him George turned to look back through the rear window.

"Please," I said, "let's ignore him. I don't want to let him spoil a wonderful evening."

I meant what I'd said, although I have to admit that Billups remained on my mind throughout dinner. Maybe George was right. Maybe I *was* taking Billups too lightly, although I was determined not to frighten myself silly worrying about him.

Still, later that night, after George followed Seth's car home, I found myself taking safety measures that were foreign to me. I've always considered Cabot Cove a safe place to live, and while I took reasonable precautions, I'd seldom taken pains to ensure that all my windows and doors were securely fastened, or deliberately left lights on in selected rooms.

But I did this night, and begrudged the need to do so.

Chapter Eight

George drove to my house early the next morning, Monday, and we had breakfast in the kitchen.

"Sleep well?" I asked.

"Yes, I did, after the good doctor and I sat up rather late solving the world's problems."

"The world owes you a debt of gratitude."

"Unfortunately, we didn't come up with any good answers. Seth is a fine man, Jessica. He has a full slate of patients today. I thought it best to absent myself. Does he ever talk of retiring?"

"All the time, but thank goodness he never gets around to it. His patients will be terribly disappointed when, and if, he does."

George insisted that I go about my usual morning routine and let him fend for himself. The day's newspapers had arrived—the *Cabot Cove Gazette*, *New York Times*,

Wall Street Journal, and *Portland Press Herald*—and he settled in the living room with them, commenting as he did, "You're obviously well read, Jessica."

"Some of my friends think I overdo it with all the papers I receive, but I'm afraid I'm addicted to them."

"A healthy addiction in any case," he said.

"It's a shame more young people don't read a newspaper every day," I said. "News reports on television or the Internet only pick up the highlights. Newspapers cover such a wide range. I've generated some wonderful story ideas for my novels from the papers."

I spent the morning going over Thursday's menu, making a grocery list of what remained to be purchased, and cleaning out the refrigerator to make room for the turkey, which was to be delivered the next day. I called Maureen Metzger and we agreed that she would make a sweet potato dish, but I left the form and the specific ingredients to her. My desire to have George experience an authentic New England Thanksgiving dinner notwithstanding, I felt I shouldn't discourage Maureen's creativity in the kitchen. She was eager to make a contribution, and despite my doubts about her culinary skills—honed I might add by several remarkable, if not entirely edible, dinners at her house—I was grateful for her willingness to help. If her concoction was not to everyone's taste, well then there would be plenty of other dishes for my guests to sample. Her friendship was more important than perfection in the kitchen.

Maureen was not the only guest contributing to the meal. Linda was bringing a pumpkin pie, and Susan

Shevlin, the mayor's wife, had volunteered to make clam chowder. The Copeland sisters, Kathy and Willie, were renowned for their cranberry relish, an old family recipe, two jars of which were already in my refrigerator, delivered by Kathy more than a week ago.

I had been baking for almost a month, which had taken its toll on the progress of my book. But my freezer already held pumpkin and cranberry breads, Parker House rolls, the makings of succotash, and both pecan and apple pies. I planned to set the table on Wednesday and would rope George into helping. For now, he was welcome to relax, at least this morning.

I managed to fit in an hour at the computer, getting up from the desk only when I heard the arrival of Newt, the mailman. I greeted him and accepted the pile of mail he handed me. On top was another letter-sized envelope with my name and address neatly printed.

George joined me at the door, and I introduced the men.

"I never met a real live Scotland Yard inspector," Newt said.

"And I've never met a real live Cabot Cove postie," George replied. "It's an honor, sir."

Once inside, George asked whether yet another strange letter had arrived.

"I'm afraid so," I said, handing him the envelope.

We went to the living room, where George carefully examined it. "Do you have a magnifying glass?"

"I do." I ran to get the lens and had to smile when I returned. There was George, frowning down at the suspect envelope, his unlit pipe clenched in his teeth. He reminded me of classic depictions of Sherlock Holmes.

"Shall I?" he asked.

"Go ahead," I said.

He slid his thumb under the flap and opened the letter; inside was the ubiquitous single sheet of paper. Pasted on it in various sizes and colors were the letters *G, L, O, T, C,* and *O.*

"The *O* is larger than the others," I commented, "the way the *C* was in the previous one."

"So I see," he said. He picked up the envelope again and examined the postmark with the magnifier. "Pennsylvania," he muttered through clenched teeth. "Anyone you know in that state capable of such a thing?"

"I don't know anyone anywhere who would engage in this sort of nonsense."

"Whoever it is obviously intends to continue until—"

"Until when?"

"Until he runs out of letters to use, or becomes tired of the game."

"It can't come soon enough."

"Your Sheriff Metzger seems sufficiently concerned about these," George said. "Frankly, I don't think his lab chaps will turn up usable fingerprints, but even if they do, whoever is sending the letters might not have his or her prints on file. In the meantime, my fearless Jessica, I suggest you begin to take some precautions."

"I have been," I said. "Last night, I double-checked every door and window, and left lights on around the house."

"Because of the letters?"

"No. Actually. I came home a few days ago and found my front door ajar."

"Don't you usually lock it before leaving?"

"I do, and I was certain I had, but it's possible I didn't. Under normal circumstances, it wouldn't have been terribly important. But I'd seen Mr. Billups across the street and—"

"You thought he might have broken in."

"It crossed my mind, but I have no evidence of it. Chances are I simply forgot to lock the door in my haste, or thought I had locked it but neglected to check."

George cocked his head and narrowed his eyes. "Here you are receiving a strange series of letters. There's some numpty across the road, possibly deranged, observing you day after day. And now the fastidious Jessica Fletcher returns home to find her door open. I'd say you have every reason to be concerned, *very* concerned."

"George, I—"

"Please, Jessica, listen to me. From this moment forward I want you to be on your guard, alert to everything and everyone around you. I know I can't demand this of you, but were I you, I would not ride my bicycle into town until all this is resolved. Doors must be firmly locked at all times, and—"

"You sound like Seth," I said with what passed for a laugh, uncomfortable with what he was saying although I knew he was making sense. "I didn't realize you'd spoken with Mort about the letters."

"Briefly, when you and his wife left us at the table for a few minutes. I must say that Dr. Hazlitt was surprised at hearing about them. He raised the topic again last night at his house."

"Oh, dear," I said, "you'll have all the back-fence gossips talking about it and worrying about me. We have an extremely active rumor mill here in Cabot Cove."

"Good," George said. "The more who know, the better—plenty of people to look out for you."

I didn't agree, but knew his intentions were good.

I settled in next to him on the couch and we shared the newspapers until it was time to head downtown to attend a dress rehearsal of the Thanksgiving pageant, which would be performed on Wednesday, Thanksgiving Eve. George drove, quite skillfully I should add, and we pulled up in front of the town hall, where the performance would take place. I noticed as I was getting out of the rental car that Willie Copeland and Archer Franklin were on their way inside. I debated warning George that Mr. Franklin might prove to be overbearing, but decided not to prejudice his opinion of the man. Maybe my initial introduction to Archer was an aberration, although Mara's comments about him rendered that possibility unlikely. I also realized that I was attempting to shield George from less-than-pleasant conversations during his abbreviated stay. He certainly didn't need such protection from me.

Once we stepped into the building, we were surrounded by a bevy of my friends, all wanting an introduction to George. Was it because he was a highly decorated Scotland Yard inspector, or because he was rumored to be my romantic interest? In any case, he was his usual charming, self-effacing self, and the look on some of my women friends' faces was pure adoration.

As the cast walked in and out in preparation for the show, Willie Copeland and Archer Franklin approached.

"I've heard a lot about you, Inspector," Franklin said.

I didn't know how that might have come about; he hadn't heard anything from me.

"A pleasure," George said after they'd shaken hands.

"I consider myself a bit of an Anglophile," Franklin said. He laughed. "Actually, more than a bit."

"Is that so?" George said. "How flattering."

"Yes," Franklin continued. "I suppose you could also say I'm a history buff."

"I'm fond of history, myself," George replied.

"So," Franklin said, "you've come to see how we celebrate Thanksgiving, hey?"

"Yes. I've heard so much about it and its—and its history. I'm delighted to share this special day with Jessica and her friends."

"Shame you don't have a similar holiday in England," Franklin said smugly.

"Well," George said, "we didn't have Pilgrims arriving in the U.K. with Indians to welcome them. Of course, we do have our own November holiday, but it's a bit different from your Thanksgiving, although it does have traditional foods."

"What holiday is that?" Franklin asked.

"Bonfire Night, or Guy Fawkes Night. It's like a combination of your Halloween and Independence Day. We set off fireworks, and leading up to it children play tricks and make stuffed figures of Guy Fawkes to throw on the bonfires."

The puzzled expression on Franklin's face testified to his lack of familiarity with George's reference. Then his face brightened. "Oh, right, Guy Fukes. He was that British terrorist who wanted to take over the country."

"Not quite," George corrected. "Actually, Mr. Fawkes was a Catholic chap who led a group that tried to blow up all of Parliament and King James the First because they were angry at what they perceived as bigotry against Catholics."

"I was there once on Guy Fawkes day," I said. "Children approached me, saying, 'Penny for the Guy?' Of course, they were looking for more than a penny with which to buy fireworks to celebrate the event."

"So those bonfires celebrate that Fukes was burned at the stake, huh?" Franklin asked, repeating his mispronunciation of the name.

"Not precisely," George said casually. "He was imprisoned, tortured on the rack, and hanged."

"Sounds like it was too good for him," said Franklin. "We're all too soft on people like that, giving them all sorts of rights and such. String 'em all up is what I say."

"As a matter of fact," George countered, "Mr. Fawkes had a point. There *was* anti-Catholic bias. Still is. To this day, under our laws a Catholic cannot be the monarch."

"Yes, I knew that," Franklin said. It was obvious to all that he hadn't.

"Actually, we do share Halloween with you chaps here in the States," George said as a parting comment. "It's becoming quite a popular day back home, much to the delight of children. They gorge themselves on candy on October thirty-first *and* rake in money on November fifth. Now you must excuse us, Mr. Franklin. I believe they're about to start."

As we walked away, George said, "Opinionated chap, isn't he?"

"I'm afraid we're in for more of his opinions on Thursday. Wilimena asked if she could bring him to dinner, and I didn't say no."

"Of course you didn't," George said. "Might be fun, hearing more about Guy 'Fukes' from the gentleman."

We both laughed and settled in folding chairs to watch the dress rehearsal.

That evening, we were dinner guests at Mayor and Susan Shevlin's home. Seth Hazlitt, Tim and Ellen Purdy (Tim is Cabot Cove's historian, and Ellen wins every statewide quilting competition), and Deputy Mayor Gus Westerholm and his wife, Birgitta, who was active in virtually every civic and charity organization in the town, were the other guests.

Gus brought up Archer Franklin during dessert. "Looks like you might have a serious challenge next year, Jim," he said to our mayor. "This new fellow, Franklin, is going around town claiming he intends to run for your seat."

"He's entitled to do that," Jim replied.

"He says he's got plenty of money to fund a campaign," Tim Purdy said.

"And he's entitled to spend it any way he wishes," Shevlin said.

This led to a spirited discussion about money in politics, and eventually to a comparison between the British and American political systems. By the time we'd exhausted that topic, it was almost midnight, a series of yawns around the table testifying to the hour.

George dropped me at the house.

"Can you find your way back to Seth's house?" I asked.

"I think so. My sense of direction is pretty sound. Come, I'll see you safely inside."

I was about to protest the need to accompany me but thought better of it. Recent events had set me on edge, and I wasn't especially keen on entering alone at that late hour. I hated to be fearful of walking into my own home at any hour of the day or night, but my pragmatic sense took over. Besides, it meant prolonging my time with George. I became acutely aware during dinner that his visit with me was fleeting.

All was quiet inside.

"A nightcap?" I asked

"Tempting," he said, "but I think it's time we both headed for bed." The double-entendre meaning of the statement wasn't lost on either of us, but we said nothing.

"A busy day tomorrow?" he asked.

"I'm afraid so. The main event is our annual Thanksgiving dinner served to our less fortunate citizens. It starts at four, although I have to be there a few hours early to help with preparations."

"Can you use an extra hand? Sounds like something I'd like to be involved with."

"Would you? I wouldn't expect that—"

He shook his head. "I can't think of anything I'd rather do than help provide a fitting Thanksgiving dinner for some poor persons, working side by side with a very special lady."

"You're pretty special yourself," I said

"Not only that. I can carve a decent turkey," he said. "I paid my way through school working at a carvery—that's a restaurant that specializes in meats."

"And you'd be wonderful, no doubt, but that's my job this year. In fact, Seth has loaned me his special carving knife for the occasion."

"Then I'll be content to do whatever is asked of me."

I walked him to the door, where we kissed good night. I watched him get into the car and start the engine. He looked back at me, and for a moment I thought he was about to get out and accept my offer of a nightcap. He didn't. He blew me a kiss and drove off.

I closed the door, leaned against it, and smiled. Despite all the recent stresses and strains, I felt truly happy.

Chapter Nine

GLOTCOY.

"What can it possibly mean?" I asked George the next morning.

"I have no idea, Jessica. I wish I did."

We'd spent an exasperating hour coming up with every possible message that the letters contained in that day's mail might represent. None of them made sense.

"It has a Boston postmark," I said.

"Chances are," he said, "these letters have been created by someone right here in Cabot Cove. This warped individual sends them to friends in other cities for mailing in order to throw you off the track."

"All right," I said, "but who would go to such elaborate means of hiding their true origins—and why?"

"Unfortunately, those are questions to which neither of us has an answer."

"Sheriff Metzger hasn't been able to help, either," I said, folding my arms and hunching forward to relieve the tension in my back.

Mort had called bright and early to report that the state crime lab had come up a cropper with fingerprints. They'd managed to detect a tiny fragment on two of the envelopes, but not enough from which to lift a traceable print.

George rose and came around behind my chair. He placed his hands on my shoulders and pressed his thumbs into the tight muscles of my back. Then he leaned down and whispered in my ear, "Do you know what I'd like to do?" he said.

"What's that?"

"I'd like to go motoring."

"You would? To where?"

He straightened but kept kneading my sore shoulders. "Anywhere. Just a pleasant drive, the two of us."

"Oh, George, I'd love to, but there's so much to do before the holiday. And we have—"

He shifted one hand from my shoulder to my neck, using his fingers to rub away the stiffness. "Show me a bit of the lovely countryside surrounding Cabot Cove, or let's stop at that lake for which you serve on a—was it a committee?"

"A commission," I said, enjoying the massage.

"It will do wonders for your psyche. And besides, I need a little practice driving on the opposite side of the road."

"The wrong side, you mean?"

"If you say so."

"You drive a hard bargain, Inspector."

George's hands stilled. He leaned over and dropped a kiss on the top of my head.

I looked up at him over my shoulder, already missing the soothing motion of his hands. "As long as we're back by two," I said, "so we can get things moving at the Thanksgiving buffet."

"I am at your service."

The ride was exactly what I'd needed. While I hadn't truly expressed to George, or to anyone, how upsetting the letters had been, they were never far from my thoughts, and had delivered a blow to my usually upbeat spirits. In my mind's eye, I saw thick fingers—they were always a man's fingers—cutting out the letters from a lurid magazine. I imagined my tormentor sniggering as he pasted them on a sheet of paper. It must be someone I had offended, someone who bore a grudge against me, but who? The face that accompanied these disturbing thoughts was always that of Hubert Billups. But I knew that was unreasonable. How could he have mailed those letters from distant cities? And why would he resent me to begin with? I didn't know the man.

We drove along the coast—is there any more beautiful place on earth than the Maine coast?—and I felt the tension subside. In town, autumn had stripped the trees of their leaves, but along the rocky shore, stately pines rose into the air like green arrows piercing the gray sky. The salt air was chilly and whipped my hair when we stopped at an unimposing seafood roadside shack for lobster rolls—luscious chunks of lobster on a toasted hot dog bun. Our timing was perfect. A sign indicated that they would close for the season the following day.

Our conversation drifted from one topic to another, nothing very weighty, but provocative discussion at times. George is one of the most balanced men I've ever known, someone who has strong beliefs but is always willing to listen to a different viewpoint and to embrace divergent philosophies. Although he'd spent his professional career in law enforcement, he'd never lost what can only be described as his gentle nature. He also had, of course, a steely side, necessary when confronting the criminal element. I'd seen that side the first time we met.

It was in London, where I'd traveled to attend a convention of mystery writers, and to visit an old friend, Marjorie Ainsworth. At that time, Marjorie, who was the reigning queen of mystery writers, lived in an imposing manor house outside London. She'd invited me to spend a few days there with her, an invitation I readily accepted.

Unfortunately, while I was there, my aged friend was found stabbed to death in her bed, and I became but one on a list of suspects. Enter Scotland Yard inspector George Sutherland, who was assigned the case because of Marjorie's notoriety. He questioned me along with the others, unfailingly polite but demonstrating an unwavering determination, and an unwillingness to accept answers he considered self-serving or evasive. As it turned out, we ended up working together to solve the murder. Our collaboration created a strong bond of mutual respect, and a developing personal interest in each other that remained to this day.

We ended our mini tour of Cabot Cove's countryside on a bluff overlooking the ocean. The water churned blue and green, with white froth riding waves that crashed against rocks below.

"It reminds me of Wick," I said as we stood side by side and soaked up nature's power and beauty.

"Aye, that it does," he said.

George was born in Wick, and his home in that northernmost tip of Scotland had remained in his family for generations. I'd visited there with a contingent of friends from Cabot Cove and was swept away by its spectacular visual splendor and the warmth of its people. Unfortunately, as with our initial meeting in London, murder would bring us together again, this time in George's ancestral home. I sighed as I thought back to that situation. Too often, murder seems to follow me when I travel, or even when I stay put in Cabot Cove. Given a choice, I'd much prefer to write about murder than experience it in my personal life, but I haven't always had the benefit of that choice.

"What are you thinking?" I asked as spray from a particularly large wave bounced off the rocks below, showering us with tiny droplets of frigid water and causing us to narrow our eyes against the briny mist.

George put his arm around my shoulders and briefly hugged me to him. "I was thinking about Thanksgiving, your special holiday. How wonderful to have a day set aside each year to give thanks for our blessings."

"It is a nice tradition, isn't it?"

"When you view the world with open eyes, you realize how much we have to be grateful for," he said.

I didn't respond, although I certainly agreed with him. My mind had wandered elsewhere—to my unfinished novel, Hubert Billups, the Thanksgiving pageant, the afternoon's event, the upcoming holiday dinner at my house, the dishes I had yet to cook, and, of course, my relationship with the handsome man standing next to me.

"Where are you, Jessica?" George asked.

"What? Oh, I'm sorry. I got lost in my thoughts."

"It's good to do that from time to time," he said. "Nice to escape the here and now."

I nodded, then shivered as another thought crossed my mind. During my brief moment of reverie I had forgotten what might be in the next day's postal delivery. Usually, I look forward to opening my mailbox, even though its contents increasingly seem to consist of what's commonly called "junk mail," the noncomputer equivalent of "spam." But I wasn't looking forward to opening tomorrow's envelopes, not with the likelihood of another message formed from letters clipped from magazines.

"Glotcoy," I said into the wind.

George laughed. "Yes, the mysterious Glotcoy."

"No such word in the dictionary," I said.

"Perhaps we'll never know what it means, unless of course the sender wishes to expose himself."

"Or herself," I said.

"Right you are. It could be a woman. In fact, Jessica, it may even be more likely that a woman is behind those letters."

"Why do you say that?"

"It's such—it's such a passive-aggressive action. Nevertheless, if it is a woman, it doesn't render this campaign any less threatening."

"I can't imagine that someone would go to so much trouble and not eventually reveal the motivation behind it."

"The perpetrator may already have achieved her objective—to unsettle you. In that case, there is no need to reveal herself. She has accomplished her mission. Staying anonymous perpetuates that goal."

"I *will* be very upset if I can't get to the bottom of this," I said.

George glanced at his watch. "Time to head back, Jessica, if you're going to be on time to serve up turkey with all the trimmings to Cabot Cove's needy."

I had only a few minutes in the house to gather up aprons and utensils before we were to head downtown, where the free turkey dinner was being served at the senior center, recently renovated through the generosity of Wilimena Copeland.

"Need this?" George asked as he picked up the box containing the carving knife Seth had loaned to me. He slowly drew it from its custom case.

"I'm reluctant to take it," I said. "It was a special gift to Seth."

"I've never seen anything quite like it," said George, holding up the ten-inch knife to better catch the light from a ceiling fixture.

"It was a gift to Seth from a wealthy Japanese businessman who'd been touring the United States with his family," I said. "They were spending a few days at the end of their trip in Cabot Cove—their son had been an exchange student here—and were having dinner at a popular Italian restaurant in town when the father suddenly clutched his chest and collapsed to the floor. Seth and I were at the next table. He immediately started cardiopulmonary resuscitation and saved the Japanese gentleman's life. The man spent time in the hospital, but thanks to Seth's quick action he recovered."

"He was fortunate to have a physician sitting at the next table."

"Yes, he was. Anyway, six months after the patient returned home to Japan, his son, the one who'd been a student here, came back to Cabot Cove bearing a gift for the doctor who'd 'given his father the gift of life.'" The knife was a handmade, carbon steel, Kounosuke carving knife that had been made in Sakai, which the son pointed out had been the home of samurai swords since the 1300s, I told George. "The case is made of paulownia wood. The son said the knife brings good luck to those who use it."

"It's magnificent."

"The handle is ivory. See those tiny pearls inlaid around the edges? That character on each side spells Seth's name. The son told him they're made from black diamonds."

"Black diamonds," George repeated. "They were formed in the heavens millions of years ago, as I understand."

"You're right," I said. "Black diamonds come from meteorites, not like the diamonds we're more accustomed to that are formed beneath the earth. I did some reading about it after Seth showed me the knife."

"It's obviously worth a lot of money," George said.

"I agree, but Seth never bothered to find out how much. I urged him to put it away in some safe place."

"Did he?"

"No. He dismissed my suggestion. Instead, he invited me to dinner and used the knife to slice a ham he'd baked for us that evening. I remember him saying: 'It might have a fancy handle and all, but a knife is made for cutting things.' He keeps it in a drawer along with his other kitchen knives." I laughed as George replaced the knife in its box. It didn't surprise me that Seth wouldn't give the gift special treatment. He's the quintessential function-over-form person. No matter how beautiful an object may be, if it doesn't perform a useful function, it isn't worth much to him.

I'd balked when Seth said that I should use his gift to carve the turkeys at this year's charity Thanksgiving dinner, but he'd insisted.

"I'd be devastated if something were to happen to it," I'd told him.

"Nothing'll happen to it, Jessica. Besides, it'll bring good luck to the folks who show up. They need it."

I added the case containing the knife to the basket I

was taking to the senior center, and George carried it out to the car. We would see if the knife lived up to its reputation, and, indeed, if it proved to be good luck to its user. I could use some good luck, I thought, as I closed the door and locked it—and checked again that I had.

Chapter Ten

The senior center was abuzz with activity when George and I arrived. A long, heated buffet table donated for the occasion by the town's leading caterer had been delivered earlier in the day, and two of its young employees were busy erecting it. Birgitta Westerholm and her husband, Gus, our deputy mayor, supervised the more than a dozen volunteers who'd already shown up. Although she wasn't old enough to be considered a "senior," Birgitta, or Gitta as she was more commonly known, was a familiar face at the center, one of numerous civic undertakings into which she immersed herself.

"Hello, Jessica," Richard Koser said, taking a break from hauling folding chairs and tables from a storage room. "Ready to do some fancy carving?"

"Ready to do my best," I said, "with George's help. You haven't met yet." I introduced them.

"Welcome to Cabot Cove," Richard said. "I've heard lots about you."

"And all of it good," I added.

"I'm relieved," George said with a wide smile. "I'm also looking forward to being a part of this worthwhile event."

"We all feel pretty good about serving up Thanksgiving meals to folks who are having trouble making ends meet," Richard said. "It seems as Cabot Cove grows, there are more of them."

Richard was right. Like so many communities across the country, we've experienced growth that while representing forward progress, at least from a financial perspective, creates its own set of problems. Not that the actual town of Cabot Cove had changed that much. The downtown—its core—had remained relatively unaffected. No national chain stores, no garish neon lights or outsized signs. Businesses were locally owned and managed, and a spirit of community prevailed. The same held true for most of the residential areas bordering the downtown, including mine.

But farther out, business had established a foothold and spawned industrial parks that had enticed many people to move to the area in search of new, well-paying jobs. When some of these start-up companies failed, their employees suffered the inevitable consequences, and many fell on hard times.

Too, there were some families who'd been residents for many years and who just never managed to make a go of it, usually through unforeseen calamities of one sort or another—catastrophic illness, business downturns, or myriad other reasons for falling into their precarious financial situations.

No matter what the reason for their misfortune, they were the people to whom the annual free Thanksgiving dinner was dedicated. Some would bring their families with them and enjoy their meal at the senior center. In other cases, meals would be packaged up and delivered to the homebound. Either way, the meaning and spirit of Thanksgiving would not be forgotten.

"Ah, my favorite writer," Archer Franklin said as he and Willie came to where we stood.

"Good to see you again," I said, sounding as though I meant it.

"Hello, Inspector," Franklin said. "Been solving any crimes while here in Cabot Cove?"

"One or two," George replied.

"Really?" Willie asked with eyes wide.

"No, not really," George clarified.

"The English sense of humor," Franklin said, slapping George on the arm. "Subtle. I like that."

"Much like the Scots sense of humor," George said, winking at me.

"Well," I said, "I think we should join the others and get ready for our dinner guests." I nudged George, and we went to the sparkling new, fully equipped kitchen, compliments of Wilimena Copeland's largesse.

"Oh, Jessica, I'm so glad you're here," Susan Shevlin said from where she checked on turkeys roasting in the large oven. "We're a little short on help. Fran Winstead is late. Wally forgot he was supposed to drop her off." Beads of perspiration dotted her forehead and cheeks, and she wiped them away with a handkerchief that was already damp.

"I'm here and ready to go," I said.

"I am, too," George said, resting our basket on a huge granite-topped prep table in the center of the room.

"It's so sweet of you to pitch in," Susan said to him.

"Wouldn't miss it," said George, removing his tweed jacket and looking for a place to hang it.

"I'll take that," Maureen Metzger said as she appeared from a back room, a large stainless-steel bowl of stuffing in her arms. She put the bowl down and took George's jacket. "I'll find a nice, safe place for it out of the line of fire." She disappeared into the room from which she'd come and reemerged a few seconds later.

"Much obliged," George said.

Josh and Beth Wappinger joined us in the kitchen. "Haven't seen you in a while, Jessica," Josh said, giving me a peck on the cheek. "How's the book coming along?"

"It isn't at the moment," I said, and introduced George to them.

"Nice to meet you," Josh said. "Say, what do you have there?" he said, noticing Seth's open knife case in our basket. He laughed. "Do you always travel with your own machete, Jessica?"

"Oh, this," I said, pulling the knife from its protective case. "It belongs to Seth Hazlitt. He insisted I use it to carve today's turkeys."

"Wow!" Beth said. "That looks like something a prince or rajah would own."

"It is beautiful," I said. "It was a gift to Seth from a Japanese businessman whose life Seth saved. I didn't want to bring it, but he insisted. You know how stubborn Seth can be."

"Seth Hazlitt stubborn?" Susan Shevlin said, looking up from giving two of the birds a final basting. "I can't imagine."

We all laughed.

I turned to Josh. "I thought you were traveling," I said.

"I was. Got back late last night."

"My traveling salesman husband," Beth said in a mocking tone. "I'd have killed him if he'd been away over Thanksgiving."

"How're things at the shop?" I asked her as I emptied the contents of my basket and placed them on the granite countertop.

"It's always a little slow before Thanksgiving. Everyone is home cooking. But it was a good excuse for me to close early so I could be here and lend a hand. I expect a big rush on Friday. Oh, and Jessica, I just got in the most adorable line of blouses you should look at. They're made for you."

"I'll make it a point to swing by," I said, "once we get through the holiday." I smiled up at George, who'd loosened his tie and rolled up his sleeves. "Ready to go to work?" I asked.

"Yes, ma'am," he replied. "Ready, willing, and I hope able."

I'd brought two aprons from home, and handed one

to George, wondering how he'd take to wearing it, but he quickly put it on. I own a collection of aprons given me by Seth over the years whenever a new book of mine was published, each carrying the name of my most recent novel. The one I wore this day read PANNING FOR MURDER. George's was of a less recent vintage: DYING TO RETIRE.

"How do I look, lass?" he asked, a bit of his brogue creeping into his speech.

"Absolutely splendid," I said, mimicking his accent.

As we walked from the kitchen to take up positions by a huge carving board Maureen Metzger had brought for the occasion, Linda Carson entered the room. I was pleased that she'd decided to come. Behind her was her husband, Victor. That was equally as pleasing to me, albeit more surprising. He lingered just inside the door, but Linda came directly to me and said, "Well, we made it. What can we do to help?"

"I'm delighted to see you both here," I said.

"I pleaded with Victor to come," she said under her breath. "It wasn't easy. He isn't very social."

"See that lady over there?" I said. "Her name is Birgitta. Call her Gitta. She and her husband, Gus, are in charge. She can put you both to work."

Linda looked down at Seth's ornate knife, which I'd placed on the carving board, and her eyes widened. "That's some knife," she said.

"It's a long story," I said. "I'll tell you later."

People started arriving over the next half hour, some alone, others with their families in tow. Knowing how difficult it must be for people attending the charity dinner to acknowledge that they'd come because of shaky finances, our committee had had discussions during meetings about how to take the onus off their situation. It was decided that all the committee members would take turns joining our guests at the tables and eating with them. This didn't sit too well with a few at the meeting who complained about eating more turkey two days before Thanksgiving, but the rest of us eventually overcame the objections of the complainers.

The turkeys coming from the kitchen were beautifully cooked, as were the side dishes, and I enthusiastically attacked my responsibility as one of two carvers, with George providing vocal encouragement. We'd decided to carve to order to allow each person to choose his or her favorite part of the bird, and George took what I'd carved and deftly placed it on plates. Seth's knife was remarkable. It sliced easily through the meat just as Seth had predicted it would, and made me feel like a professional.

"Well done, Jessica. You can get a job at any London carvery now," George said after a half hour had passed. "Like me to take over for a bit, to give you a wee rest?"

"That would be great," I said. "I'm supposed to join some of the guests. I won't be too long."

I placed some food on a plate and surveyed the room, which by now was three-quarters full. Everyone seemed to be having a good time. Families that shared some of the larger tables were engaged in spirited conversations. Maureen Metzger had joined one such table, Willie Copeland and her sister, Kathy, another. I looked for Willie's new romantic interest, Archer Franklin, but he apparently had left. Linda Carson had elected to help in the kitchen. Her husband, Victor, had joined a group of men clearing tables and carrying empty dishes and used silverware to the kitchen, where a clean-up crew was busy trying to keep up with the flow.

I spotted a table at which a family of four had settled after going through the serving line. As I headed in their direction, Fran Winstead, who'd recently arrived, slipped into a seat joining them.

As I turned to see if another table needed me, Sheriff Metzger and Seth Hazlitt came through the door.

"How are things, Jessica?" Seth asked.

"Great," I replied.

"No problems?" Mort asked.

"Problems? No, why would there be?"

Mort nodded in the direction of the door, where Hubert Billups had entered and taken a seat at an empty table. He was dressed as usual, red-and-black mackinaw, scarf, and black wool cap. The only discernible change was his red beard, which looked as though it had grown a little longer

"Oh, I see," I said. "No, no problems, Mort. Excuse me."

I went to Billups and asked, "Mind if I join you?"

He looked up at me through deadened, watery, unblinking eyes.

I sat.

"I've been wanting to meet you for quite a while now," I said, smiling. "I'm Jessica Fletcher. I know you're new to

Cabot Cove and—well, I wanted to welcome you to our town."

He spoke without making eye contact with me. "I, ah—that's okay of you," he said, eyes fixed on the tabletop.

"I have to admit," I said, "that seeing you so often on the road across from my house had me wondering whether you—whether you had some sort of interest in me."

He silently shook his head.

I realized that he hadn't gotten any food. "I don't want to keep you from enjoying some turkey," I said. "Go ahead and get a plate."

He left the table and took his place at the end of the serving line.

I looked at Seth and Mort, who'd been watching, and smiled. Seth shook his head. Mort looked puzzled. As they headed in the direction of the buffet table, Victor Carson, in a great rush, passed my table and disappeared through the door. *How odd*, I thought, *he wasn't here that long.* But I didn't have time to dwell upon it because my eye caught Billups holding a tray with his dinner and a cup of iced tea. It looked as if he was debating whether to return to the table at which I sat, but when he saw me watching him, he shrugged, took the seat he'd previously occupied, and immediately began to eat.

"I'm so glad you could come today," I said. "As I was saying before, I've noticed you on my road, Mr. Billups, and I—"

"Don't mean no harm—to you," he said. He spoke slowly, taking care to enunciate each word.

"Oh," I said, "I didn't mean to imply that you did." I stopped talking for a minute to allow him to enjoy his dinner. "Is there any way that I can be of help in getting you settled here in Cabot Cove?" I asked. "I know how a new place can be daunting and thought maybe I could make the transition easier for you."

I watched him as he processed what I'd said. When he had, he finished what was in his mouth, dabbed at it with his napkin, used his fist to cover a small burp, and said, again in his careful, deliberate way of speaking, "There's not much you could do for me, missus."

"Jessica Fletcher. Please call me Jessica."

"I figure I have to work things out for myself."

"And I'm sure you're capable of doing just that, Mr. Billups. Do you have any family near here?"

Another slow shaking of his head. He finished the small portion of turkey and stuffing on his plate.

"What are you doing on Thanksgiving?" I asked. The minute it was out of my mouth, I knew what I would end up saying next.

He shrugged. "Excuse me," he said, getting ready to leave.

"Mr. Billups," I said, reaching and touching the sleeve of his mackinaw, "if you don't have any place to go on Thursday—for Thanksgiving dinner—you're welcome to come to my house. I have room at the table and—"

He stood and looked down at me. "Thanks," he said. "That's okay of you."

"Come at three?" I said. "You obviously know where I live."

"Thanks," he repeated, and gave what amounted to a small bow. "Thanks."

He was gone.

I sat there stunned at what I'd just done, my thoughts jumbled. Joining him had been, at best, an impetuous act, although it struck me as the perfect time to engage him face-to-face. It occurred to me immediately after sitting at the table that I might be breaking bread with a man who held some perverted sort of grudge against me. But that was pure conjecture on my part, and any concern I might have had quickly dissipated. After all, I was in a room with dozens of friends, including Cabot Cove's sheriff.

But if deciding to join Billups represented an impulsive gesture on my part, inviting him to my home for Thanksgiving dinner was a rash, irrational act, at best. I don't know what possessed me—I certainly hadn't planned it—and I suppose it stemmed from a combination of sincerely wanting to provide Thanksgiving dinner for a lonely man, coupled with an ongoing obsession to know more about him. No matter what my motives, I was now faced with the reality of his possibly showing up. Had I created a scenario in which my other guests would be made uncomfortable at having Billups share their holiday table? A man who seemed to own only one outfit, and that one none too clean? Had I put Billups in an awkward position?

I'm not terribly proud of the fact that the moment he left the senior center I assured myself that he probably wouldn't show up on Thursday because he wouldn't want to be made more uncomfortable than he already was. It was a rationalization, but it was my out.

I carried our plates, his and mine, to Linda Carson,

who took them from me and set them on the counter behind her.

"I saw your husband leave," I said. "Was there a problem?"

"He just remembered an appointment," she said, brushing her lips with her hand. "I really have to go, too. I wish I could stay but—" She untied her apron.

"Don't worry about it," I said, sensing that she was upset. "You run along. Thanks for all your help. See you on Thursday."

I watched her gather her purse and jacket and head for the door. What was going on with them? I wondered. It must have beeen a troubled marriage. I felt sorry for her, as I would for any couple facing difficulties, but I also experienced a more self-serving feeling, and that had to do with Thursday's holiday dinner. Would their problems carry over to the gathering? Would he, or they, even show up? Would they bring their troubles and resentments to the table?

I certainly had made a muddle of my guest list, inviting complete strangers to my house without any thought to how they would get along. I had wanted George to experience a "traditional" Thanksgiving at my home, but the dinner was becoming less traditional by the moment. Food was the easy part, but my mix of guests promised either very lively conversation, or a miserable atmosphere. My musings were interrupted by Gus Westerholm.

"Jessica, we have a problem," he said.

"Oh? What's the matter?"

"Two of our people who were supposed to deliver meals can't do it. Wally dropped off Fran, so she doesn't have a vehicle. And Rena is having car problems. Do you think that you could take over—?"

"Gus, you know I don't drive."

"I know, but your friend has a rental car. I thought maybe the two of you could do the deliveries, him driving and you showing the way. I'd offer to do it myself, but I really can't leave here yet. There are only nine deliveries to make. The birds have all been carved."

"Of course," I said. "I'll ask George."

"You trust me to drive on the other side of the road all over Cabot Cove?" he responded when I broached the subject.

"You did very well earlier today. I'll be right by your side."

"Whatever you say, my dear," he said. "I have to retrieve my jacket. It won't take a jiffy."

I managed to say goodbye to a few people, but our departure was hurried and hectic as we relayed dinners heavily wrapped in foil to George's rental car.

"You go on and run," Birgitta said. "Those meals get cold fast. And enjoy the rest of the evening together." She gave me a sly wink. "He's very handsome, Jessica, and so charming."

It took us more time than we'd anticipated to drop off the dinners. We couldn't just hurry away when those who were homebound wanted a little socializing. George was especially popular with the elderly ladies who lived alone. In some cases we had to help reheat the dinners. After the last platter had been delivered, George asked, "What's next?"

I couldn't help but laugh. "What's next," I said, "is going home, giving my aching feet a rest, and relaxing with you. You are an absolute trouper, George Sutherland. I don't know anyone else who would have thrown himself into our annual charity event as you did."

"It was fun. And I'll do anything to stay close to you, Jessica. I want to share as much of your life as possible."

At home, snifters of brandy in our hands, we toasted the success of the event.

"I noticed you chose to sit with that Billy-no-mates who's been loitering outside," he said.

"Does that mean someone without a friend?"

"Yes."

I nodded. "He does seem a sad soul, and it was a perfect time to approach him," I said. "I've wanted to do that for a while but for some strange reason never got up the courage."

"What did he have to say for himself?"

"Not much."

"How much?"

"He said I was 'okay.'"

George smiled. "I'd certainly agree with his assessment."

"George, I invited him to Thanksgiving dinner."

He moved to speak, but nothing came out of his mouth. Whatever he had intended to say, he decided to keep it to himself.

"I know, I know," I said. "I shouldn't have. But the idea just came to me and—"

George placed his hand on mine. "I'm not surprised," he said. "You're just being Jessica."

"Is that good or bad?"

"Oh, it's decidedly good," he said.

"He didn't say he would come. He probably won't. And to be perfectly honest, there's a part of me that hopes he won't."

"Whether he does or not, the invitation has been extended. You'll just have to wait and see."

I changed the subject. "Did you get an opportunity to sit down at one of the tables?" I asked.

"Not officially. But the turkey was excellent. I managed to nip a piece now and then."

"I hope it doesn't spoil your appetite for Thursday."

"Not a chance, Jessica," he said, turning toward me. He reached out and touched my cheek. "One of my favorite dishes."

There was a brief pause in the conversation. I wouldn't say it was awkward—I've never felt awkward with George—but I broke the mood by asking: "Did you happen to speak with my new neighbor, Linda Carson, or her husband? I introduced you to her in town."

George settled back on the sofa. "Briefly," he said. "She's a nervous little thing, isn't she?"

I nodded. "I have a feeling their marriage isn't a very happy one. Her husband came with her and pitched in a little, but he didn't stay long. She scooted out right after him."

"Oh, well," he said, "that's what makes this an interesting world, its people, everyone different, everyone with their own pains and pleasures, triumphs and failings."

We sat silently for a while, content with our individual, unstated thoughts. I couldn't help being happy that our relationship had grown into one this comfortable and accepting, neither of us feeling the necessity to keep the conversation going, just sitting together, feet up on an ottoman, content, at least for the moment, as the rest of the world passed by.

But my peaceful thoughts were jarred by a less happy one. George sensed it.

"What's wrong?" he asked.

"Tomorrow's Wednesday," I said.

"I believe you're right."

I sighed. "There'll be another mail delivery."

"Ah, yes. Will there be another upsetting letter? Perhaps there won't be, Jessica."

"I wish I were certain of that."

Another period of introspective silence followed until I suddenly sat up and dropped my feet from the ottoman. I gasped. "Oh, good heavens!" I said.

"What's the matter, Jessica?"

I moaned. "I have to go. Right now. George, please. Get up! We have to go."

"For goodness' sake, lass," George said, his Scottish brogue thickening, "are you all right?"

"We have to go. I can't believe I forgot all about it."

"Whatever it is you forgot, I'm certain we can resolve it tomorrow."

"No, you don't understand," I said, frantically pushing my tired feet into my shoes. "We have to get it now."

"What do we have to get?"

"Seth's knife."

Chapter Eleven

Rather than rush back to the senior center, which would have been locked up for the night, George suggested I make a series of calls to the people who'd worked there with me. I couldn't in good conscience ask anyone to leave their home to open the building for me at this hour, but perhaps I could find reassurance that the knife was safely stowed away. Susan Shevlin momentarily raised my spirits. "I saw the box," she said. "I put it on a shelf in one of the kitchen cupboards."

"Was the knife in it?" I asked, holding my breath.

"Afraid not, Jessica. It was empty. I thought you'd probably taken the knife but overlooked the box."

"If only that were the case," I said. "Thanks, Susan."

My other calls didn't fare any better.

"I never thought of it in the rush to leave with the dinners to be delivered," I said to George after I'd exhausted my list of people to call.

"I didn't either," he said.

"I can't believe I did this," I said.

"I'm sure it will turn up," he replied.

"What if it doesn't? I didn't want to use it—it's more a piece of art than a kitchen knife—but Seth was so insistent."

George took my hand. "We'll look for it first thing in the morning," he said.

"How am I going to tell him?"

"Seth? You don't have to tell him right now. Chances are we'll find it in a drawer and you'll put it back in its case and return it, no one the wiser."

"But if it's gone, I should be the one to break the news."

"Of course. However, I'm confident you won't have to be passing along any bad news."

Try as I might to adopt George's positive outlook, I had a bad feeling about the knife. It was a valuable object, one that conceivably could fetch a lot of money if someone desperate for funds had taken it with the intention to sell it. My mood turned somber, and George took it as a cue to leave. When I realized that he'd picked up on my unhappiness, I apologized and asked him to stay longer. But he said, "It's been a long day, Jessica. I'd best be getting back to Dr. Hazlitt's house, my home away from home. Don't worry, I won't mention the knife to him, and in any case, you'll be returning it to him safe and sound tomorrow."

I walked with him to the car. "I owe you an apology," I said.

"Whatever for?"

"For the way your visit is turning out. It seems that all I've had to offer since you arrived is a series of problems, *my* problems—weird letters, Mr. Billups setting me on edge, thinking someone broke into my house, and now the missing knife. I can't believe I was so careless as to leave it behind. It's just not like me."

"Stop beating yourself up, Jessica. We all make mistakes."

"True," I said, smiling up at him. "Still, that doesn't make me feel any better."

"We'll face all your problems together, lass—at least we will tomorrow. I'll be here first thing, before the mail delivery I know you're dreading. We'll look at the next letter together, providing there is one. We'll find Seth's knife at the senior center and return it unscathed. Any dragons that come along, I'll slay. And, oh yes, I'm sure you have a full day on tap preparing for your Thanksgiving dinner."

"I've put that out of my mind; I'd better bring it back to the front burner, so to speak. And we mustn't forget the Thanksgiving pageant tomorrow night."

"I'll be happy to pitch in with your preparations for dinner, Jessica. Put me to work. I know how to Hoover a rug. I don't claim much expertise around a kitchen, but I am good at scrubbing pots and pans, and I look quite spiffy in your aprons, if I do say so."

I laughed.

"And as for your Mr. Billups, if he does decide to accept

your invitation, we'll welcome him with open arms the way Native Americans did when your Pilgrims arrived in their new world."

I was overwhelmed at that moment with appreciation for this wonderful man who seemed to take everything in stride, who always had a reassuring word, and provided a subtle touch of humor when needed. I threw my arms around him and squeezed tight.

"I don't know what I did to deserve that," he said when we disengaged, "but I intend to do it again as quickly as possible."

First on my agenda the following morning was to find Seth's carving knife. Once I accomplished that—and I hoped that I'd be successful—it promised to be a day spent in the kitchen, as well as getting the dining room table set with my best china and silverware. I counted a dozen other chores to get ready for Thanksgiving dinner. There was a large tablecloth to be ironed, along with matching napkins. I'd pulled them out before going to bed and was relieved, and surprised, that I had fourteen of everything, although thirteen was all that was required.

Since Linda Carson hadn't called, I assumed that she and her husband would be joining us as planned. I had mixed emotions about that. Victor had struck me as a strange duck, possibly antisocial, surely difficult. Could it be I'd misjudged him? True, I hardly knew the man. Maybe he was simply shy. I preferred the latter description, and decided that having him at Thanksgiving dinner would give me a chance to get to know my new neighbor better, and hopefully put him more at ease.

At a quarter to nine, George picked me up and we drove to the senior center, arriving just as the doors opened to admit a contingent of elderly ladies intent on a morning of Texas Hold'em. The longtime friends used to play bridge or canasta, but the popularity of big-money poker tournaments on TV had prompted them to change their game. They played with a vengeance, no-holds-barred, collecting pennies instead of chips and contributing the day's winnings to the senior center refreshment fund.

George and I went to the kitchen and began our search for Seth's knife. We opened every cupboard door and every drawer. We found nothing except the empty box that had contained the knife. We expanded our search to the main room, where the dinners had been served, but didn't find it there either.

"Someone must have taken it," I said as we walked out to the parking area in front of the building, the empty box in my hands.

This time, George said nothing, and I knew his optimism of the previous night had waned.

"I'm feeling terribly guilty," I said.

"Don't give up hope yet," George offered, his optimism returning. "Maybe someone in your favorite food shop will know something."

"Mara's," I said. "Yes, let's check there."

The luncheonette was the town's Grand Central Station of gossip, rumors arriving daily and dispersing like so many trains to the far reaches of Cabot Cove. A knife like Seth's would hardly go unnoticed if someone attempted to sell it locally. And that news would make its way to

Mara's. The only problem was: Just asking if anyone had heard anything about the knife would start the talk on the tracks. I'd have to work fast if I didn't want Seth to hear about it from someone other than me.

"All set for turkey day?" Mara asked as we walked in.

"Still lots to do," I said. "Mara, has anyone talked about finding an ornate carving knife used at the senior center yesterday?"

"Doc Hazlitt's knife?"

"You already know about that?"

"Somebody said you'd been calling around looking for it."

"I borrowed it from him and . . . it doesn't matter." Chances were that Seth had now heard about it, too. "If you do hear anything," I said, "you'll call me?"

"Sure will. Coffee? Tea?"

"Two cups of tea would hit the spot," George said, looking at me for approval. I agreed.

"I can't spend the day looking for it," I said. "For one thing, I'm not sure where to start. And for another, there's so much to do at home to get ready for the holiday."

"It sounds as though the entire village knows by now, Jessica. My suggestion is we relax with our tea, then return to your house and hope someone calls."

We finished our tea—I can't say it helped me relax; my mind was buzzing—said goodbye to Mara, and stepped into the chilly fall air. At the end of the dock, where it meets the sidewalk, a scene was being played out that stopped us. Archer Franklin and Hubert Billups stood nose to nose, glaring at each other. It was Archer's voice we heard as he boomed, "Lowlifes like you deserve to be put away, exiled to some godforsaken island where decent people don't have to see or smell you."

Whatever Billups said—he spoke too softly for us to hear—his words enraged his opponent even more. Franklin's face had turned crimson. He shoved his index finger into Billups's chest, sending him backward against a railing. Billups brought up a hand in a defensive gesture, but Franklin swatted it away, sending his fist flush against Billups's cheek. Billups fell away to one side, grasping at the railing to keep from landing on the pavement. He scrambled to his feet and put up his fists, as if preparing to box. "These fists . . . are . . . lethal weapons," he finally got out.

"You ever come near me again," Franklin said, "and you'll wish you were never born."

Billups tried to advance against Franklin, but his gait was unsteady.

As Franklin poised to strike again, George sprinted forward and grabbed the man's wrist in midflight. "Enough," George said, bringing Franklin's arm up behind him.

"Let me go!" Franklin demanded, struggling against George's grip.

"Only if you calm down," George said, his voice low.

Franklin whirled around when George loosened his grip. "Oh, it's you," he said, brushing off his sleeve.

George stepped around Franklin to block him from attacking Billups again. He rested his fingertips against Franklin's chest. "There's no need for fisticuffs," he said.

"I'm sure you two gentlemen can resolve whatever differences you have in a peaceful manner." He risked a glance at Billups.

Shielded from Franklin, the ragged man had leaned against the railing, holding on with one hand while the fingers of his other hand shifted his jaw from left to right, testing to see if it was broken.

Franklin forced a smile. "That *gentleman*, as you called him, assaulted me."

"The only assault I saw came from you," George said, as I caught up to them.

The sound of a siren drew everyone's attention. We all turned as Mort Metzger's marked sheriff's car came to a screeching halt. Mort assessed the scene and slowly climbed from the behind the wheel. "Guess I missed the action," he said, ambling to where we stood, his eyes flicking from Billups to Franklin and back. "What's going on? Mara called to report a fight."

"Nothing of the sort," Franklin said, stepping forward. "This—this *bum* assaulted me and I defended myself." He waved a hand at Billups, who inched along the railing.

Mort grabbed him before he could walk away. "Are you making trouble again?" he asked.

Billups replied, "I didn't do nothing to him. I swear it."

Mort turned to Franklin. "You want to press charges?" he asked.

"No, that won't be necessary," he said, puffing out his chest. "But I do suggest that you do a better job of ridding the streets of scum like this. If you can't efficiently carry out your responsibilities to keep the citizens of this town safe, then we should consider finding a replacement who will." He looked around at the few people who'd gathered to watch what was going on. "Isn't that right?"

Anger flared in Mort's eyes, but he didn't respond. Instead, he turned to Billups. "You want to press charges against Mr. Franklin?"

The red-bearded man shook his head.

"Really, Sheriff," Franklin growled.

"You okay, Mrs. F?" Mort asked me.

"I'm fine."

"You, Inspector?"

"We're both fine, thank you."

"Well, then, I suggest everyone go on their way," Mort said, turning in a circle. "All of you. We don't need this sort of nonsense the day before Thanksgiving."

The small crowd melted away and we watched Billups shuffle up the street and disappear around a corner. Without another word, Mort got back into his car and drove off, leaving George, me, and Archer Franklin standing at the end of the dock.

"I'm sorry that you two were spectators at this unfortunate episode," Franklin said to me, conveniently forgetting George's role in preventing him from throwing the next punch. "The sheriff is right. With a festive dinner at your home tomorrow, Jessica, it's best that we all forget it. Isn't that right, Inspector? I just hope that both of you won't think poorly of me for defending myself against an obvious madman."

I wasn't sure that Billups was the madman here, but

Franklin's suggestion that we all put the incident behind us felt right.

"Can I drop you two anywhere?" Franklin asked. "My car is down the street. It would be no trouble at all."

"Thank you, no," George said. "I have a car."

"How do you like driving on the right side of the road for a change?" Franklin asked, laughing.

"I'm enjoying it very much, thank you," George said, taking my arm. "Coming, Jessica?"

"Yes. Goodbye, Mr. Franklin."

"Looking forward to tomorrow," he called after us.

"Wait until he finds out who's sitting at the same table with him," I said so only George could hear.

George chuckled.

We didn't turn to acknowledge Archer, simply climbed in the rental car and drove home, where, after leaving a message on Seth's answering machine, I tried to put the missing knife, and the altercation we'd just witnessed, out of my mind as I focused on getting ready for the next day's festivities.

I was well into it, with George lending a hand, when I happened to spot Newt walking toward the mailbox. George accompanied me to the door.

"Morning, Mrs. Fletcher; Inspector."

"Good morning, Newt," I said.

"Here you go," he said, handing me that day's mail. Right on top of the pile was another neatly addressed letter. I must have gasped because George placed his arm over my shoulder and said to Newt, "Have yourself a wonderful Thanksgiving, sir."

"Oh, I expect to," Newt said with a broad smile. "Got my brother and his wife coming in from Texas; should arrive any minute now. You folks have a good one, too."

We opened the latest missive in the kitchen. Sure enough, an eighth letter had been added, a tiny pink, lowercase *b*. The postmark was Bangor, Maine.

"GLOTCOYB," I said through a sigh. "At least tomorrow won't bring another. There's no mail on a holiday."

"Something else to give thanks for," George said. He got to his feet and went to the window. He pulled aside the curtain, and stood quietly looking out. After a few minutes, he said, "Come here, Jessica."

I joined him at the window. George put his arm around my shoulder and together we watched Hubert Billups walking up the road in the direction of the Carson house. After he'd passed from our view, George commented, "At least he isn't standing there staring at your house. Come on, lass, time to get back to work. Thanksgiving will be here before we know it."

Chapter Twelve

The words to a Thanksgiving ditty by the country's first children's poet laureate, Jack Prelutsky, were part of a package of printed material that Tim Purdy handed out to those attending the previous evening's pageant. As the event's host, our town historian gave a fifteen-minute presentation that wove amusing stories in with some little-known facts, as well as myths, about Thanksgiving.

"Your Mr. Purdy is quite an entertaining chap," George said as we worked together to get ready for the three o'clock arrival of our guests.

"He's a delight," I said. "I hadn't realized that our annual tradition of having the president pardon a turkey may have begun with Abraham Lincoln, if the folklore is true."

"That's one lucky turkey," said George. "What I found

interesting was what Tim said about the National Day of Mourning."

Tim had pointed out that while Thanksgiving was to celebrate the coming together of the Pilgrims and Wampanoag Indians in 1621, many Native Americans have used the occasion to commemorate what they call their "Day of Mourning" to point out how they'd been mistreated over centuries. According to Tim, Wampanoag leader Frank James had been invited by the Commonwealth of Massachusetts in 1970 to deliver a speech at the top of Coles Hill that overlooks Plymouth Rock. They expected a positive, uplifting speech from the Native American leader. But they discovered prior to the event that he intended to deliver an angry protest on behalf of his people, and they canceled his appearance. But on every Thanksgiving Day since, members of his tribe gather on Coles Hill to commemorate what they consider to be the holiday's true history.

"A very different take on the holiday's meaning," George said as he dripped candle wax into a candleholder to keep one of the long, tapered orange candles from tilting.

"And unfortunately true," I said from the kitchen, where George joined me. "I washed the long-stemmed white-wine glasses," I told him. "Care to dry them?"

"Of course."

By one, things were in pretty good shape. Of course, I would have been happier had Seth's knife shown up. But it hadn't, and I had to resign myself to the nasty fact that someone had taken it from the senior center. Naturally, before he'd had a chance to listen to my voice mail message, Seth had heard from Cabot Cove's virtual "water cooler" that the knife had gone missing. He'd mentioned it to me at last night's pageant.

"Oh, Seth, I am so sorry," I'd said after the performance had ended and we'd gathered outside. "We looked everywhere. My only hope is that someone took it home inadvertently and will return it when they discover their error."

"Not to worry, Jessica," Seth said, a hand on my shoulder. "Such things happen, and you shouldn't fret over it. After all, it's just a knife."

"Oh, no," I'd said, "it was more than that, Seth. It was a special gift to you for having saved a man's life."

"Do you think his is the only life I've saved?" he replied, feigning having been insulted.

"Seth, I—"

"Not another word, madam. I assume your own carving knife will do nicely tomorrow."

"I'm sure it will."

"You'll be doing the carving honors, Inspector?" he asked George.

"If called to duty."

"A good soldier, huh? Well, keep in mind if your arm tires, there's an experienced carver who can step in as backup. Remember, I've had training in surgery."

At two, it seemed that everything was set. The table was laid, the pies, cakes, and breads on the sideboard with a space left for Linda Carson's contribution. An empty space on the stove awaited Susan Shevlin's clam chowder. The turkey was roasting in the oven, with an occasional basting by George. He'd set up a bar in the living room and was prepared to play bartender, along with being the designated carver.

"I'll keep thinking of that ditty Mr. Purdy handed out while slicing up the bird," he said through a smile.

"Just don't slice a piece off your finger," I admonished. "We don't need a thumb on the platter."

We took a brief break and sat with our feet up until two thirty when I announced, "Battle stations!"

"Yes, ma'am."

Seth was first to arrive, which was no surprise. He's a stickler for being on time, which benefits his patients, who seldom are kept waiting. Following close on his heels were Wilimena and Kathy Copeland, accompanied by Willie's new boyfriend.

"A pleasure meeting you, Dr. Hazlitt," Franklin said after I'd introduced him to Seth. "I hear that you're the best sawbones in town."

Seth winced but shook Franklin's hand and said, "I've been at it awhile."

After a few minutes of aimless chitchat, Franklin said, "I assume you keep up with newer advances in medicine."

"Actually," said Seth, "I still use leeches for bloodletting. They're coming back in style. Excuse me while I see what's going on in the kitchen."

George, who wore another of my aprons bearing the

name of one of my novels, *Margaritas & Murder*, greeted Seth as he came into the kitchen and asked if he wanted a beverage.

"Ayuh," Seth said, "but nothing alcoholic. I ended up spending the morning at the hospital. One of my patients thought her oven was off and took a peek inside, using a match to see better. Her hair and eyebrows should grow back in a few months. I promised I'd check back later today."

George went to the living room to serve drinks, mostly wine and a punch I'd whipped up from a recipe that had been in the family for generations.

"Do you think I'm getting too old to keep up with new discoveries in medicine, Jessica?" Seth asked.

I looked up from the succotash casserole I'd taken from the oven. "Why would you ask that, for heaven's sake?"

"Just curious," he said.

"I've never heard anything so ridiculous in my life," I said, returning to my chore.

The doorbell heralded the arrival of more guests, this time Mayor Jim Shevlin and his wife. Susan had brought her famous clam chowder, a particular favorite of mine and Seth's.

"I brought a little corn bread to serve with it," she said, heaving the pot onto the burner. "And some crumbled bacon and parsley. Those go in at the last minute."

"So what's new at the mayor's office?" Franklin asked Shevlin after they'd been introduced.

"Nothing much, Mr. Franklin. I've heard a lot about you. Welcome to Cabot Cove."

"Thanks. I think I'm going to enjoy it here, especially after meeting this ravishing creature." He smiled at Wilimena, who hung on his arm.

"Willie's a treasured newcomer to the town," Shevlin said. "Of course, we've had the pleasure of her sister, Kathy, for many years."

"The dynamic duo," Franklin said. "You know, Mr. Mayor, I've been meaning to get in touch with you for quite a while. I'd like to find some time to sit down and give you my thoughts on solving some of the town's more pressing issues. I'm afraid I'm a little tied up right now, but I'll try to find an hour or two over the next few weeks."

"That's good of you," Shevlin said, being nice enough not to add that Franklin wasn't the only one pressed for time. "We have a monthly 'Ask the Mayor' breakfast. You'll have to join us for one of those occasions."

Everyone had settled in the living room with their drinks when the Metzgers came through the door, Maureen carrying her sweet potato casserole. I divided my time between my guests and the kitchen, where Maureen had stationed herself. She'd donned one of my aprons—*A Question of Murder*—and looked very much at home. "You go mingle," she told me. "I've got everything under control." She had taken ownership of the kitchen, which made me smile.

I was about to suggest that we all take seats at the table when the doorbell rang. It was Linda and Victor Carson, my new neighbors. I greeted them warmly, my senses attuned to Victor's response. Although he didn't smile, he thanked me for inviting them and followed us inside the house. Linda was dressed smartly in a blue pantsuit and white blouse, and carried a foil-covered pumpkin pie. Maureen appeared briefly by my side to relieve Linda of her package. "Everyone loves pumpkin pie," she whispered to Linda and was gone.

Victor wore a slightly wrinkled pair of khaki slacks, white shirt, and maroon cardigan sweater. I was again aware of what a big man he was, with wide shoulders, a bulging chest, and arms that were defined even beneath the fabric of his shirt and sweater. He towered over everyone in the room, although George came close to his height. I couldn't help but notice his reaction when shaking hands with Mort. I had the feeling—and that's all it was, a feeling—that they already knew each other. Silly notion, I told myself as I headed back to the kitchen to see how Maureen was doing.

"Ready to go," she announced. "I checked the bird. He's done to perfection. And I added a few things to the giblet gravy."

"What things?" I asked.

"My secret ingredient."

"Great," I said, hoping the gravy tasted like the giblet gravy to which I was accustomed. "Let's get everyone seated and serve the clam chowder and salads."

Because I was aware of seating certain people apart from each other, I'd done what I'd never done before at Thanksgiving, set out handwritten place cards with everyone's names at their seats. While the table was set for fourteen people, I'd left two place settings at the end without cards. I had, however, made up one that read "Hubert Billups" in the event he decided to show. I was now confident that he wouldn't.

Despite my concerns about pairing certain people, the mood at the table was appropriately festive and friendly. Conversation flowed easily as Maureen and I ladled the chowder into bowls, sprinkled on the garnishes, delivered salads, and joined the others.

"You'll say grace," Mort said to Seth.

"*Ayuh,*" Seth said. "I usually do."

Seth delivered what had become his standard prayer, with appropriate religious references combined with more secular expressions of thanks for the gathering of good friends, newcomers who would become good friends, and of course, for the bounty we were about to enjoy.

When he finished and people picked up their soup spoons, George asked if he could speak.

"Please do," I said.

He stood and cast a wide smile across the table. "It is a rare privilege to have been invited to join you for this most American of celebrations, and so I wish to propose a toast. It's said in Britain that it takes three people to properly offer a toast—one to hand the glass to the toaster, the toaster to drink from it, and the third to defend the drinker whilst he's otherwise distracted."

There were laughs; Archer Franklin's was the loudest and most prolonged. Victor Carson's was brief and forced. It took Mort a few seconds to get the humor. Once he did, he joined in.

"But since I'm the only Brit here—a Scotsman, actually—I'll have to fend for myself. You've welcomed me to Cabot Cove with open arms, and the warmth I've experienced will stay with me for a very long time." He raised his wineglass. "To my friends in Cabot Cove, Maine, good health, good fortune, and may we dine together again soon."

Other glasses were raised and a few said, "Hear! Hear!"

"Maybe we can get together for Guy Fukes Day in England," Franklin suggested.

"A splendid idea," George said, sitting, tossing me a sly smile and sipping his wine.

As we enjoyed our chowder and salads, Linda Carson commented on the two unoccupied place settings.

"I like to leave a place in case a last-minute guest arrives," I said.

"What a nice gesture," she said.

She was seated next to Mayor Shevlin, who engaged her and her husband in dialogue about their lives prior to settling in Cabot Cove. I eavesdropped on their conversation with one ear while listening to Maureen Metzger and Kathy Copeland compare their approaches to making turkey stuffing. While Kathy wasn't as obsessed with cooking as Maureen was, she had a skilled hand in the kitchen, and an even better one when it came to gardening. Maureen was impressed that Kathy was building an elaborate stone wall on her property.

"You're doing it all by yourself?" Maureen asked.

"Sure," said Kathy.

"Mort started one a few years ago," Maureen said, "but gave it up."

"Too much work," our sheriff said. "Besides, every time I'd put in a few rocks I'd get called down to headquarters."

"Being sheriff is a full-time job," Jim Shevlin offered.

"What do you do, Victor?" Franklin asked.

"I'm in the process of looking for a job."

"What sort of work?" I asked.

"I'm, ah—I used to be in the restaurant business. A manager. Casinos, too. I figure I'll find something in a restaurant around here."

That led to a flurry of suggestions as to where he might look, with others at the table coming up with names of people to approach.

"Is everyone done with their chowder and salads?" Susan asked, getting up to help me clear.

It appeared that they were. I'd just picked up the first empty bowl when the doorbell sounded. I handed the bowl to Susan and went to the door, wondering as I did who would be stopping in unannounced on Thanksgiving.

The answer came to me as I reached for the knob. I opened the door and my realization was confirmed.

"Happy Thanksgiving, Mr. Billups. Please come in."

Chapter Thirteen

I walked into the dining room and announced, "We have another guest."

Conversation stopped and everyone looked at me, and then beyond to Billups, who stood in the archway between the living and dining rooms.

"Mr. Billups—I'm sure he doesn't mind being called Hubert—is a little late, but that's certainly no problem."

Billups remained motionless, a blank expression in his eyes. He'd obviously washed up, and had trimmed his red beard a little. I was pleased that he'd shucked his usual uniform and wore a yellowed, slightly stained, double-breasted white dinner jacket, gray shirt, skinny black tie, tan cargo pants, and low black sneakers, a proud man who'd tried to dress for the occasion.

I grabbed his place card from a small basket on the breakfront, set it down at one of the two unoccupied spots at the table, and said, "Please sit down, Mr. Billups. I'm sure no one will mind waiting until you've had your clam chowder and salad."

Seth had a wry smile on his face as he said, "Welcome, Mr. Billups, and happy Thanksgiving."

Across from him, Mort was in shock, his face a wrinkled question mark as he looked at me, then back at Billups, who'd taken his seat. Susan Shevlin ladled chowder into the new arrival's soup bowl and placed a salad next to it.

"Jessica, can we talk?" Wilimena whispered in my ear.

We went to the kitchen.

"Jessica, what have you done?" she asked in a low, panicked voice.

"Inviting him? He's new in town and alone. Besides, I have my reasons for wanting to get to know him better."

Wilimena sighed deeply and crossed her arms in front of her. "This is terrible," she said.

Her comment surprised me, and I asked why Billups's arrival had upset her so.

She replied with great gravity, "It makes thirteen, Jessica."

"Thirteen *what*?"

"Thirteen people at the table."

I couldn't contain the laugh that erupted from me. "Are you really that superstitious, Willie?"

"Oh, you can laugh all you want, Jessica Fletcher, but having thirteen at the table can only result in tragedy."

"Well," I said, "we'll just have to weather that storm.

Why don't you go back and join the others? I'm sure everything will be fine."

Her face was set in a concerned scowl as she grabbed her cane from where she'd hung it on the counter and squeezed past Mort, who was coming into the kitchen.

"Are you having some kinda breakdown, Mrs. F?" he asked.

"Of course not," I said.

"What's *he* doing here?"

It would have been easy to pretend that I didn't know which "he" Mort referred to, but I simply said, "Enjoying Thanksgiving dinner with us."

"I don't know, Mrs. F. Don't you think it's taking a chance, inviting a guy like that into your home? He . . . he . . . could be a killer, for all we know. I still don't have a lot of information on the guy and I've been asking around for weeks."

"He's alone on a holiday and I'm offering him dinner and a bit of kindness. What kind of chance am I taking? I've got the sheriff on one side of the table and a Scotland Yard inspector on the other. If I'm not safe with the men in this house, I never will be."

Mort shook his head. "You're always full of surprises," he said, and departed the kitchen. I followed him and saw that Billups had finished his chowder and salad, and was listening to something Jim Shevlin was saying.

"Everyone ready for Tom Turkey?" I asked brightly.

The main part of the meal went smoothly despite the unexpected presence of Billups. He wasn't talkative, although he did respond to comments and questions from others at the table. And when we were making toasts—to everyone's health, to the hostess and her visiting Scotland Yard inspector, to welcome new neighbors—he raised his glass and called out, "Down the hatch." Everyone laughed except Linda, who had swallowed too quickly and coughed; her husband helped by pounding her on the back.

George sampled every dish and condiment, complimenting the various chefs who had contributed to the meal, and saving his highest praise for Maureen's praline sweet potato casserole, an opinion shared by everyone else, including me.

"It's a Southern recipe," she told him shyly. "I know Jessica wanted to have a classic New England menu for you, but I figured she wouldn't mind if we had sweet potatoes from another part of the country. It's still American."

"I don't mind where the recipe comes from when it's as delicious as this," I said, smiling at her.

Mort grinned and winked at his wife. I was willing to bet that he'd be delighted to eat these sweet potatoes another day, but I doubted there would be any leftovers for him to take home.

After the turkey and its accompanying dishes had been consumed and the plates and silverware removed to the kitchen, I suggested we take a break in the living room before coffee and dessert. As was usually the case at Thanksgiving dinner, everyone had eaten too much and needed a respite before attacking the array of pies and cakes provided by the guests, and by yours truly.

As I'd done at the table, I found myself interested in the interaction between people. Contrary to what I'd expected, Archer Franklin had kept his ego in check. For the most part he ignored Billups; an expression of disgust crossed his face each time he glanced in the direction of the newcomer, but he refrained from making any comment. Wilimena had spent most of the dinner looking concerned, as though a calamity would ensue at any moment. Her sister, Kathy, poked her with her elbow and whispered admonitions to stop being a baby. Mort kept his distance from Billups, and did the same with Victor Carson, who rivaled Billups as a noncommunicator. Linda Carson's spirits were high throughout the meal, chatting constantly while stealing peeks at Billups. She must have been wondering why I'd invited him. Seth staked out his favorite chair, a plump, overstuffed one where he fought to keep his chin from dropping to his chest. I sympathized with him. The heavy meal had made me drowsy, too.

"Coffee, Mr. Billups?" I asked.

"No, thank you. I'll be going."

"But you haven't had dessert."

"Thank you for the dinner. You're okay. G'bye."

I walked him to the door. He said nothing else as he went down the front steps, walked across the road, and disappeared from my sight. An odd man, to be sure, and I wondered what his life had been like prior to coming to Cabot Cove. My intention to learn more about him hadn't been successful, but maybe others at the table had gleaned information.

I returned to the living room, where George was in a discussion with Mort, Mayor Shevlin, Archer Franklin, and the Copeland sisters. I picked up snippets of their conversation as I gathered empty glasses to take to the kitchen, where Maureen, Susan, and Linda helped with the cleanup. Franklin was pontificating about what was wrong with Cabot Cove and what he'd do to fix it—provided, of course, that he was in a position to do anything. Seth had dozed off. Victor Carson stood at the window, his attention on anything but the room and those in it. He turned and intercepted me.

"Enjoying yourself?" I asked.

"Huh? Yeah, very much, only I'm not feeling too good."

"Oh, I'm sorry. Can I do anything for you, get you something, an aspirin or—?"

"I think I'd better leave," he said.

"If you'd feel better at home, I certainly understand."

I turned toward where the guests were talking. Mort's focus was on us, a frown on his broad face.

Victor went to the kitchen to tell his wife that he was leaving. Her expression immediately fell. I could see that she was torn: stay, or go with him?

"You stay," he said, and without a parting word he was gone from the house.

With two down, the eleven remaining guests enjoyed dessert and even livelier conversation than before—Willie had cheered up considerably—until fatigue set in and it was time to end the day. As I said goodbye to my friends at the door, I looked across the road and saw Hubert Billups pacing back and forth. Was he waiting to talk with someone? I wondered.

"I'll see if he wants a lift into town," Seth said. But

Billups waved Seth off when he stopped the car. Perhaps he would have accepted if the weather had been foul, but it was a lovely, unusually mild November evening, with plenty of stars and a full moon.

Once back inside, George suggested we finish the cleanup. The lure of the couch and the urge to let everything slide was powerful, but I knew he was right. An hour later, a little after nine, the house was put back together, and the only reminder of the earlier feast—apart from the aluminum foil packets in my fridge—were the delicious aromas that still lingered in the air.

"In the mood for a walk?" George asked.

"Good idea," I said, "get rid of some of these excess calories."

We went along the road in the direction of town, arm in arm, and all was well with the world. Dinner had been a rousing success, especially since it was clear that George had gotten a taste of the holiday traditions and its food, exactly what I had hoped for him.

"Happy?" he asked.

"Very. You?"

"Verra much," he said, the Scots accent clear. He squeezed my arm and smiled.

We covered what I judged to be a mile or a little less, and turned around. I was enjoying the crisp air and the company, so when we reached the house, I suggested that we continue to the end of the road, where the Carsons' home was located.

"Not the friendliest fellow," George commented when I mentioned the Carsons.

"He seemed terribly uncomfortable, but his wife certainly enjoyed herself," I said. "It was almost as though she seldom gets to go out and felt free for the first time."

"About your Mr. Billups," George said as we slowly strolled along the shoulder of the road, "not a bad chap. His presence seemed to unsettle the sheriff, although everyone else took it in stride."

"Not Wilimena Copeland. Billups was the thirteenth person at the table, which really bothered her. I had no idea that she was so superstitious. But I agree with you. Mort was on edge the minute he walked in. I'm sorry if Billups took away some of the pleasure of the holiday for Mort. I didn't stop to think of the run-ins he'd had with Billups, including the fight we witnessed between him and Archer Franklin. I really can't blame Mort for being uneasy."

Clouds had begun to roll in and obscured the moon during much of our postprandial stroll.

"I should have brought a flashlight," I said.

"Let's head back," George suggested.

We'd reached the Carsons' house. Lights shone through the windows. Their cat, Emerson, suddenly sprang out of a bush and ran across our path, causing me to jump. George pulled me close. "At least he's not a black cat," he said, chuckling.

"Now don't tell me you're superstitious, too."

"Not a bit. I'll even walk under a ladder to prove it to you."

"There's no need for extreme measures," I said.

We retraced our steps, the moon playing hide-and-seek with the clouds. When we were halfway home, they parted and the full moon came to life, shedding light over the swath of weeds that ran alongside the road, the feathery heads of dried grasses rippling in the breeze.

We were within yards of the house when George stopped. "What's that?" he said, pointing to an area of tall grass to our right.

I squinted to see what had captured his attention. Something in the grass now glistened in the moonlight, tiny specks of brilliance twinkling like earthbound stars.

It wasn't until I was ten feet from it that I recognized what it was.

The hilt of Seth's knife!

That should have been cause for celebration.

But there would be no celebration.

The elaborately crafted carving knife protruded from a body—a man's body from the glimpse I saw of his clothes. The moon had washed out the colors. It wasn't until George knelt beside the victim and swept aside the wispy grass that we saw the lifeless eyes of Hubert Billups.

Chapter Fourteen

George stayed with the body as I ran to the house and called 911. Within minutes police and medical personnel started to arrive, their flashing lights, blaring sirens, and crackling radios penetrating the night. Mort Metzger eventually joined his officers and took charge of the scene. They used crime-scene tape to create a wide off-limits area around Billups's body. George and I stood next to Mort's squad car and watched as his deputies performed their official duties. An officer videotaped the body from a variety of angles, as well as the surrounding area. Another of Mort's deputies took measurements. When Mort felt that things were appropriately buttoned down, he came to us.

"Well, he's definitely dead. You called it in, huh, Mrs. F?" he said.

"That's right. George and I were taking a walk and

spotted the handle of the knife sticking up. I was elated at first, thinking we'd found Seth's missing knife, but then we saw Mr. Billups."

"Before you found the body, did you notice anything out of the ordinary or see anybody else while you were walking?" Mort asked.

George and I looked at each other. "No," I replied. "There were cars that passed us, but no one on foot."

We turned as the medical examiner's ambulance arrived. The tape was pulled back to allow it to get close to the body, and two men in white coats placed Billups inside. I noticed that the knife had been carefully secured in a brown evidence bag by an officer wearing latex gloves.

Residents of other houses had ventured forth to see the cause of the commotion. Included among them were Linda and Victor Carson. They stood apart from others. She leaned against him, and he had his arm around her. I was pleased to observe their closeness, even though my instinct that theirs was a troubled marriage hadn't abated.

"I'd like you two to come down to my office in the morning and make formal statements," Mort said.

"Of course," said George.

"In the meantime, I suggest you lock up tight. Looks like we've got a homicidal nut running loose in Cabot Cove."

George and I returned to my house, where I made coffee, and we sat in the kitchen discussing what had just transpired. I'd been reluctant to express what I'd been worrying about since coming across the body, and George sensed I was holding something back. "Tell me what you're thinking, lass."

"I know it's an outlandish notion, but it has been running through my mind."

"What's that?"

"Do you think it could have been someone who was here tonight?" I said, chilled by the very thought.

"I can't imagine that anyone close to you would be capable of such madness," he said.

"I agree," I said, "but there were others here who aren't close to me, like Archer Franklin and Victor Carson. I really don't know them."

"Then it's not unreasonable to consider them suspects, Jessica, but what about the women? You mentioned that Ms. Copeland was upset at his arrival."

"Just a silly superstition about having thirteen people at the table. She was afraid it would result in tragedy. And look what happened. Now she'll be convinced she was right."

"Is she—?" He hesitated, patting the patch pockets on his jacket.

"Is she what?"

"Is she mentally unbalanced?"

His question took me aback. "No. Not at all," I said. "Willie can be quirky, but I don't see her as a murderer. As I said, I don't know anything about Victor Carson, and the same holds true for his wife, Linda. Archer Franklin certainly didn't have any love for Billups. We saw them fighting, and he'd made a number of comments about ridding the town of men like Billups."

"True, but he behaved relatively rationally tonight. And he's a wealthy businessman. Such men don't usually stoop to stabbing people in the chest with a carving knife."

"Ruthless ones stab competitors in the back now and then," I said.

George grunted, pulled his pipe from his jacket pocket, and stood up.

"Where are you going?"

"Thought I'd go outside and take a pull on my pipe. Helps me to think."

"You can do your thinking right here," I said.

"You don't mind?"

"I've always been partial to the aroma of a pipe."

George settled back in his chair. "What about your neighbor, Victor?" he asked as the flame from his match ignited the tobacco and sent a cloud of fragrant smoke into the air.

"I've been thinking about him. He probably represents the great unknown among people who were here, but why would he kill someone like Billups?"

"I don't have an answer," George said. "I'd say it's highly unlikely that anyone gathered around your table today is a murderer. Let's put that notion aside for the moment and step back. Billups was likely to have been killed by one of three people: someone he knew who bore him ill will, someone he may or may not have known, a deranged person, say." He took a puff on the pipe.

"And the third?" I asked

"Someone he didn't know at all, perhaps someone passing through, who selected him at random."

I remembered Mort telling me about a man at Billups's rooming house with whom Billups had had altercations. And there was Wally Winstead, a notorious Cabot Cove hothead consumed by jealousy over his wife, and who'd physically assaulted Billups. Who knows how many others he'd offended or enraged since his arrival in town?

George was right. There were ample avenues to follow to Billups's murderer without turning a suspicious eye on those who'd shared our Thanksgiving table. It had to have been someone from town with a grudge against Billups, or he'd been slain during a chance meeting with his killer.

It was almost midnight when George announced that he was leaving. I walked him to his rental car.

"Okay to drive to Seth's house?" I asked, aware that he'd had two short drinks of Scotch and water.

"I'm fine," he said. He placed his hands on my shoulders and gave them a squeeze. "I'm sorry, lass."

"Sorry about what?"

"That you've ended up close to another murder."

"That seems to be my fate."

"Sure you'll be all right alone? I've slept on many a couch in my day."

"I'll be fine. I'll lock up. We'll go to Mort's office first thing in the morning?"

"I'll be here at eight."

"I'll be ready."

We kissed good night and I watched him drive away. The mild night had turned chilly—or was it an inner chill I felt? I went to the house, ensured that the doors and windows were locked, poured myself a glass of cranberry juice, and settled behind the desk in my study. I'd forgotten about my novel and how far I was falling behind with each passing day. I stared at the computer screen on which the last page I'd written reminded me that I'd neglected to build upon it, advance the story, continue to lead my characters in the direction I intended for them.

"Go to bed," I told myself, and reached to turn off the desk lamp. But the last of the letters I'd been receiving over the past eight days stopped me. "GLOTCOYB," I said aloud.

Was there any connection between them and the fate that had befallen Billups? My earlier happiness had faded. I felt very much alone at that moment, impotent, unable to write my book or to make sense of anything—of unwelcome letters from a stranger, or the murder of a man who'd been watching me for weeks and who'd enjoyed dinner at my house only hours earlier.

I quickly undressed for bed and climbed beneath the covers. The full moon that had illuminated our grisly discovery was now positioned in the sky so that it was fully visible through one of the bedroom windows. Despite its beauty, it was too much of a reminder of what had occurred that evening. As I got out of bed and approached the window, intending to close the drapes, the honey-colored moon seemed to turn bloodred. I snapped the drapes together, scurried back to bed, and waited for sleep to deliver me from reality.

Chapter Fifteen

"Appreciate you folks coming in so early," Mort said after George and I had given our statements. "Nothing more you can remember?"

"Nothing I can think of," I replied. "We were taking a walk and came upon the body." I picked up a photo of the crime scene from Mort's desk and examined it.

"You, Inspector?"

"I think we've covered everything, Sheriff."

"Did you notice how the angle of the knife is straight in?" I said, turning the picture sideways to see if it made a difference.

George leaned over to see what I was looking at. "Whoever killed him slipped that knife between two ribs straight into his heart."

"Do you have any leads, Mort?" I asked.

"Too soon for that, Mrs. F. I'm heading over to that

rooming house where he lived. I sent one of my deputies there to make sure nobody disturbs it."

"Mind if we tag along?" I asked.

"Now, why would you want to do that, Mrs. F?"

"I feel very much a part of this," I said. "He'd been a guest at my dinner table hours before he was murdered, and had been spending an inordinate amount of time standing across from my house. Besides, there's the matter of the knife that killed him. It belonged to Seth, and I lost it."

"*We* lost it," George corrected.

"I suppose there's no harm in having you come with me," Mort said, "provided you stay out of the way."

"You have my word," I said.

Mort's expression said that he'd heard that from me before and didn't necessarily buy it.

We drove to the rooming house in Mort's marked vehicle. I'd not seen the building before, or at least hadn't noticed it. I admit to having a stereotypical expectation of what it would look like. I was wrong. Instead of being run-down, it was a nicely kept, very large older house that probably once had been home to multiple families. A small garden in front was neatly tended, and a fresh coat of yellow paint glowed in the morning sun. An unoccupied Cabot Cove patrol car was parked to the side of a wide driveway.

We stepped up onto the porch that ran the width of the house and Mort knocked on the front door. A woman immediately peered out from the carpeted entrance hall.

"I'm Sheriff Metzger, ma'am," Mort said, touching the brim of his Stetson.

"This is terrible," the woman said, wringing her hands. I'd seen her before around town, although we'd never had an opportunity to speak. She was in her sixties, with salt-and-pepper hair that flowed freely over her shoulders and down her back. She wore a black leather jacket over a red turtleneck sweater, and a black skirt that almost reached her ankles. "To think that a tenant of mine was murdered gets my blood boiling. A person isn't safe in this town anymore."

"Yes, ma'am," Mort said. "Where was Mr. Billups's apartment?"

"Apartment? We don't have apartments here, just rooms, but nice ones I can assure you. Never had no trouble with the law. I run a respectable establishment, check on my people before I let them stay. I don't like havin' a cop up there, I can tell you. Upsets the neighbors."

"The room's up there?" Mort asked, indicating the staircase.

"That's right, second floor, third door on your left."

"May we?" Mort said.

"Just make sure you wipe your feet," she said stepping back to pull the door wide. "I just cleaned up there."

We did as instructed. Mort didn't bother introducing George or me to the landlady, which was just as well. We followed the sheriff up the stairs to where a uniformed officer leaned against the wall next to an open door. A short strip of yellow crime-scene tape was draped across it. He snapped to attention upon seeing Mort, who said, "Relax, Joey. Nobody's been in there?"

"No, sir. I made sure of that."

"Good job."

The officer removed the tape and we followed Mort into the room. I'd arrived with another conventional notion, that Billups's room would be messy, and maybe even dirty. It was anything but. Neat as a pin, although I didn't know if that was Billups's doing or his landlady's. The bed was made, and no clothing was visible. The wastebasket was empty, except for a torn piece of newsprint. I reached down and pulled it out. Nothing was written or printed on it. I dropped it back in the basket.

Mort opened the only closet, in which the few pieces of clothing Billups possessed were neatly arranged. I went to a table next to his bed. On it were three small silver frames holding color photographs. I picked one up to examine its picture, but Mort said, "I'll be the one to do that, Mrs. F."

I replaced the frame on the table and took a few steps away to allow Mort to get close to the table, but not so far back that I couldn't see the photos along with him.

The first showed a man I assumed was a beardless Billups at a much younger age. He stood next to a beautiful woman on a beach. Both wore bathing suits. He had his arm around her shoulders, she had hers around his waist; they looked very much in love.

The second photo was more recent Billups, again minus his red beard. He stood in front of a storefront window next to another man; both wore suits and ties. There seemed to be a strong resemblance, and I surmised they were related.

Mort placed the second photo on the table and picked up the third.

"Mind?" I asked as I retrieved the second picture and studied it more closely. Behind the two men—the two brothers?—was a sign above the window, DOWN-THE-HATCH. It wasn't a very good photo, and had faded over time. But from what I could tell, Down-the-Hatch was a restaurant or bar.

"I suppose you want to take a look at this one, too," Mort said, handing me picture number three. This shot was of Billups being presented something by a white-haired gentleman. I had no idea who that man might be, but the setting had all the trappings of a politician's office.

"Interesting," I said, placing it next to the other two.

"What's interesting?" Mort asked.

"The pictures. I wonder where they were taken."

"No idea, Mrs. F. Never found out where he was from."

"Wherever it was, he could have made an enemy there," I added.

Mort sniffed as his eyes roamed the room but said nothing.

George had stood silently in the doorway, obviously not wanting to appear to be intruding on Mort's turf. Finally, he said, "I'd say that the victim had a confrontation with someone last night."

Mort turned. "I'd say that goes without saying, Inspector."

George smiled. "That he'd been stabbed in the chest means he'd faced his attacker, as opposed to someone sneaking up from behind. That's all I meant."

"You mentioned that he'd had an altercation with someone here at the rooming house," I said to Mort. "Have you spoken with him?"

"Not yet, but I will." He poked his head out the door and instructed his deputy to bring the landlady to the room.

She arrived, and not at all happy at being summoned. "You know my business doesn't stop just because you're up here, Sheriff," she said. "I've got more rooms to clean and dinner to get on for my tenants, and that means a trip to the market. Thanksgiving emptied the shelves, as it is. If I don't get there soon, the best produce will be gone. I don't imagine you're going to hang around and explain to my tenants why I can't put a decent dinner on the table. And don't tell me to go. I'm not leaving this house until you do."

"Can't be helped, ma'am," Mort said, doffing his hat. "Sorry to inconvenience you. We'll try not to keep you too long."

"See that you don't," she said, but Mort's courteous manners had disarmed her and her voice had softened.

Mort asked about the roomer who'd accused Billups of having stolen his things.

"That'd be Mr. Catalana. Pain in the neck, but not a bad sort." Her voice dropped to conspiratorial level. "He's paranoid, you know. Hears things, I think. But he always paid his rent on time. That's what matters to me, and that they act respectful and don't make a mess."

Mort pointed to his deputy. "Write down the name Catalana," he said. "We have to find this guy and bring him in." He turned to the landlady. "First name?" he asked.

Her brows shot up. "Beverly," she said, smiling and pulling a lock of hair across her shoulder, curling it around a finger.

"Not yours. His."

Beverly's face flooded. She dropped her hands to her side, where they fluttered like a bird unsure where to land. "Oh. Um. Pete. I mean, Peter J., I believe. Anyway, that's what he wrote in the register."

George rescued her from her embarrassment. "You said he always 'paid' his rent on time," he said gently. "Does he no longer live here?"

She swiveled toward him. "Left this morning," she said, recovering her poise. "Paid me for the week, packed his suitcase, and was gone." Her face twisted in thought. "You don't think that—"

"He leave a forwarding address?" Mort asked.

"No," she said. "They never do."

"We'll want to see his place, too, in a few minutes," Mort said, turning over items on the small desk that was among the sparse furnishings in Billups's room.

"Then you can call me when you're ready," the landlady said crisply, her limited supply of patience evidently having been exhausted. "I can't stand here waiting around for you. I've got chores to do." She bustled out the door, making a show of staring down the deputy to get him to move out of her way.

Mort's attention stayed focused on the desk. He opened its only drawer and pulled out the contents. On top of the pile was a menu, its edges frayed, the paper yellowed with age. He discarded it to the side, but I stepped closer to get a better look. Printed in fancy script at the top was DOWN-THE-HATCH. Below it was the establishment's Boston address and telephone number.

Mort finished going through papers from the desk, slipped them into a plastic bag he drew from his pocket, and handed them to the deputy. "I don't see anything here, but I'll look them over again in the office in case I'm missing anything."

"What about that menu?" I asked. "He might have had something to do with the restaurant it came from. One of the photographs has him posed in front of it."

"Oh, yeah, I noticed that, Mrs. F, but the shot could've been taken when he was on vacation. We got a lot more to find out about what he was into in Cabot Cove before I go digging into what he did who knows how many years ago. I doubt it's got anything to do with what happened here last night. I'm going to check out this Mr. Catalan's room and head back to the office."

"Catalana," I corrected softly.

"Whatever. I gotta hurry. I've got Wally Winstead coming in at nine thirty."

George looked quizzically at me.

"A fellow in town who accused Mr. Billups of flirting with his wife," I explained.

"Coming?" Mort asked.

"May I take this menu with me?" I asked.

"You collecting old menus now, Mrs. F?" Mort asked, snorting. "From the looks of it, it's from the Revolutionary War. Might be worth a fortune."

"A new hobby," I said with a smile.

"Suit yourself."

"While I'm suiting myself, may I borrow one of these photos for a few days? I promise to return it."

"Take 'em all," Mort said, his patience with me finding its limit. "But if some next of kin shows up, you'd better be prepared to bring them right back."

"Of course," I said. "They'll be on your desk Monday morning."

He grunted and I refrained from saying any more in case he changed his mind. Mort has welcomed my assistance in the past, but he was clearly not pleased at the moment. Perhaps the presence of a Scotland Yard inspector was intimidating. George would never interfere with Mort's investigation nor comment negatively on his analytical skills, but I could understand where having such an internationally experienced detective peering over his shoulder—so to speak—might make Mort ill at ease.

Mr. Catalana's now-unoccupied room provided nothing of interest, and we returned to headquarters, where Wally Winstead was pacing out front. Judging from his crimson face, Winstead was angry at having been kept waiting. "It's not like I got nawthin' better to do except sit around here twiddlin' my thumbs while you're rammin' around the countryside," he told Mort as we walked into headquarters.

"Ran a little late," Mort said, motioning for Winstead to follow him to his office. We trailed along.

"I gotta get to work. How come I've been brought down heah?" Winstead demanded. He was a big, beefy man with a large, round face and head, with a series of corkscrew blond curls sprouting from his pate at odd angles.

"It's about the murder last night," Mort said.

"Murder? What murder?"

"Hubert Billups."

"Who's he?"

"The man you attacked about your wife, the old guy with the red beard."

"That homeless bum? He got 'imself killed? Well, I'll be."

"Tell me about it," Mort said.

Winstead squirmed in his chair, and for the first time seemed to notice that George and I were also in the room. "What are you doin' here, Mrs. Fletcher?" he demanded.

"Don't worry about them," Mort said. "Where were you last night?"

"Now don't jump down my throat. I don't hafta answer your questions," Wally said. He faced me again. "You writin' some stupid story about this?"

"I suggest you lower your voice, sir," George said.

Winstead turned to Mort. "If you want to know the truth, I was home last night with the wife." His voice had increased in pitch.

"All night?" Mort asked.

"That's right. A man oughta be able to spend a night with his wife." He turned to me again. "If somebody killed that foolish old bum, he had it coming. Write that!"

"Who can vouch for your whereabouts last night?" Mort asked. I was impressed at how he maintained his composure, keeping his voice even and well modulated despite Winstead's provocative manner.

"My wife."

"Wives' alibis don't count," Mort said. "Who else? You have Thanksgiving dinner with other people?"

"You chargin' me?" Winstead said, standing and hitching up his trousers.

"Not at the moment," Mort said.

"Well, then, I'll be leavin'. All I did was pound up the fella, and he weren't dead then. I don't hafta be here."

George and I expected Mort to stop him, but he didn't say or do anything as the increasingly agitated Wally stormed from the office.

"I don't figure he'll go very far," Mort said.

"It may not be my place to interject, Sheriff," George said, "but I believe the man was lying about where he was last night."

"Oh? What makes you say that?"

"He had all the physical signs in his voice and his face. His eyes opened wider than usual, and his pupils were dilated. That suggests to me that he suffered more tension than if he'd simply been telling the truth. He was thinking hard about what to say. That tension showed up in his voice, too. Did you notice how much higher it became when he had to come up with an answer to your question?"

"And he didn't answer your question right away," I added. "He asked me a question first. That gave him some extra time to think of an answer to your question, Mort."

"I picked up on those things, too," Mort said. "I'm going to let him stew in his juices a bit, then get him back in here for further questioning. I know what I'm doing."

"Without doubt," George said. "Very sound thinking."

"And it's time for us to leave," I announced. "Thanks,

Mort. I appreciate your allowing us to come with you this morning. Oh, did Seth's knife provide any useful information?"

"Not yet. It's at the state lab. I expect some preliminary info later today." He seemed to relax now that we were making our departure. "By the way, Mrs. F, dinner was terrific yesterday. Best yet."

"I'm glad you enjoyed it, Mort. And please thank Maureen again for me. Her sweet potato casserole was superb."

Mort chuckled. "Yeah," he said, shaking his head. "It was. Whaddya know?"

Chapter Sixteen

We'd intended to go straight home, but when we passed the street on which Beverly's boardinghouse was located, I asked George to turn in.

"Forget something?" he asked.

"I just want to ask her a question. You can wait in the car. I won't be long."

George pulled his pipe from his pocket. "Take your time," he said.

Beverly recognized me when she answered my ring. "Did you leave your hat or something?"

"Didn't have a hat," I said. "I know how busy you are and I apologize for intruding on you again, but I did forget to ask you a question. I hope you don't mind."

"Might as well come in. With all these comings and goings, I'm not getting much done today anyway."

"Beverly, I'm afraid I don't know your last name."

"It's Shotwell."

"Well, then, Ms. Shotwell."

"You can use Beverly. I don't mind."

"And I'm—"

"I know who you are. Think there's anyone in town don't know who Jessica Fletcher is?"

While that news didn't come as a complete surprise, I can't say I was exactly pleased, but I simply said, "And you must call me Jessica."

"Okay. *Jessica*."

She led me into a small parlor that was not unlike my own, with a wooden rocker and an upholstered wing chair pulled up to a fireplace, and a faded settee nestled in the curve of a bay window. The room smelled like beeswax.

I perched on the settee and she took the rocker. "Ms. Shotwell, Beverly," I began, "I noticed how clean the rooms were upstairs, and here as well, of course."

Her eyes scanned the room. "I take great pride in keeping this place up," she said.

"And you've done a wonderful job."

She gave a sharp nod.

"Tell me," I said. "Did you clean up Mr. Billups's room this morning?"

"I did, although I didn't have to make up the bed."

"Ah, yes. Of course not. But when you were cleaning, did you happen to notice anything different? Was anything missing? Or was anything there that you hadn't seen before?"

"Not that I saw."

"Was Mr. Billups a neat man?"

"Pretty much like the rest. Not neat. Not messy."

"Did you empty his wastebasket?"

"Always do."

"What was in it?"

"I don't snoop on my tenants, Jessica."

"Of course not," I said quickly. "But as an observant person and someone accustomed to straightening rooms and emptying baskets, you would be aware if there were anything unusual or—"

"Nothing interesting. It was only yesterday's newspaper. That was all."

"Do you still have it?"

"Believe so. Haven't taken out the trash yet."

"Would you mind giving it to me?"

"You can have the whole trash bag if you want."

"That won't be necessary."

She left the room and a moment later returned with two folded newspapers. "He used to buy a paper every day. Big reader, I guess. Don't know which was his."

I examined then both. When I found the one with a small piece torn away from the front page, I knew I had Billups's newspaper. It was the *Boston Globe*. If he bought the *Globe* every day, it confirmed for me what I suspected, that he might have lived in Boston at some point.

"You said you check up on your tenants. Did you do that with Mr. Billups?"

"Well, I check up as best I can. He said he didn't have no arrest record. Sounded legit, and paid me the first week in advance."

"But he didn't provide you with any other background information, like where he was from?"

"No. And that's a whole bunch of questions. That it?" she asked.

"One more thing. Mr. Billups's room didn't have a bathroom."

"None of them do. They have to share the one in the hall."

"I didn't see a toothbrush or comb in his room. Did he leave them in the bathroom?"

"Probably. He's got his kit on a shelf. Each roomer has a shelf in the bathroom. Don't want anyone leaving their mess on my sink."

"May I see his kit?"

"You can have it. I got someone interested in the room. Already stopped by to see it after you left. She's going to call me later. I need that shelf cleared off for the new tenant. Of course, she didn't look like someone who would want to stay here, and I'm not sure I want a woman anyway. They're too much trouble."

Beverly trotted up the stairs and returned with a plastic bag holding the toiletry items belonging to the late Hubert Billups.

I thanked her for her time and patience, and returned to the car. George had rolled down the windows, so there was only a faint aroma of pipe tobacco when I settled in the passenger seat.

"Learn anything new?" he said, starting the engine.

I sighed. "Nothing useful, I imagine."

As we drove back to my house, I remembered that

there would be a mail delivery waiting. I mentioned it to George.

"One hopes there won't be another GLOTCOYB letter," he said.

"Yes," I said, giving him a small smile. "One hopes."

Our hopes were rewarded. The bundle in the mailbox did not contain another of the telltale envelopes.

"Perhaps your torment is over," George said as I sorted through the correspondence on the kitchen table. "The sender may have gotten bored."

"If it's so, I'm grateful for that, but it doesn't answer the question of why those eight letters were sent to me in the first place."

"You may never know, lass," George said. "Some people get their jollies by sending anonymous missives and never revealing their identity."

"That would be a shame," I said, tearing up an advertising circular.

George laughed. "What do we have planned for the rest of the day?"

"I haven't really thought about it. I assume Mort will be questioning the others who were at dinner yesterday, both the men and the women."

"An equal-opportunity investigator."

"Appropriately so," I said. I opened my shoulder bag and took out the plastic bag Beverly Shotwell had given me with Billups's toiletries. I peered at the contents—a comb, a frayed toothbrush, an almost empty tube of toothpaste, and a rusty pair of scissors—nothing that gave any hint of the man or insight into the crime.

Sighing, I unfolded the menu taken from Billups's room, laid it on the table, then set the three photos next to it. I studied the face of the victim as a young man. Was there anything in these photos that could give us a clue to his life—and his death? Or were they simply mementos of happier days?

"I have the feeling that your mind is shifting into high gear, Jessica. You get a certain look in your eye when the hunt is on."

"What look is that?"

"Now don't get offended, dear lady. It's a look I take great pleasure in seeing. When you're presented with a puzzle, it brings all your concentration into focus, sparks that famous inquisitiveness, and displays the uniqueness of your intellect. It's a rare talent, and one I'm enjoying seeing you apply to the unfortunate soul who met his Maker last evening."

I sat back and directed a stream of air at my forehead. "I simply can't accept that Mr. Billups was killed by some stranger. Wally Winstead is a hothead, it's true, but how would he have gotten hold of Seth's knife? The same is true for the other tenant from the rooming house, although his disappearance following the murder *is* suspicious." I paused.

"Go on," George said. "What else are you thinking?"

"Billups's behavior since arriving in Cabot Cove was strange, to say the least—hanging around on the road across from my house, showing up where I happened to be in town, even accepting my invitation for Thanksgiving dinner. Then there are those letters with that indecipherable message. And I don't believe that someone like Archer Franklin, with all his braggadocio, is capable of murder, despite his dislike of Billups and others like him."

"Why not?"

"This is an awful thing to say, but somehow I don't think Mr. Franklin would stab someone who stood facing him. Now, if Mr. Billups had been stabbed in the back . . ." I trailed off.

"What about Mr. Carson?" George asked. "He's not a known quantity to you. He lives on the road where the murder took place, *and* was at your senior center when the doctor's knife was stolen."

I nodded in agreement. Everything George said was correct. But the set of circumstances he'd voiced didn't add up to any tangible reason to suspect Victor Carson or his wife, Linda. "He might be an antisocial sort of fellow, but that doesn't necessarily translate into being a murderer," I said. And even though my new neighbors had been at the senior center, whoever used the knife to kill Billups could have gotten it or stolen it from someone else.

At George's encouragement, I spent the next half hour trying to get back into my novel. It wasn't a successful attempt, which I knew would be the case when I sat down. I'm not very good at writing in fits and starts, and that had been the situation for the past few weeks. My friends know that once I settle in for full days of writing, I'm in a hibernation of sorts and best left alone. That's what I needed: a two-week stretch of uninterrupted time to immerse myself in the novel and not be distracted by bizarre letters, a lost knife, men being stabbed to death across the street, or holiday preparations. My writing required time with no phone calls and no visitors—even the wonderful man currently sitting in my living room reading my day's pile of newspapers.

The ringing phone didn't bother me because I was getting ready to call it quits anyway.

"Jessica, it's Archer Franklin."

"Hello, Archer," I said warmly, thinking how nice it was that he was calling to thank me for dinner. It *had* been a lovely Thanksgiving, the subsequent events notwithstanding.

"I need to see you."

"Oh? About what?"

"About this pathetic excuse Cabot Cove has for a sheriff."

"Oh!" My hackles went up. Although Mort Metzger and I had had our run-ins now and then, he was a fine law enforcement officer, and I didn't take kindly to slurs about him.

"He wants me to come in for questioning."

"Ah," I said. "It must be about the murder. I assume he wants to interview everyone who was at dinner with the victim. George Sutherland and I gave our statements at police headquarters this morning."

"And someone of your stature allows this buffoon to drag you to his office?"

"I don't know why you're calling me about this. Sheriff Metzger is doing his usual good job, and I suggest that you should do what he asks."

There was an energetic snort on the other end.

"Mr. Franklin?"

"Our law enforcement officers should be ridding our streets of bums like the one who was killed, and not harassing leading citizens."

Leading citizens? I doubted that this newcomer to Cabot Cove could claim that status.

"Mr. Franklin, I really must go. I have—"

"What's with this Mr. Franklin business, Jessica. It's Archer. Remember?"

"Yes, of course. Sorry, but I really have to run. Bye."

What nerve, I thought as I rejoined George and recounted the conversation.

"A wee bit full of himself, isn't he?" George commented.

"Worse than that," I said. "I can't imagine what Wilimena sees in him."

"Dollar signs?"

"I prefer to think she's got more character than that. I certainly hope she does. But I don't know why she doesn't see through him."

"People tend to see what they expect to see, Jessica."

"True." I stopped, staring off into space.

"What is it, Jessica?"

"George, I have an idea."

Chapter Seventeen

George listened intently as I told him what I wanted to do. When I finished, he sat back, closed his eyes, and his lips formed a small, wry smile. His eyes opened. He leaned close to me and said, "I can understand why your crime novels are so successful."

" 'Crime novels,' I repeated. "That's right. You don't call them 'mystery novels' in England."

"Call them what you will," he said, "your success has everything to do with the way your mind processes grisly matters like murder, to say nothing of your tenaciousness and inherent curiosity."

"You sound like Seth."

"Not a bad person to emulate."

"But you do think I'm right."

"Yes. Frankly, I'm surprised that your sheriff doesn't

share your belief that knowing as much as possible about the victim's past can be pivotal to solving his murder."

"Mort deals very much with the here and now," I offered in defense of our sheriff, "and he sometimes jumps to conclusions prematurely. I'm afraid that's what he's doing here, treating Mr. Billups's murder as having to do with a recent event or random incident. He may be right, but I can't help feeling there's more to it than that."

"Your instincts have been solid ever since I first met you, Jessica. By all means follow them."

I'd decided to find out as much about Hubert Billups as possible. I knew that it might prove to be an academic exercise, turning up nothing that would bear upon his murder. Then again, I've always been a believer in the past influencing the present. Or, to put it more plainly, we are who we were. It seemed at first blush that Billups's past was unrelated to his arrival in Cabot Cove, and to his death. But things on the surface often cover up deeper truths, like finding an artistic masterpiece beneath a less valuable painting.

George was scheduled to leave from Boston on Sunday for his flight back to London. I suggested instead that we travel to Boston the next day, Saturday, and do a little snooping into Hubert Billups's background in search of something, anything, that might help make sense of his vicious murder. George readily agreed.

I called Jed Richardson to see whether he could change his schedule and fly us to Boston tomorrow. He said he could accommodate us, and we booked him for a nine-o'clock departure.

"I'd like to make Seth aware of our change in plans," George said, looking at his watch.

"He's invited us for dinner tonight, and I accepted on our behalf. You can let him know then."

"Yes, I can. But I planned to bring him a little gift as thanks. Would you care to accompany me into town to pick something out?"

"Mind terribly if I don't? I have a little catching up to do."

"Working on your novel?"

"Perhaps."

"I'm guessing you have another sort of computer work in mind," he said, kissing my cheek. "I shouldn't be too long. I'll ring you up when I'm on my way back."

George knew me too well. I'd already dismissed any notion of trying to work on my novel. Instead, I booted up the computer again, went to Google, and typed in "Down-the-Hatch." Four sites came up, and I clicked on the first, the official Web site for a restaurant and bar. According to its self-serving blurb, it was one of Boston's oldest eating and drinking establishments in the Back Bay area, and further billed itself as "the real answer to *Cheers*." Two color photographs were posted. The shot taken of the exterior, although updated, was unmistakably the same setting that appeared in the picture of Billups and the man I thought might be his brother. The interior photograph showed a large masculine room with a long bar running along one side, and tables filling up the other. The bill of fare hadn't changed significantly; it reflected the same options as the menu Billups had saved, offering what can only be described as pub fare—chicken wings, burgers, salads, soups, and "pies affectionately baked on the premises." There was no listing of owners or managers.

A second posting was a review of Down-the-Hatch in the *Boston Globe*. It wasn't a particularly positive one, although the reviewer did say that the establishment had been at its location for sixty-six years and served a loyal clientele.

Posting number three was simply a listing of Boston pubs that included Down-the-Hatch.

The fourth was decidedly more interesting. It was a brief article taken from the *Boston Herald*. According to the reporter, Down-the-Hatch had been shuttered during an investigation of the finances of its new owners, who were alleged to have ties to organized crime. I printed out that story before scrolling through the next two dozen entries in search of a follow-up but found nothing, nor did the name "Hubert Billups" together with "Boston" produce anything on Google.

Before shutting down the computer, I typed in the name Archer Franklin on a whim. The only thing I knew about his background came from Wilimena, and her knowledge was based upon what he'd told her. Of course, I'd also experienced firsthand his bravado and heightened sense of self-importance. While links to several "Franklin Archers" popped up, I couldn't find anything on Archer Franklin, the man who claimed to be an expert in the commodities market.

Strange, I thought, that a man with the level of business success he claimed to have wouldn't have had anything written about him, not even a mention in the well-known business magazines, nor the obscure ones for that matter. Was Archer Franklin his real name? If not, why would he have chosen to assume a new identity?

Further research yielded nothing more and after an hour, I was too fidgety to stay chained to my desk. I'd wished I hadn't encouraged George to go into town alone. His trip was coming to an end, and all the events of the past few days had dashed my hopes of a leisurely visit, with quiet times to catch up on our respective lives. Thinking he may have preferred to present Seth with his gift in private, I called the house.

"Stopped by a bit ago on his way into town," Seth said when I asked for George. "I've been busy with patients. He did tell me that he'll be leaving tomorrow instead of Sunday. What brought that about?"

I considered what to tell Seth. If I said I was going to Boston to dig into Hubert Billups's background, he'd undoubtedly be critical of me for poking my nose into what is a police matter. So I said instead, "I thought George would enjoy a day and night in Boston, Seth. He seems pleased with the idea."

Seth laughed. "I'll miss having him here," he said. "He's a fine gentleman."

My face lit up. I'd been nervous about George staying with Seth, based upon tensions that seemed to have existed between the two men during previous meetings. How nice that Seth agreed with my assessment of George.

"We'll have to get him back here again soon," I said.

"Ayuh, that we will, or visit him across the pond."

"I like that idea even better," I said. "If George comes back, Seth, please ask him to call."

"Happy to, Jessica. See you this evening."

I realized with horror that I'd sent George off without even offering him lunch, and decided to head into town on the off chance I'd run into him, and we could grab a bite together. It was a beautiful, sunny day, with mild temperatures still dominating the region. Despite George's admonition not to ride my bike until the GLOTCOYB matter was resolved, I elected to do just that. I needed the exercise, wanted to stretch my legs and breathe in some fresh air.

I noticed that the front tire on my bicycle was low on air, used my trusty hand pump to fill it up, and headed downtown. I looked for George's rental car along the way but didn't spot it. I parked in the bike rack in front of the clothing shop that Beth Wappinger had opened. She was already decorating her store window for Christmas. When she saw me, she waved me inside. I hadn't intended to stop in, but couldn't be rude.

"I knew you'd want to see those new blouses," she said to me just as another customer called out to her. Beth raised a finger to indicate she'd be with me in a minute. I'm not an avid shopper and never have been, although there have been times when I've enjoyed picking out a new outfit for a special occasion, especially when I had travel plans. Idly, I looked through the rack of new blouses Beth had gotten in. Although they were pretty enough, I wouldn't buy one. While I do love bright colors, I'm more of a traditionalist than drawn to modern styles. I insist on comfort, and lean toward classic designs that will wear well for many years, my New England taste coming to the fore.

The other customer left—without purchasing anything, I noticed—and Beth joined me. "Aren't they beautiful?" she said, touching the blouses. "He's a hot new California designer. I was lucky to get on his list."

"They're lovely," I said, meaning it, "but not really for me, Beth."

"They are a little, well, lively," she said. "What brings you downtown?"

"Just out for a ride. It's a lovely day."

"And how is that handsome Scotland Yard inspector of yours?"

"George is fine, although it hasn't been the sort of visit I envisioned for him. Too much going on."

"Like a murder," she said.

I nodded. "Yes, like a murder."

"I noticed that you and the inspector were down at the sheriff's office this morning. Does he have any leads on who killed that old man?"

"Afraid not, at least none that he shared with me. How was your Thanksgiving?" I asked.

"Nice. Josh was home—for a change." She rolled her eyes up toward the ceiling. "I wish he'd get a job where he's not traveling so much."

"Maybe he'll get tired of being on the road and settle into a job here in Cabot Cove."

"That would be heavenly. How's your book coming?" she asked with a mischievous grin.

"Slow, but getting there. Thanks for asking."

"We're all rooting for you to finish it," she said.

"And I'm sure all that 'rooting' will help."

"Sure you don't want to try on one of these blouses? The bright colors will bring out the color in your cheeks and—"

"Thanks, no, Beth. We'll catch up again soon."

I walked down to Charles Department Store, where I thought George might have shopped for a gift for Seth, and inquired about him. David, one of the owners, said he hadn't been in. As I was leaving, Kathy Copeland, Wilimena's sister, came through the door. She was dressed as she usually was, in jeans, a flannel shirt, and boots. Kathy is an inveterate gardener. Thanksgiving was one of the few times I'd seen her this year when she hadn't been wearing gardening clothes. But beneath that rough-hewn garb is a pretty, feminine woman who's never found the right man to marry. Or perhaps she prefers to remain single. The contrast between Kathy and her sister is marked. Willie is an inveterate consumer, whether it's high fashion, face-lifts, expensive cosmetics and perfumes, or diet products. She would never be caught with dirt under her fingernails. Unlike Kathy, she's had several husbands, and is almost never without masculine company.

"Great dinner yesterday," Kathy said. "The turkey was cooked to perfection."

"I thought so, too," I said. "I had a lot of help and it was an interesting mix of people."

She laughed. "It certainly was." Her face became serious. "I was sorry to learn about Mr. Billups. And just as we might have gotten to know him."

"Yes, I was sorry, too."

"Well, I'll see you soon." She started to move toward the stairs leading to the second floor of the landmark store, but I stopped her. "Kathy, do you have a minute?" I asked.

"Of course."

"Let's go outside."

She looked at me quizzically but followed me to the sidewalk.

"Kathy," I said, "I know this might not be any of my business, and if I'm intruding where I shouldn't, stop me."

"Okay."

"What do you and Willie know about Mr. Franklin?"

She fidgeted with a button on her shirt. "Know about him? What do you mean?"

"What I mean is, just what do you *really* know about him?"

She looked down while gathering her thoughts. When she looked up, she said, "Gee, Jessica, I suppose we don't know very much about him aside from what he's told us. Why do you ask?"

"Oh, you know me, Kathy, always asking questions and looking for answers. It's in my writer's genes, I suppose."

She cocked her head. "Come on, Jessica, level with me. Do you have suspicions about Archer?"

"Frankly, yes."

She looked left and right before saying, "So do I."

"Care to share them with me?" I asked.

"Let's go over there," she said, pointing to one of Cabot

Cove's many pocket parks created by Mayor Shevlin and his administration.

"He's too full of himself," she said after we'd shooed two pigeons from a bench and claimed their seats. "He's all bluster and boasting about his business success, how much money he has, the houses he's sold, things like that."

"And you don't think he's telling the truth?"

"I don't know for sure whether he is or not. But that's not what bothers me. For someone with all his alleged money, he's a sponger."

"Sponging off you and Willie?"

"Right. She ends up paying whenever they go out to eat, and he's even borrowed money from her."

"For what purpose?"

"Some business deal he said he had to act upon quickly but didn't have immediate access to his funds. It really worries me, Jessica. You know Willie when it comes to men. She needs their attention and approval, and that's gotten her into so much trouble over the years. She came into that money from the gold in Alaska, and it's a lot. But it can go fast—and is."

"I understand your concern," I said.

"And now he's staying with us."

"Oh? When did that happen?"

"Two days ago. He said it's only temporary until he closes on a house he plans to buy. He said he doesn't feel safe on his houseboat, that there have been break-ins at the marina. I haven't heard about any break-ins. Have you?"

"No, I can't say I have."

"You know how Cabot Cove is. I find it hard to believe we wouldn't have heard about any criminal activity in such a well-to-do neighborhood. Do you know what I think?"

"Tell me, Kathy."

"I think—I think that somebody's after him and he's hiding out with us."

"The law?"

"Maybe. Or somebody else he's conned. I can't sleep at night worrying about it."

"Have you discussed your feelings with Willie?"

"I tried, but right away she jumps to his defense. She says I don't understand the way big business works and the pressures someone like him suffers." Kathy gave a soft snort. "The problem is I think I understand only too well. Please don't tell her about this conversation, Jess. She'd be furious."

"I won't," I said. "I promise."

She stood. "I'd better go. I need to buy a new coffeepot at Charles. Willie burned the one we had last night. She left it on the stove and forgot about it until the living room got smoky. It's ironic, really."

"Why's that?"

"We'd been talking about Archer when the pot burned, and I'd been telling her to wake up and smell the coffee."

Chapter Eighteen

My search for the missing Scotland Yard inspector was not successful, and realizing that I was famished—and would never make it to dinner without something in my stomach—I stopped in for a quick bowl of minestrone at Peppino's, where its owner, Joe DiScala, greeted me at the door. A lively crowd had gathered in the bar and I opted for a small table there. Friends greeted me as I settled in. Unlike those who like to get a jump on the holiday season and fill the stores in search of bargains, I take the Friday after Thanksgiving as a day of relaxation. The planning and preparations for the big Thursday meal are but a happy memory; it's time to relax and enjoy a "down" day. There would be plenty of leftover dishes as the weekend progressed, which might explain why a decidedly nonturkey dish had its appeal.

As I savored my soup and freshly baked hot bread,

Joe joined me. After the requisite conversation about our respective Thanksgiving dinners—Peppino's had been closed on Thursday in honor of the holiday—he mentioned Hubert Billups's murder and asked if I knew anything about the investigation.

"Absolutely nothing, Joe," I said. "What have you heard?"

He nodded toward the bar, where a spirited discussion was taking place about how Cabot Cove was changing, and not for the better. I picked up snatches of the conversation: that Franklin guy was right; the police weren't doing their job; the mayor had lost touch; and there were too many outsiders arriving.

I shrugged. "There are bound to be changes," I said, "but that doesn't necessarily mean they're bad for the town. It's still relatively crime free, and—"

I turned to see Archer Franklin and Wilimena Copeland come through the door, Franklin leading the way, with Willie leaning on her cane, bringing up the rear. Joe got up to accompany them to the main dining room, but Franklin spotted me and came to the table.

"Ah," he said, "my favorite writer."

"Hello, Archer. Hello, Willie."

"About that call I made to you regarding the sheriff," he said. "I went down there and gave my statement. I still think it's outrageous that an upstanding, law-abiding citizen is hauled into police headquarters like a common criminal. I gave that bozo of a sheriff a piece of my mind that he'll not soon forget."

"I'm sure he appreciated your input."

Willie shifted her feet, an expression of discomfort on her face. I asked how she was doing.

"All right," she said, sounding as though she was unsure. To Franklin: "Let's get a table. I'm hungry."

"Can't have my honey suffering hunger pangs, now, can I?" Franklin said. "I'm still looking forward to getting together with you to discuss my works."

"Oh, I am, too, Archer," I said.

After seating them, Joe returned carrying an espresso demitasse for me.

"Do they come in often?" I asked.

He nodded and leaned across the table. "He's a good customer and all, but so difficult. He sends everything back. He chooses a wine, sniffs the cork, swirls it around in his glass, tastes it, and says it's no good. The pasta is never al dente enough, the sausage too spicy. You'd think he was paying the bill."

"She pays?"

"Always. She's a nice lady."

He didn't have to finish his thought. He obviously felt that Willie was being used by Franklin, which mirrored her sister's view.

I paid and stepped outside. During the time I'd been inside Peppino's, the blue sky had changed to ominous gray, with towering black cumulus clouds moving west to east, carrying with them potent thunderstorms. A few raindrops had already begun to fall, but by the time I'd pedaled halfway across the parking lot, the sky opened and rain came down in sheets, instantly soaking me.

I considered going back to the restaurant and waiting

it out, but I was already a soggy mess; better to head for home, a hot shower, and change of clothes.

There were times as I moved slowly along the road leading to my house that the rain was so dense I had trouble seeing. Apparently drivers had difficulty seeing me, too, since so many of the passing cars splashed water on me. It really didn't make much difference. I couldn't get any wetter.

Standing water covered portions of the road where drainage was poor. Some of it was quite deep, and I was concerned that I might take a tumble while pushing through it. That fear became reality when I was halfway home. A car, driving too fast for the conditions, went whizzing by, its side-view mirror coming dangerously close. I swerved in a nervous reaction, lost traction, and fell on my derriere, leaving me sitting in a foot of water. I pulled myself up, relieved that the only damage was to my ego. I picked up my bike and decided walking might be a safer choice for the next portion of the trip. I'd taken a few steps when I heard a horn. I turned. George pulled up next to me. He cranked open his window and said, "Need a ride, lass?"

"George!" I shouted. "Thank goodness."

He put on the car's flashers, popped open the trunk, jumped out, and helped wedge my bike into the "boot," as he called it. By the time he'd gotten back into the car, he too was soaked, and we both made a "whooshing" sound as we settled on the seats.

"What possessed you to try and bicycle home in this downpour?" he asked, shifting into gear and pulling away.

"I thought that—no matter. I'm just glad you came along."

"You look absolutely beautiful with water running off that fine nose," he said.

"I'm a mess."

"All in the eye of the beholder, Jessica. You'll soon be warm and dry." He hummed "Singin' in the Rain" as we continued the trip. We passed the spot where we'd come upon the lifeless body of Hubert Billups, and the chill I experienced had nothing to do with the clammy clothing pasted against my body.

Once home, I gave George a sweat suit to change into—three sizes too big for me, it had been a recent gift that I hadn't found time to return—while I took a hot shower and put on another sweat suit that was my size. With our wet clothes in the dryer, George lit the logs in the fireplace and while we sat in front of the flames and enjoyed steaming cups of tea, I told him of my conversations with Kathy Copeland and Joe DiScala about Archer Franklin.

"If what they say is true," George said, "I feel sorry for Ms. Copeland."

"I thought for a while that she'd latched onto him because he was rich," I said, "but it now looks as though it's the other way around. I Googled him and found nothing under the name Archer Franklin."

"For a man of his alleged successes, I find that strange."

"And he moved in with Kathy and Wilimena a few days ago."

"Another bad sign."

"Wilimena isn't a stupid woman," I said. "Surely she's capable of seeing that Archer isn't all he claims to be."

"One would hope so, although you've said she craves male attention. I suppose that could explain the blinders she's wearing."

"Did you find a gift for Seth?" I asked.

"I certainly did. In our conversations, Seth revealed that, like me, he's an avid reader of history."

"No wonder you got along so well."

"We did, in fact. Anyway, I noticed that Seth had the first and second volumes of Edmund Wilson's excellent series of diary entries from the last century, spanning the twenties through the sixties. I found a bookstall outside of town that stocks rare and used books, and bought him the editions he was missing."

"He'll love it. He's always been a fan of Wilson."

"A crusty chap with an outsized ego, and intellect."

"Edmund Wilson, or Seth?"

He laughed. "Wilson, of course. I'll give Seth the books at dinner tonight."

We decided to leave early for Seth's to allow George to change into a fresh set of clothing. Scheduled to join us that evening were Jack and Tobé Wilson, who were running late, something to do with emergency surgery Jack had to perform on someone's pet. Seth had been busy in the kitchen when we arrived, prepping a dinner of fresh brook trout dusted with oatmeal; broccoli; small Yukon Gold potatoes baked with onions, garlic and green peppers; and for dessert a pineapple upside-down cake fresh from Charlene Sassi's bakery. With culinary matters under control, and with George off changing his clothes and finishing packing for our departure the next morning, Seth and I sat in his living room.

"I'll be sorry to see him go," Seth said.

"So will I. I feel as though I've barely seen him."

"I have a feeling, Jessica, that Inspector Sutherland might be close to asking you a question."

My raised eyebrows invited him to explain.

"He's in love with you, you know."

I looked down at my hands folded in my lap.

"But I'm sure that doesn't come as a surprise."

I looked up at my friend of so many years, who was smiling. "I assume you and George have been discussing me," I said.

"Your name did come up a few times."

"And you think, based upon those conversations, that he's about to ask me a question?"

"Ayuh, and I'm sure I needn't elaborate on what that question will be."

"Are you telling me this, Seth, to warn me?"

"That's a little harsh, Jessica."

"If you are, I'll consider it positively, as trying to spare me a surprise."

"Well, now, if George Sutherland should propose marriage to you, there would be no surprise in that. I suppose I'm curious as to what your response might be."

"And I don't have an answer for you, Seth. It isn't as if I haven't thought about it many times since meeting George, but—"

"Ah, there he is, all garbed up," Seth said as George entered the room.

"Have I missed anything?" George asked.

"No, just catching up," Seth said, casting a sly smile at me.

Jack and Tobé arrived, and Seth poured drinks.

George, who's usually in good spirits, was absolutely ebullient this evening. He isn't what you would term a chatty man, not one for small talk, but he quickly fell into a storytelling frame of mind and entertained everyone with tales of cases on which he'd worked, especially those involving dumb criminals.

". . . and so this bloke stands there blinking furiously and scratching his nose, sure signs that he's lying. It's called the Pinocchio Syndrome. There's even a theory that blood rushes to the nose when you tell a lie, making it itchy. But the kicker, of course, was that he'd written his stickup note on the back of his business card. There's a right turnup for the books, wouldn't you say?"

With Jack and Tobé encouraging him, George continued to tell amusing stories during dinner. While I enjoyed them as much as others at the table, I couldn't stop thinking about what Seth had said. Was George about to propose marriage to me? Seth had been right when he said that a proposal would not come as a surprise. George and I had discussed the subject of marriage on more than one occasion, although none of those conversations had involved a formal proposal. Rather, they revolved around our individual lives and whether marriage was in the cards for either of us. George had left little doubt that were I receptive to a proposal, he would offer one. But he was also well aware that I was not ready to commit to such a dramatic change in my life, and that I might never be.

Had he decided that by formally proposing marriage, it might break through my resolve to not alter my life? Was he planning to do it in front of my friends in the hope that they would pressure me to accept? Or was it Thanksgiving that prompted him to choose this time and place to pop the question?

I thought of that famous bit of folklore involving Captain Myles Standish, the Pilgrims' military leader, who though fearless in battle was hopelessly shy when it came to women. He'd fallen in love with Priscilla Mullens but couldn't muster the nerve to ask for her hand in marriage. He enlisted the aid of his friend John Alden to approach her on his behalf, which Alden did. Priscilla was reported to have replied, "Why don't you speak for yourself, John?" Alden took her suggestion, and he and Priscilla were married soon after.

Seth might have meant well in forewarning me, but all it accomplished was to set me on edge throughout dinner. I kept looking at George for a sign that he might actually be poised to propose, but he gave no indication of it.

Following dinner, and after we'd helped clear the table and tidy up the kitchen, we returned to the living room for coffee and after-dinner drinks. If it were going to happen, I decided, it was now. My heart skipped a beat when George, a glass of Seth's vintage brandy in his hand, asked for everyone's attention. I closed my eyes and waited.

"My visit here has been a wonderful one," George said. "I haven't had the pleasure of spending much time with Dr. and Mrs. Wilson, but I intend to rectify that the next time around. I'm especially grateful to Dr. Hazlitt, who opened his home for me and has been a splendid host." George left the room, returning seconds later carrying the neatly wrapped books he'd purchased. He handed the package to Seth, whose expression indicated he was truly surprised.

Seth tore off the paper and removed Edmund Wilson's volumes one by one, admiring each as he did. "This was certainly unnecessary, George," he said, "and I'm touched by your generosity, as well as your taste in literature."

George laughed. "I thought you'd enjoy having the complete set."

"That I do, and I intend to read every word," Seth said. He got to his feet, reached behind his chair, and came up with another package, this one wrapped in silver paper. "Seems to me," he said, "that this might be a good time to become a gift giver, too." He crossed the room. "For you, Jessica," he said.

"What is this for?" I asked, turning the small but surprisingly heavy package in my hands.

"Open it and find out," Tobé said.

All eyes were on me as I pulled on the red silk ribbon and the wrapping fell away to reveal a gleaming marble statue of a man holding a writing tablet and quill pen.

"What's it supposed to be?" Jack Wilson asked.

I found the answer by reading what was inscribed on a brass plate at the base:

"Be thou the tenth Muse, ten times more in worth
Than those old nine which rhymers invocate."

William Shakespeare, Sonnet 38

"It's lovely, Seth," I said. "Thank you."

"I figured since you've been having trouble finishing your latest book, your regular muse might have skipped out on you, so I came up with this new one, compliments of Willie Shakespeare."

"Where did you have it done?" I asked.

"Up in Portland. Remember Regina Gormley?"

"Of course I do. She's a wonderful sculptress. I was sorry to see her leave Cabot Cove after her husband died."

"She moved to Portland. We've kept in touch, so when I had this idea to get you a new muse, I called her. She came up with Shakespeare and that quote. Flew up with Jed Richardson to pick it up personally."

I kissed Seth's cheek and said, "I have a feeling, Seth, that this new muse is exactly what I need. With him looking over me, I'll have that book written in no time."

At ten thirty, with Seth nodding off, we called it a night. I was still waiting for George to do what Seth had indicated he might, but to my relief it didn't happen. Although the Wilsons offered to drive me home, George insisted it was his pleasure. I had mixed emotions about that. On the one hand, I wanted to extend the evening with him. On the other, I was afraid that he would use our time alone to raise an issue that I wasn't ready to face.

"You were full of wonderful stories," I told him as we drove.

"I had a wonderful audience," he said. "I felt very much as though I was with family."

"You've been adopted," I said lightly.

"Lucky me."

We pulled into my driveway. George shut off the engine and walked me to the door.

"As much as I love your friends, Jessica, I admit I'm looking forward to our trip tomorrow, just the two of us."

"It will be a busy time," I said. "I hope you don't mind that I'll be spending much of it trying to fit pieces into the Billups puzzle."

"Correction," he said. "*We'll* be looking for those missing puzzle pieces. Besides, what would a trip with Jessica Fletcher be without a hefty dose of intrigue?"

I laughed. "What a reputation to have," I said.

"Just one of many things I—I love about you, lass. Go on, now, get yourself inside. Have you packed?"

"No."

"Then get to it. What shall I do with the car?"

"You can give it to Jed at the airport. People do that all the time."

"Very good. What time would you like me to collect you?"

"Come by at seven thirty. We can have breakfast here before heading for the airport."

George wished me a good night's sleep, waited until I locked the door behind me, and left.

I dressed for bed and came back downstairs to place my newly acquired muse next to the computer. "I expect you to do your thing, William Shakespeare," I said, patting his marble head.

I dropped into my chair and thought of the evening, thought of everything that had happened recently: my unfinished book; the busy time leading up to Thanksgiving; the GLOTCOYB letters that sat on my desk, their origins as mysterious as the reason behind them; and, of course, my plans to get on a plane to Boston the next morning. Would the trip shed light on Billups's death and on who might have killed him? Perhaps not, but that wouldn't deter me from finding out all I could about his past, and how it might be connected with his murder.

But all those thoughts took a backseat to George Sutherland.

Seth had been wrong about George planning to propose that night. Had George decided not to inject that potentially awkward situation into his final night at Seth's house? Would he consider our trip to Boston a more suitable time and milieu? Or had Seth simply been hazarding a guess based upon conversations they'd had?

My final question on the topic, with Shakespeare watching over me, was whether Seth had inadvertently slipped into the role of John Alden, speaking for George but unwilling to approach the subject on his own behalf?

Had the "muse" of Thanksgiving descended upon us all?

Chapter Nineteen

Jed was standing next to the Cessna when we arrived. "Drive their car over to the rental agency down by the dock," he instructed his young helper. "They'll give you a lift back."

We climbed into the aircraft, with me in the left-hand seat, so I could log some additional piloting time—I hadn't flown this much in a very long time—and George wedged into one of two rear seats. A few minutes later I pushed the throttle to the wall and we picked up speed down the runway. There was a stiff crosswind, which necessitated some pressure on my part to hold the plane's nosewheel on the white center stripe, but we soon lifted off and were headed for Boston.

"What's the drill?" Jed asked after we'd landed at Logan Airport. "When do I pick you up, Jess?"

"Sunday afternoon," I replied. "Is four okay with you? George's flight to London leaves at three."

"Sure. Not a problem." He shook George's hand. "Travel safe, Inspector," he said, "and come back soon."

"Oh, I intend to do that," George said. "Many thanks for the smooth flights."

We got into a cab in front of the terminal. "The Lennox Hotel, please," I told the driver, "on Boylston at Exeter."

I'd stayed in this charming Back Bay hotel on previous visits to Boston and enjoyed its European feel coupled with modern amenities. It had opened in 1900 but fell on hard times. Recent renovations had brought it up to four-star excellence. There was an added attraction to staying at the Lennox. Down-the-Hatch was also located on Boylston Street, not far from the hotel.

I'd booked adjoining rooms, including a corner unit that featured a working fireplace. I assigned that room to George. After a bellhop had delivered our luggage, we agreed to meet in the lobby in a half hour. George was sitting there when I stepped off the elevator.

"What's first on the agenda?" he asked.

"A stop at Down-the-Hatch," I said.

"Ah, haven't gone pub crawling since my early days with the metropolitan police."

"Just one pub, George. I have no idea what Billups had to do with Down-the-Hatch, but there was that photo of him posing in front of it, and the menu found in his room. There has to be some connection."

"A little early for a pub to be opening, isn't it?"

"It's getting close to noon," I said. "There must be people there setting up for lunch."

"Lead the way, lass."

Boylston Street was bustling with shoppers. Back Bay had changed considerably from its nineteenth-century origins, when it was created from landfill dredged from the Charles River and the sea. It was transformed from an odorous industrial area to the city's most prestigious address, with stately Victorian homes along treelined streets. Those golden days were gone, however. Back Bay had morphed from Victorian elegance to twentieth-century modern, to a twenty-first-century home to office towers, condominiums, shops, and restaurants and bars, including Down-the-Hatch.

We lingered outside the restaurant for a few minutes and peered through the window observing the activity inside. The staff scurried about setting tables and readying the long bar for the first customers of the day.

"Nice-looking place," George commented, "very welcoming. Reminds me a bit of home."

Down-the-Hatch appeared to be the quintessential bar and grill frequented by neighborhood residents and other regulars who knew one another and looked forward to whiling away a few hours over an ale.

"Shall we?" George said.

"Yes. Let's."

"You take the lead, lass. You know better than I what it is you're looking for."

When we opened the door, a young woman approached.

"Afraid you're a little early for lunch," she said, a smile on her wide, freckled face, "but you can get something at the bar." She looked to where a bartender was dumping plastic pails of ice into sinks. "I think he's ready," she said.

We took stools at the bar; the bartender indicated with a wave that he'd be with us in a few minutes. "No rush," I said.

We took the opportunity to take in our surroundings. George was right. It was a nice, welcoming place. There was lots of wood, although the lengthy bar top was zinc. The tables were set with black-and-white checkered tablecloths, with silverware wrapped in napkins at each place setting. A small vase with a single rose sat in the middle of each table. An older waitress in one of six booths lining one wall wrote that day's specials on a chalkboard. Low-level music from unseen speakers was of the modern variety, pop music or rock and roll I suppose was the proper description. I'm afraid I don't keep up with such things, the proof of which is my trouble with crossword puzzles that include those references.

George remarked on the ambience of the place, comparing it to British pubs, until the bartender came to where we sat and asked what he could get us. He was a young man with bushy black hair and an elongated face.

"Just a glass of seltzer for me," I said.

George looked at his watch. "Make that two," he said.

The bartender, who'd not initially struck me as friendly—was it because we'd ordered only soft drinks?—

seemed to warm up when he delivered our order. "Visiting Boston?" he asked George.

"I am," he replied.

"It was the accent. Could tell you weren't local." He looked at me. "Where are you from?"

"I'm from Maine. My friend here is from London."

"I was in London last year," the barkeep said. "It's a cool city."

"This is a nice bar," I said. "Who owns it?"

He mentioned two names. "Husband and wife," he added. "They own a couple of spots around the city."

"Have they owned it long?" George asked.

"Five years, maybe six."

"I suppose you don't remember a fellow named Billups," I said. "Hubert Billups."

His blank expression said that he didn't.

"Probably before your time," I said. "Anyone been around here long enough to remember back to, say, ten or twelve years ago?"

He laughed. "Damon goes back that far, even longer."

"Damon? He works here?"

"Nah. He's a customer, been coming in for as long as I've worked here, and that's only a year. But he's one of the regulars from way back. You're sitting in his place."

"I am?" George said.

"Sure, read that little plaque on the edge of the bar."

George and I leaned over to read the tiny inscription: RESERVED FOR DAMON O'DELL.

"He must have been a very good customer," I said, "to warrant his own barstool."

"Never misses a day unless he's sick. He's a nice old guy, lives alone a few blocks from here. A real gentleman." He smiled. "And a good tipper."

"Do you think he'll be in today?"

"I'd bet my life on it. Two o'clock sharp. Bowl of chowder with extra crackers, sliced tomatoes with mayonnaise, and a Rob Roy."

"I like his choice of drink," George said.

"He's got taste," the bartender said. "Always dresses nice and neat. Like I said, a real gentleman. Excuse me." He moved down the bar to serve a couple who'd just arrived.

"This Mr. O'Dell might be able to tell us something," I said to George.

"It sounds as though he goes back far enough," he said. "Shall we stay for lunch?"

"I'd like to. Maybe we should vacate his reserved spot. We wouldn't want to upset him when he walks in."

George and I took a booth and ordered one of the day's specials, Reuben sandwiches with salads on the side. The place had begun to fill up, and by a few minutes before two there wasn't a table or booth to be had. Although the bar was busy, too, no one had opted to sit in O'Dell's spot.

At a few minutes past two, the door opened and a dapper gentleman, whom I judged to be well into his seventies, came through it. He wore a camel-hair sport coat with leather-covered buttons under which was a brown vest over a yellow windowpane-check button-down shirt and maroon tie. Tan slacks and brown loafers completed his fashionable attire. His hair was gray and close-cropped, his complexion ruddy. He went directly to the O'Dell stool and slid onto it.

"That must be him," I said.

"How do you plan to approach him?" George asked.

"Look, the person next to him is leaving."

We left the booth and approached the bar, where I took the now-vacant stool. O'Dell glanced at me, smiled, and returned his attention to the Rob Roy the bartender had prepared moments before his customer's arrival. George stood behind me.

"Drink?" I was asked.

"Oh, yes, please. That's an interesting-looking drink," I said, indicating O'Dell's Rob Roy. "I think I'll try one of those."

"You, sir?" the bartender asked George.

"I believe I'll join in as well," George said.

"What's it called?" I asked O'Dell.

"A Rob Roy," the bartender said.

"Oh, Jimmy, you know better than that," O'Dell said.

"He's right," the bartender said. "It's actually a Bobbie Burns."

"Is that after the Scottish poet?" I asked. "What makes it that?"

O'Dell turned to me. "Quite simple," he said. "You take the classic Rob Roy, which was named for the Scots folk hero Robert Roy MacGregor, but add a dash of Benedictine. Gives it a nice honey flavor."

"Make it that way, please," I told the bartender.

"Yes, ma'am."

O'Dell returned his attention to his drink, and to the plate of tomatoes slathered with mayonnaise. Judging from his complexion and vitality, his arteries hadn't suffered too much.

"By the way," I said, "I'm Jessica Fletcher, and this is my friend George Sutherland, visiting from England."

O'Dell's eyes opened wide, and he smiled. "*The* Jessica Fletcher?"

"I'm the only person I know with that name," I replied.

"The writer," he said. "I've read most of your books. I like mysteries."

"I'm flattered." I was also pleased that a rapport had been so easily forged.

He cut a tomato slice into small pieces, ate it, and sipped his drink. "What brings you to Boston?" he asked. "Promoting a new book?"

"Actually, no," I said. "George and I are looking into the background of someone."

His eyebrows went up. "Sounds intriguing," he said. "Anyone I know?"

"I'm not sure," I said, "but here. Take a look."

I handed him a copy of one of the three photos I'd taken from Billups's room. I'd used my computer to make scanned copies, returning the original photos to their frames ready to be delivered to Mort on Monday morning. I pointed to Billups in the picture of the two men posing in front of Down-the-Hatch.

"It's Hubie!" he said.

"Then you know him."

"Of course I do, or did. Haven't seen him in a dog's age."

I looked up at George and smiled.

"May I ask how and where you knew him?" I said.

He took another stab at his tomatoes, and sipped his Rob Roy.

"Did you have a close relationship with him?" I asked.

He slowly turned to face me. "It seems as though I should be asking you the questions," he said firmly but without an edge.

The person to the other side of me left and George took his place.

"Please do," I said to O'Dell.

"Why are you carrying around a picture of Hubie, and why are you asking about him?"

I wasn't sure how much to reveal, but decided there was no reason to hold back. "It's difficult to have to tell you this, but Mr. Billups is dead. He was murdered in front of my house," I said.

My blunt statement caused O'Dell to flinch, as though I'd punched his arm.

"Hubie's dead?" he said.

"I'm afraid so."

"Murdered, you said?"

"Yes."

"Oh, boy," he muttered, and took a big gulp from his glass.

"I'm sorry to break that news, Mr. O'Dell."

"Oh, no, it's okay. Just a momentary shock, and I shouldn't be shocked."

"Why's that?"

"I knew Hubie would have a bad end after what happened."

George leaned in to me to better hear what O'Dell was saying.

"I don't understand," I said. "What *did* happen to him?"

He shook his head and continued eating. I glanced at George, who shrugged.

O'Dell asked me, "Are you writing a book about what happened to Hubie?"

"No. My only interest is to do what I can to help find his killer. He'd moved recently to Cabot Cove—that's where I live in Maine—and he was a guest at my Thanksgiving Day dinner. He seemed to be a very lonely man and, well, a little strange."

"How could he not be?"

My silence invited him to say more.

"Hubie got beat up pretty bad," he said, "especially around the head. Folks didn't think he'd pull through. He did, but he was never the same. His brain didn't work so well after that. His speech was affected, and his eyesight. He kept forgetting things. Really sad. Then he just disappeared."

"He was in an accident?" George asked.

"More a case of being in the wrong place at the wrong time, with the wrong people." He squinted at George. "Are you a writer, too?"

"No, sir. I'm with Scotland Yard in London."

The bartender delivered our drinks and slid a bowl of

clam chowder in front of O'Dell. Apparently, he'd overheard what George said and showed interest in where our conversation was now going.

"Scotland Yard, hey?" O'Dell said, impressed with George's credentials. "Why would Scotland Yard be interested in Hubie?"

"They aren't," George said. "I'm just tagging along with Mrs. Fletcher."

O'Dell's gaze came back to me. "Enjoying your Bobbie Burns?" he asked.

"I haven't even tasted it yet," I said. I lifted my glass and took a sip. "It's good, very good. As you say, it has a hint of honey."

"Yes," George agreed. "Very tasty."

"Glad you approve," O'Dell said, blotting his lips with a napkin. "That's about all I can tell you about Hubie. I'm sorry to hear what happened to him. They haven't caught the culprit yet?"

"It happened only two days ago," I explained.

I reached into my purse and pulled out the old menu from Down-the-Hatch. "I found this in his room," I said. "That's why we came here. The picture of him was taken in front of this place, and with the menu we thought there might be a connection between him and the restaurant."

O'Dell finished his drink and asked the bartender for another.

"Two today, Mr. O'Dell?" the bartender said with a smile.

"I've had bad news, Jimmy. Bad news calls for another balm to the soul," O'Dell said.

I was hoping to get answers to my questions before Mr. O'Dell was no longer able to think clearly. I cleared my throat. "I was saying that—"

"I heard you," O'Dell said. "You thought there might be a link between Hubie Billups and Down-the-Hatch."

"That's right."

"Well, I'd say there certainly was."

George and I looked blankly at him.

"Hubie used to own the joint."

Chapter Twenty

"Sir, your bill!"

The hostess stopped us as we were leaving with Damon O'Dell.

"Sorry," George said. "We were busy talking at the bar and forgot about our lunch." He gave her his credit card and left a good tip.

We had paid for the drinks at the bar with O'Dell despite his protestations, and he invited us to continue our discussion at his apartment, which he said was just around the corner. Having had two Bobbie Burns cocktails hadn't seemed to affect him. He walked steadily and with purpose as we went down Boylston Street, turned on to a treelined side street, and soon stood in front of an older apartment building nestled between two tall, recently built condo structures. O'Dell looked up at one. "A monstrosity," he proclaimed.

His apartment was on the first floor of the older building. It was a one-bedroom, with a sizable living room that was more like a library. Floor-to-ceiling bookcases covered three walls, with a rolling ladder allowing access to the higher shelves. Books were also piled everywhere, on tables and chairs, and stacked on a window ledge that obscured the lower half of the windows themselves.

"Please excuse the mess," he said, shifting piles from two chairs for us. His personal chair was a large, tan leather recliner next to a goose-neck floor lamp.

"You have quite a collection," I said.

"I love books!" he said loudly. "Yours are over there, right-hand bookcase, third shelf from the bottom."

I went to where he'd indicated and saw that he did, indeed, have virtually every one of my books, including the first as well as the most recent.

"Would you be good enough to sign them for me?" he asked.

"Of course."

While I signed, he and George engaged in a conversation concerning a section of his library dedicated to Scottish history. I heard him say through a laugh, "I'm Irish, but I've always admired the Scots. They hold their liquor better."

When I joined them I guided the topic back to Hubert Billups. "Do you know the other man in the photo with Mr. Billups?" I asked.

"I sure do. That's Hubie's brother, Harry."

"I thought they might be related."

"Another sad tale, I'm afraid," O'Dell said. "Harry was killed the same night that Hubie was beaten up."

"You say he was 'beaten up,'" George said. "Victim of a robbery?"

"No. That would have made more sense. Hubie was beaten up by members of a gang here in Boston."

"Gang?" I said.

"You know, mobsters, organized crime."

"Why?" George asked.

"Well," O'Dell said, "Hubie was a real hard-nose, stand-up sort of fellow. He wasn't very big—you already know that from having met him—but he made up for his lack of size with a fierce temper." O'Dell shook his head at the memory. "Oh, yes, Hubie was some tough guy, feisty, hardheaded, afraid of no one." He smiled at this vision of Billups. "I used to say to him, 'Hubie, you're going to get yourself killed one of these days. You don't mess with people like them.'"

"Them?"

"The mob, the wiseguys. I used to watch them come in to Hubie's place, strutting around like they owned it. I'm convinced that's what they wanted—to own it. The problem for Hubie and Harry—they were partners—was that these hoods *demanded* they give them their business, wouldn't let the brothers run the place their own way. They kept putting the pressure on the boys, buy linens from this vendor, use this window washer, get your tomatoes from this guy, pay another one a king's ransom to collect the garbage, things like that. And, of course, they tried to shake down Hubie and Harry to pay them a monthly fee for their 'business advice,' and to keep someone from burning the place down."

"And Hubie and Harry resisted," I said.

"Oh, did they ever. I warned them. I told those stubborn brothers that they'd better go to the police, blow the whistle, get some sort of protection. Know what Hubie said to me?"

George and I shook our heads.

"Hubie said, 'Damon, I'd rather boil in hell than give in to those mugs.' Well, I doubt whether Hubie's in hell, more likely causing trouble in heaven, but it looks like he got what he wished for."

"Tell us about how Harry was killed, and Hubie beaten up," George urged.

"It happened one freezing winter night. I remember how cold it was. Had snowed the day before. I wasn't there when it took place, of course. I only go to Down-the-Hatch during the day, although if the conversation is good I'll stick around, maybe have dinner now and then. Anyway, I heard about it the next day when I went for lunch. The place was closed, crime-scene tape everywhere. Lil—she was a waitress at the time—she was standing out front crying like a baby. I asked her what had happened, and she told me that Harry had been murdered, and that Hubie had been beaten and wasn't expected to live."

"Must have been quite a shock," George said.

"It certainly was. Took me a long time to get over it, and I'm not sure I ever have. Was months before I ever went back."

"You mentioned that these mobsters wanted to take over Down-the-Hatch," I said. "What happened regarding ownership once the Billups brothers were out of the picture?"

"It got complicated," said O'Dell, "and I never really did understand the machinations that went on. But it seems that the ones who killed Harry and beat Hubie claimed that the brothers had sold the restaurant to them, and produced some sort of forged documents. It didn't hold up as I remember, and they never did take over."

"Were they ever charged with the murder and beating?" I asked.

"Eventually. From what I heard, the screws were put to the gangster behind the takeover, and to save himself, he ratted out his own goons who did the deed. They went to prison."

"What about the man who ordered the killing and beating?"

O'Dell shrugged. "I have no idea what happened to him. Anyway, Hubie survived, although he was never the same. I only saw him once after he came out of the hospital. I couldn't believe the way he looked and acted, his speech slurred like he was drunk, walking funny, you know, like an old man. It was really sad to see this tough little guy reduced to that."

"And that was the only time you saw him?" George asked.

"That's right. Folks told me that whatever money Hubie got from the sale of Down-the-Hatch went to pay his hospital bills, and what was left went to his wife."

"He was married?"

"Oh, yes, he was. She was a beauty, and a real spitfire. She used to come in the place now and then, and everybody liked her. Hubie used to say that she had to be a saint to put up with him, and he was right. They got along fine. At least it seemed that way to me."

I fetched the scanned copy of the photograph of Billups and a woman that I'd taken from his rooming house and showed it to O'Dell.

"That's Connie, all right."

"Is she still alive?" I asked.

"I believe so. You can give her a call. I have her number—if she's still there."

He rummaged through a bulging address book until he found it.

"Speaking of pictures," I said, "can you identify what's in this one?" I handed him the photograph of Billups receiving a plaque.

O'Dell nodded. "That was the Boston mayor giving Hubie a citizenship award. Hubie used to sponsor amateur boxing here in Boston, gave kids from the poorer parts of town something positive to do. Hubie probably would have been a pretty good fighter himself if he'd pursued that, probably in the lightweight or welterweight division. He loved those kids he trained, always said it was better for them to punch each other in the ring than in some back alley." He sighed at the memory. "Can I get you folks some coffee and cake? I've got a nice pound cake in the freezer, defrosts in no time flat."

"I think we've taken enough of your time," I said. "You've been very gracious, Mr. O'Dell."

"Please call me Damon," he said. "If you want to try calling Hubie's wife—I suppose she's his widow now—you can do it from here." He pointed to a phone half buried beneath books.

I took him up on his offer and dialed the number. It rang quite a long time before it was picked up.

"Hello?" a female voice said.

"Hello. Mrs. Billups?"

"I was. Who's asking?"

"My name is Jessica Fletcher. Damon O'Dell was kind enough to give me your number."

"Damon! A blast from the past. Say hello to the old rascal for me."

"I'll do that. Mrs. Billups, I'm here in Boston with a friend from London. We're trying to find out what we can about your husband, Hubert."

"I wouldn't know anything about him," she said in a strong voice. "Haven't seen him in years. Not since the divorce."

She obviously didn't know of his death. I hated to be the one to break it to her, but I felt I had to. I told her that he'd died in Cabot Cove, Maine, on Thanksgiving evening.

Her reaction was delayed. When she finally did speak, she simply said, "I didn't know." Then she asked, "How did it happen? He'd been sick?"

"No," I replied. "Mrs. Billups, could my friend and I

come visit? We're here in Boston only overnight—my friend flies back to London tomorrow—and I would very much appreciate being able to talk with you in person. I promise not to take too much of your time."

"I guess so," she said. "Poor Hubie. He never was the same."

I suggested that we come to her home, but she vetoed that.

"Would you like to meet us at Down-the-Hatch?" I asked.

There was a long pause. "Haven't been there since it sold. Probably wouldn't know anyone anymore." She sighed. "All right. Wouldn't hurt to see what they've done to the old place."

I offered to buy her dinner, but she turned me down. We agreed to get together at six. It was now four o'clock, two hours to kill.

After thanking O'Dell profusely, and promising to send him a signed copy of my newest book when it was published—assuming I'd ever finish it—we left and walked slowly along Boylston Street in the direction of Boston Common, one of the loveliest public gardens and parks in America. We'd intended to stroll the common, but the weather had turned increasingly wintry, and after a half hour of brisk walking, we opted to stop in a pretty tearoom and bakery.

"What do you think?"

"I'm not sure what to think, George," I said. "We know that Billups once owned Down-the-Hatch with his brother, Harry, and that the mob tried to muscle in on their business. They balked and Harry paid with his life. What I'm not clear about is what happened to Hubert after his hospitalization. His wife—actually, his former wife—might be able to fill in the gap between his injuries and his arrival in Cabot Cove."

"That's a lot of years to cover."

"I know, but it doesn't make sense to me that he just happened to end up in town. Why Cabot Cove? He must have come there for a reason."

"Maybe, maybe not," George said. "Men like that are apt to wander without specific destinations. If he left Boston and traveled north along the coast, eventually he would hit Cabot Cove. He may have lived somewhere else to the south for a time until he got the urge to move."

"True, but—"

"Jessica."

"Yes?"

"You do realize that what we find out from his former wife, and what we've learned from Mr. O'Dell, may make an interesting story but may have absolutely no bearing on why Billups was killed."

I drew a deep breath. He was right, of course. Our trip to Boston a day ahead of his scheduled departure might end up being nothing more than a wasted exercise, a self-serving trip for me. But despite silently acknowledging that possibility to myself, I knew I'd do it again should a similar situation develop.

I turned and looked at George, who smiled. Was he thinking behind that smile that I might not be the woman he thought I was, that my compelling need to get to the bottom of a mystery bordered on obsession? Did he think

I was wasting the precious little time we had to be together, squandering our chance for some intimacy by chasing a red herring? I hoped not.

My thoughts then naturally shifted to what Seth had told me, that George was likely to propose marriage. He hadn't as yet, and frankly I hoped he wouldn't. I'd braced myself ever since Seth mentioned it, mentally forming the words that would allow me to decline as graciously as possible to spare him hurt feelings. But those words had never truly gelled. Did that mean that my resolve to maintain my single status wasn't as set in stone as I thought it was?

"Jessica?"

"What?"

"Your mind is elsewhere again."

"Oh, yes. I'm sorry. Do you think this trip is pure folly?"

"Of course not."

"I'd understand if you did."

"Well, I don't."

"We could have been seeing the sights in Boston on your last full day here."

"Your face is the sight I most prefer, lass," he said. "I never was one for doing the tourist route." He checked his watch. "Maybe we should be going."

I nodded, and motioned for our check.

"How will we know her?" George asked after we'd stepped outside and looked for a taxi.

"She said she'd be wearing a red beret and a black cape."

George laughed. "Quite an outfit for an older woman."

"Maybe she was a child bride. Maybe Mr. Billups robbed the cradle."

"I hope not."

"There's a cab," I said, sending George off the curb to hail it.

The bar at Down-the-Hatch was overflowing with patrons when we returned. It was a convivial crowd and loud, most of them standing and talking and laughing, happy to be in out of the cold and celebrating Saturday night. I stood on my tiptoes and scanned the faces, looking for someone who might be Connie Billups. George tapped my shoulder and indicated a small table against the wall and away from the throng. A woman in a red beret, black cape folded over the back of her chair, was alone, a drink in front of her.

"Are you Connie?" I asked, coming up to her. At her nod, I said, "I'm Jessica Fletcher. This is George Sutherland."

She took us in with heavily made-up, wary eyes. "Hello," she said.

It was difficult to guess her age; her face was unwrinkled, her skin glowing, and her hair was a shade of copper that didn't exist in nature.

"Would never have recognized the place, you know, if it weren't for the sign over the door."

"Has it changed that much?" I asked, taking the seat opposite hers. George dragged a chair over from an adjacent table.

"A bar gets a lot of wear and tear, especially the floor," Connie said, eyeing the Mexican tile beneath her feet.

"Ours was wood." Her gaze roved over the room, taking in all the details. She looked up at the pressed-tin ceiling. "And of course every owner has a vision of how they want it to be. At least they kept the name. That's nice."

A waiter with a long, drooping black mustache came to the table. "You having dinner, folks?"

I looked at Connie and she shook her head. "No, thank you," I said to the waiter, "but you can bring us something to drink."

With glasses in front of us, Connie took charge of the conversation, condemning the demise of family-owned bar-restaurants in Boston, complaining about the overflow of students in the city, expressing her political philosophy, and bemoaning the long, bleak winter ahead. George and I listened attentively, waiting for an opportunity to change subjects.

"Would you excuse me a moment?" Connie said.

I hadn't realized how tiny she was until she stood up and walked quickly toward the hall to the kitchen and the restrooms. She returned a few moments later. "Just wanted to see if my name was still carved in the wood back there," she said, smiling softly.

"And is it?" George asked.

"It is. I guess you always want to leave a permanent mark on a place you've owned. Hubie and I picked out the lintel over the kitchen door, figuring it would last a long time, and it has."

She had given us the conversational opening.

"It was good of you to find time for us," I said. "I know this must be distressing for you, but—"

"It's okay," she said, and I thought of how her late husband often used the word "okay."

"You say Hubie's dead. How did he die?"

George answered. "He was murdered," he said.

Her eyes widened. "Hmmm," she said. "Murdered? How?"

"Well," I started to say.

"Someone stabbed him to death," George said.

"Oh. Who did it?"

"We don't know," I replied. "That's why we're trying to come up with an answer."

"Are you cops?"

"No," I replied.

"Well, if you're not, what are you here for?" she asked. "What are the police doing?"

"They're doing all they can," I said, "but—"

"Who are you?"

"I'm a writer, and George is with Scotland Yard."

"Scotland Yard? Did Hubie do something *really* wrong?"

George grinned. "No. I'm just along as Jessica's friend."

Her narrowed eyes said she thought we were more than that.

I started to ask a question when she summoned the waiter and ordered another drink. "You're paying, right?"

I nodded.

"Okay, what do you want to know about Hubie?"

An hour and a half later, George and I stepped out of a taxi in front of our hotel.

"Hungry?" he asked.

"Maybe a little. What I'd really like is a quiet place to talk."

We had two choices in the Lennox: an Irish pub, Sólás, or the less crowded City-Bar. We opted for the latter.

". . . and according to her, Mr. Billups just disappeared from Boston and from her life," George said, nibbling at our shared Maine lobster salad.

"I had the feeling that she wasn't particularly unhappy to see him go."

"I had that feeling, too. Of course, he wasn't the same man she'd married, not once those thugs scrambled his brain."

The former Mrs. Billups had also told us that the little money she'd received from the sale of Down-the-Hatch hadn't gone very far. Hubie, unable to work, had taken off. She was left almost destitute and had made ends meet by working as a waitress in restaurants around Boston. She'd attempted during the first few years of his absence to find out where he was, but eventually gave up and resigned herself to never seeing him again. She filed for divorce based upon abandonment and it was easily granted.

"She certainly is no fan of law enforcement," George said.

"I suppose you can't blame her, George. The two thugs who killed her brother-in-law, and who beat her husband nearly to death, ended up in prison, but the man behind it beat the rap."

I pulled a slim reporter's notepad from my purse on which I'd made notes during our conversation with Connie. "That would be . . . Here it is: Vincent Canto, nicknamed 'the bear' because he was so big. She claims he cut a deal with the authorities, turned state's evidence against Hubie's assailants, and got a free pass."

"Chances are he's in your Witness Protection Program, never to be seen or heard from again."

"Do you have that program in England?" I asked.

"Oh, yes, patterned after your own. Yours was extremely well thought out, and works quite efficiently, including all its subtleties, the way identities are kept secret, funding families that are entered into the program, rules concerning the role of local law enforcement and its responsibilities, down to such things as choosing new names for informants who go into witness protection. We always recommend that they choose a name with the same first and last initials as their real name, or at least retain their first name."

"You do?"

"Oh, yes. Every detail is thought out."

"I suppose it has to be to assure their safety."

"Do you know what I think, Jessica? While all this is interesting from a human drama perspective, I'm beginning to doubt it has anything to do with Mr. Billups's demise."

"You may be right," I said sadly.

We fell into an easy, comfortable conversation from that point forward about a variety of distinctly less weighty things. It was after George had assigned the bill to his room, and we were about to head for the elevators that I gasped and grabbed his arm.

"What's wrong?" he asked.

"I don't think this was a wasted trip after all."

Chapter Twenty-one

On Sunday afternoon, George and I sat in Terminal E at Logan Airport trying to squeeze in a few more minutes together before his flight to London. We didn't have much to say at this juncture. I was terribly sorry to see him go, and he'd expressed his unhappiness at leaving. Now it was just a matter of watching a large wall clock tick off the minutes before he would walk through security, board the 747, and be gone.

Last night, after leaving the hotel's City-Bar, we'd gone to his room, where we started a fire in the fireplace and continued our conversation. Boston's lights twinkled outside the large window, and the moon looked as though it was perched atop a distant high-rise.

George had, of course, wanted to know why I'd said that the trip to Boston hadn't been a wasted one. I'd explained to him the scenario I'd conjured, which prompted him to question every aspect of it.

"What will you do?" he asked.

"I'll call Mort Metzger and tell him what I think might have happened."

"Do you think he'll listen to you?"

"Oh, Mort will listen, but he might not agree with me."

"You really have little concrete to offer, Jessica."

"Except a strong hunch. My hunches haven't always been right, but they haven't always been wrong either."

"If the conclusion you've come to is correct," he said, "you'll be stepping on some pretty big toes."

"Which isn't nearly as important as getting to the truth about Billups's murder. Funny how my view of Billups has changed over the past few days. I started out being wary of him, even fearful. Now it's as though I knew him, a friend who's been killed in a brutal way, someone who deserves to see his killer brought to justice."

"I admire your tenacity," he said.

"Some, like Seth, consider it a character flaw."

George laughed. "I suspect, Jessica, that the good Dr. Hazlitt has great respect for that so-called character flaw."

We talked until midnight when I announced that I was sleepy and was going to retire. "What time would you like to meet?" I asked as I walked to the door.

"As early as possible," he said. "Let's squeeze every last minute out of the time we have left."

* * *

George's flight announcement came through the PA.

"The time went so quickly," I said, walking with him to the row of people waiting to get through security.

He took my elbow and led me away from the line to a quiet area off to the side. "I hate to leave, lass," he said, drawing me into his arms. "It will be too long till I see you again. I know this may not be the best time, but I've been meaning to ask you a question."

"You have?"

"Yes. I've given it a great deal of thought and there's something I wish to propose."

Propose? In an airport terminal as he's ready to wing away?

"George, I—"

"I know, I know, your head is filled with thoughts of murdered men, ruthless gangsters, and abandoned women. But I feel the pressure of time."

I said nothing. I didn't know what to say.

"I was going to propose that—" He looked away, his face creased as though reconsidering.

I waited.

"Would you consider coming to London for Christmas this year?"

"Christmas?"

"I know, it's a very special time of year for you here in the States, wanting to spend it with family and friends, but we do quite a nice job of celebrating it in Britain."

The large smile that broke out across my face was purely involuntary.

"Will you at least consider it?"

"Yes, I will consider it very seriously," I said, aware that

I suffered from a clash of emotions at the moment—relief and disappointment.

"That's all I can ask," he said.

We hugged, parted, hugged again, and I watched him walk through security and disappear with a wave down the hall leading to the departure lounge.

I stood at the huge windows overlooking the airport until his plane was pushed from the gate and taxied out of sight. I wiped away a tear that had formed, walked away, and went outside to call Signature Flight Support for a car to take me to the side of the airport where Jed Richardson would be arriving. As I waited, I called Mort Metzger's home number, which was stored in my cell phone.

"Mrs. F," he said. "Where are you?"

"In Boston, but I'll be home early this evening."

"What are you doing down there in Beantown? Oh, that's right. Seeing the inspector off?"

"Yes, but that wasn't the only reason for my being here. Mort, I think I might have information that will lead to Hubert Billups's murderer."

"You do?"

"Can I drop by the house tonight?"

"You're always welcome, Mrs. F, but I have to tell you, you're a day late and a dollar short."

"Why do you say that?"

"I've already solved the case."

"You have?"

"That's right. I arrested Wally Winstead yesterday for the murder of Hubert Billups."

Chapter Twenty-two

Although the arrest of Wally Winstead had taken place only a day earlier, news of it had spread quickly. Jed Richardson mentioned it the moment we were airborne and en route to Cabot Cove.

"Wally's always been a hothead," he said, "an accident waiting to happen."

"Do you know what evidence Mort has against him?" I asked.

"I heard that he lied about his whereabouts the night the old guy was killed. Mara said she heard someone say Wally's wife was screaming at him when Mort came to take him in. Said that was the last time she'd lie for him. Said it served him right, that jail was too good for him. She hoped they'd put him away forever. She was that mad."

I climbed over the clouds, with Jed's permission, and set the dials for automatic pilot. My first reaction to Mort's announcement that he was charging Winstead with Billups's murder was surprise and disbelief. Did the fact that the arrest dashed the theory I'd come up with play a role in my response? Undoubtedly. Although Mort and I had butted heads on occasion, he was a good lawman who wasn't known to go off the deep end and charge people without having enough evidence to back it up. Still, I was confident that the conclusion to which I'd come had merit, and I was anxious to share it with Mort.

I walked into my house, flipped on lights, and laid Saturday's mail on the kitchen table. There were no more mystery envelopes containing cutout letters pasted on a page. Thankfully, the *B* had been the last one. GLOTCOYB. I wondered if George was right, if I might never find out what it meant. I tossed two advertising circulars into the recycle bin and took the remaining correspondence into my study. Even though George hadn't stayed at my house, it seemed oddly quiet, as if something—or someone—important wasn't there. I felt out of sorts now that the man who had contributed so much to my holiday happiness had gone home. But had I made him happy, too, with my frantic preparations for Thanksgiving, dragging him thither and yon, and then pushing him to Boston to satisfy my need to get to the bottom of a case? Talk about a busman's holiday! The man works at Scotland Yard, and I use his days off to involve him in a murder investigation. It was a wonder he wanted to see me again so soon.

Christmas! I had to laugh at Seth, so broadly hinting that George was going to propose to me. He did indeed make a proposal, but not one that either Seth or I was expecting. Did I want to spend Christmas with George? That decision would have to wait until I finished my book. I looked at the computer, then at my watch. It was too late to start writing now. It would be better to attack the manuscript on Monday morning—doesn't every project start on Monday morning? But what now? My hand hovered over the telephone, and finally I picked it up and dialed Mort's number.

"Hi, Mrs. F. Back safe and sound?"

"Yes, thank goodness. Mort, you said I could stop by. Does the invitation still hold?"

"Sure does, Mrs. F. Maureen whipped up a new dish. It was pretty good. We have some left over, if you're hungry."

"Sounds nice," I said, my growling stomach testifying to not having had dinner. "I'll be there in twenty minutes."

I hung up and sat back, trying to collect my thoughts so that I could present a concise, compelling case to Mort. As I was about to leave the study, my eyes rested on the pile of GLOTCOYB letters on my desk. I pulled out a new file folder, put the letters in it, and dropped the folder into a file drawer. I pushed thoughts of them from my mind as I called for a taxi.

Mort and Maureen had just finished cleaning up after dinner, but offered me a bowl of an experimental fish stew Maureen had made, along with a salad and French bread. They joined me at the dining room table.

"Now," Mort said, "what's this you say about having come up with something to do with the Billups case?"

"I'm eager to run it by you," I said, "but first tell me about Wally Winstead. You're sure he's the killer?"

Mort nodded gravely. "You bet I am," he said. Then he grinned. "I hate to admit it, but I had a little help from Scotland Yard."

"Really? How so?"

"Well, you remember when you and the inspector were in my office while I questioned Wally?"

"Yes."

"I kept thinking about what George said, that Wally was lying about where he'd been the night Billups got it. Remember? He said his eyes opened wide and his pupils got dilated, and that his voice got higher."

"George has been studying signs of when a person isn't telling the truth," I explained to Maureen, finishing the last of her stew, which, I had to admit, was very good.

"I might study up some more on that subject myself," Mort said. "Anyway, I decided to do some serious asking around about Wally's whereabouts that night. He said he was with his wife, who confirmed it when I asked her. I didn't believe her either. Her eyes got wide and her pupils dilated, and her voice got all high and squeaky."

"Go on."

"So I stopped in places I know Wally likes to go, that bar down on Shad Street, and the billiards parlor next to the movie theater. Bingo! It took some hard questioning, but I finally got the truth out of a couple of regulars in those places. Seems that Wally showed up at the bar about nine o'clock on Thanksgiving evening after getting into a row with his wife, had a lot to drink, and started talking about her, about how she was no good anyway, let other men make eyes at her. Then he starts up about Billups, about how he was following her around, and how no bum was going to flirt with his wife, the usual crazy stuff from Wally. According to the ones I questioned, the more Wally drank, the madder he got, railing about bums like Billups. He left the bar mad as the devil, still squawking about Billups and how he'd teach him a lesson."

He sat back, arms crossed over his chest, a satisfied smile on his face.

"That's it?" I said.

He came forward. "No, Mrs. F, that's not it," he replied, clearly irritated. "I brought him in and gave him a chance to deny he'd done it. He never did deny it. Claims he can't remember where he was that night, but still says how Billups got what he deserved, nutty things like that. Winstead lied about where he was. He doesn't have an alibi for the time the murder took place. He made threats against the victim. And, Mrs. F, he sure had the motive."

I didn't argue because what Mort said was obviously correct. But that didn't necessarily mean that he had the right man.

"Have you charged him?" I asked.

"Not yet. I'm meeting with the DA tomorrow to discuss it. I think he'll agree with me and go along with a formal charge."

"What about the knife, Mort?" I asked.

"What about it?"

"Were his fingerprints on it?"

Mort shrugged. "Lab is still working on it."

"I don't remember seeing Wally at the charity dinner. Seth's knife was taken from there."

Mort's smile was smug as he said, "You're wrong, Mrs. F. After you and George took off to deliver the meals, Wally showed up. At least that's what Archer Franklin told me."

"Archer Franklin? How would he know? He left early."

"Doesn't mean he didn't come back. He says he saw Wally come in toward the end. Didn't stay long, according to Franklin, but he didn't have to. Just hung around long enough to grab the knife he used to kill Billups." He put up his hands in mock self-defense. "I know, I know, Franklin is a pain in the butt, sure not my favorite fellow. But that doesn't mean he'd lie about Wally."

"Unless he wanted to frame someone else for something he did himself," I said.

Maureen had retreated to another part of the house during my conversation with Mort. She returned to offer me coffee and a slice of blueberry pie she'd baked that day. I passed on the pie but took the coffee.

"Look, Mrs. F," Mort said wearily, "we checked everyone else out, including that other boarder, Catalano. Found him not twenty miles from here. He had a solid alibi for the time of the murder. Wally doesn't. I'm sure it's him. I can't believe you still want to present this theory you've come up with."

My enthusiasm for what I'd put together had waned in the wake of Mort's belief that he had his man. Still, I couldn't leave without justifying my visit.

"Mort," I said, "what do you know about Victor Carson?"

He stared at me and shook his head.

"Mort?" I said.

"You know, I hate to say this, but I think we've discussed

this enough," he said. He stood, picked up his empty pie plate and went to the kitchen, leaving me stunned and confused. When he returned, I tried to resurrect the topic again, but he shut down all conversation. "Hate to be rude, Mrs. F, but it's been a long day, and I have an even longer one tomorrow. Sorry to shoo you out, but I'm sure you understand. Want me to call you a cab?"

"All right," I said, surprised that he hadn't offered to drive me home.

The taxi arrived a few minutes later.

Mort didn't see me to the door. Maureen did. "Did you really enjoy the stew?" she asked.

"Oh, yes, Maureen, it was excellent, very tasty."

"Don't mind Mort, Jessica. He was so excited when he solved the murder, he was singing when he got home yesterday. I guess he just isn't ready for anyone to take away that satisfaction."

"I'm sure you're right, Maureen. Thanks. Talk to you tomorrow."

Chapter Twenty-three

To say that I was taken aback by Mort's refusal to discuss Victor Carson is a vast understatement. In all the years since becoming Cabot Cove's sheriff, Mort's been unfailingly polite and willing to listen. That's not to say that he's always concurred with my analyses. Far from it. But he'd never before shut me off so abruptly, and I pondered late into the evening why he'd done it on this particular night.

I'd flown home from Boston after having conjured up what I considered to be a credible scenario that would explain why Hubert Billups was in Cabot Cove, and the reason for his murder. George had reminded me that my theory was just that, more supposition than substantiation, but that it was as plausible as any other explanation, and might be a reasonable path to pursue further. This was hardly the ringing endorsement I was hoping for, but I was willing to admit to Mort that the explanation of events was pure speculation on my part. All I wanted was for him to hear me out, and to possibly provide some validation based upon what he knew about Victor Carson.

Billups had owned Down-the-Hatch in partnership with his brother, Harry. Local mobsters had put the squeeze on them, not only to pay for various services, but with the intention of eventually taking over the place. Hubert and Harry balked, which led to Harry being killed, and Hubert suffering a life-threatening beating that left him mentally and physically challenged.

According to Damon O'Dell and Connie Billups, the thugs who did the deed had been ordered to do it by a higher-ranking gangster named Vincent Canto. Canto, it seems, had turned state's evidence against his underlings and been cut some sort of a deal by the authorities. His whereabouts were unknown, at least to O'Dell and Connie. George Sutherland's assumption was that he'd disappeared into the Federal Witness Protection Program, his identity changed to protect him and his family from retribution by fellow mobsters.

When George had talked about the Witness Protection Program, I'd begun to see pieces of the puzzle fall into their slots. What if Victor Carson was, in fact, Vincent Canto, and had been relocated to Cabot Cove as part of his plea deal? George had said that it's recommended that the people going into the program use the same first name as their real ones, or choose first and last names that start with their initials.

Victor Carson.

Vincent Canto.

V and *C*.

Carson was an enigmatic man, at best. Initially, I'd chalked up his behavior to being shy and socially unsure of himself. He was certainly a bear of a man, which matched Canto's nickname according to Connie Billups. It seemed to me that he behaved like someone who was hiding a past, not exactly antisocial, but pretty close to it, and certainly a man of few words. Flimsy, I know, but given what Billups's former wife had said, coupled with what I'd learned from O'Dell, the picture led me to wonder whether there wasn't a less sanguine reason behind Victor's reclusive manner.

Could Billups have learned through some source that Canto, aka Carson, was in Cabot Cove? If so, he'd taken that information with him to his grave. But whether he knew in advance or simply happened upon his former tormentor, once he found Carson, Billups may have planned to seek revenge. If so, it's not too far a stretch to think that Carson recognized Billups and killed him to protect his new identity and life.

It was a neat solution even if there were some gaping holes in it, and I was sorry our sheriff didn't want to hear it. However, the more I reflected upon Mort's unusual behavior, the more I was able to cut him some slack. He'd arrested Wally Winstead for the murder, and was confident that he'd solved the case. I've known my share of law enforcement officers over the years who, in their zeal to break a case, rushed to judgment, focusing on the closest and most accessible suspect. There's no defending that behavior, of course, not when innocent people end up convicted while the guilty go free. But I suppose it's only human nature to want to succeed as quickly as possible and to take the easiest available route. With that in mind, my compulsion to get to the truth in the Billups murder—the *real* truth—was about to pick up steam.

I'd sent George an e-mail before retiring for the night. In it I'd voiced how much I hated to see him go, assured him I'd give serious consideration to spending Christmas in London, and told him of my disappointing meeting with Mort Metzger and that he'd made an arrest in the case, Wally Winstead, whom George had sensed was lying. I added, of course, that Mort had credited George for pointing that out. Archer Franklin also came to mind. He'd placed Winstead at the charity dinner at the senior center, which would have given Winstead access to the murder weapon. Had Franklin told the truth? It would be easy enough to confirm that Wally came to the senior center simply by querying the others who'd been in attendance. I had no reason to doubt Archer's word, except for my inherent dislike of the man. Had he given Mort that useful bit of information in order to cast suspicion away from himself?

George's return e-mail the following morning fueled my resolve to go forward.

My dear Jessica—The flight home was pleasant and uneventful. I miss you already, and hope you'll venture across the pond for Christmas. The more I think about your theory of the Billups case, the more it appeals to this Scotland Yard inspector. Your sheriff's reaction can be explained, I feel, by the rules of the Witness Protection Program as practiced here and in the States. When someone is relocated through the program, local law enforcement officers must be told of their presence in the community. Of course, they are bound to secrecy unless circumstances warrant a breach. Certainly, murder would constitute such a circumstance. Have to bob down to a meeting. Always a dashed meeting it seems. Fondly, George.

Of course! That had to explain Mort's reaction to me when I mentioned Victor Carson. I'm not a betting person, but I was now confident that what I'd suspected was true. Victor Carson *was* Vincent Canto, and Mort was duty bound to conceal his identity.

My elation was short-lived, however. I needed Mort's cooperation if I were to proceed, but his hands were tied by regulations. Unless, as George pointed out, unusual circumstances justified a breach of the secrecy rule. Murder! Could there ever be a more ironic state of affairs than a criminal under government protection killing someone?

I settled in my home office and decided upon my best approach to Mort. I was aware, of course, of my promise to myself to work on my unfinished novel, and even though I'd filed away the GLOTCOYB letters, they were still a loose end I intended to pursue. But neither of those issues seemed important enough to trump the Billups murder.

I was about to pick up the phone to call Mort when it rang.

"Jessica, it's Beth Wappinger."

"Good morning, Beth. How are you?"

"I—am—wonderful!"

Her glee came through the line and caused me to join in her laughter. "What's happened?" I asked.

"Josh is changing jobs."

"Oh?"

"He's getting off the road—finally! He's been hired by King Industries here in Cabot Cove to be their new national sales manager. There'll be some travel involved, but nothing like he's been doing for the past eight years."

"That's really great, Beth. Congratulations to you and to Josh."

"Thanks. I just received a new line of sweaters. One of them has your name written all over it."

"How nice of you to let me know, but it'll be a couple of days (I was really thinking weeks) before I can get to your shop."

"Just don't take too long. I'd hate to see them gone before you take a look. How's the book coming?"

"It's coming—fine. Just fine. Speaking of that, I'd better get back to it."

"Go to it, girl. Don't waste those creative juices. Bye."

The phone rang again before I could call Mort. "How was your weekend in Boston with George?" Seth asked.

"Wonderful, Seth. I was sorry to see him leave, of course, but it was nice getting away together for a day. How are you?"

"I'm doing well, Jessica. I'll tell you why I'm calling. Mort stopped in this morning."

"Oh?"

"Yes. He came by to tell me that you'd dropped over to his house last night and were acting strangely."

"Strangely? Why in heaven's name would he say that?"

"Now, don't get your feathers ruffled. You know Mort. He has your best interests at heart. He said you were, well, not making sense, maybe because you were fatigued from your Boston fling."

"That's ridiculous, Seth. I wasn't at all tired and . . . did he indicate what I said that led him to the conclusion that I was 'acting strangely'?"

"No, nothing specific. You are all right, I take it."

"Of course I am. Thank you for asking, but I'm fine, just fine."

"I know it's not my business, but I thought maybe your conversation with George might have unsettled you."

"What conversation? Oh, I know what you're getting at, Seth. Did George propose to me? The answer is no."

"He didn't? Well, that's interesting. Guess I didn't read the fellow right."

"Did George ever tell you he was planning to ask me to marry him?"

Seth cleared his throat. "Not in so many words, but—"

"But you just assumed he would."

"Well, I'm pleased that you're feeling well. I'll let you get back to your novel, Jessica, now that you don't have any more distractions."

That devil, I thought after hanging up. He'd put me through the wringer warning me that George planned to propose when it was simply a guess on his part. And now he'd called because he was curious about whether he'd been right. Was Seth happy that George hadn't proposed, or disappointed for me?

And what about Mort, telling Seth that I'd acted *strangely* at his house? What was he doing, setting up a situation where if I further pursued the Victor Carson matter I would be viewed as unstable? I hated to think that of him, but I couldn't assign any other motive.

I decided that it didn't matter what Mort was thinking. It was entirely possible that I had a former mobster living just down the road from me, a man who ordered that the Billups brothers be beaten and killed, and who might well have murdered the survivor of that attack after leaving Thanksgiving dinner at my home.

At a little before noon I pulled out a shopping bag and put in the photos I'd taken from Billups's room at the boardinghouse, intending to return them to Mort. When I dialed his number, however, I was informed that the sheriff was out and wouldn't be back until four. Good, I thought. I'd devote the next four hours to my novel. Hoping to pick up where I'd left off, I spent the first hour reading the most recent three chapters in order to capture the flow and rhythm I'd established. Confident that I had, I went to the kitchen to make tea and a light lunch of crabmeat on Ritz crackers. As I waited for the kettle to boil, I went to the living room to retrieve the day's newspapers and happened to look out the window. The sky had turned gray, and there was a mist in the air, but I could easily see Victor Carson standing across the road, at the same place where Hubert Billups used to station himself.

It occurred to me with a jolt that, despite my fears, Billups probably hadn't been watching my house at all. No, he'd likely been there keeping an eye on the Carson house, out of my line of sight because of the road's curve, but visible from where Billups had been, and where Carson now stood. Why was Carson there now? Was he returning to the scene of the crime, or was he keeping an eye on my house? Had word gotten back to him of my trip to Boston and the questions I'd asked? Impossible. That left only Mort as a viable source of such information. As his local "handler," Mort might have mentioned to Carson my having expressed interest in him last night, and that my question obviously had to do with the Billups murder. Mort would never deliberately expose me that way, but then why was Carson there? I couldn't come up with an answer that made sense.

Carson saw me standing at the window and headed back toward his house. His unexpected presence sent a chill up my spine. If my supposition about him was correct, he was capable of anything, including murder.

I tried to work on my novel, but my mind kept drifting to Victor Carson, aka Vincent Canto if I was right, and Hubie Billups. Finally at four, I called Mort, who'd just returned from a meeting of Maine law enforcement officials.

"I don't have time to talk," he said curtly.

"It doesn't have to be this minute," I said, "but I must speak with you, Mort."

"Give me a call tomorrow, Mrs. F."

"Mort," I said sternly, "this is extremely important. I've never known you to put me off this way."

There was silence on his end.

"I think you've arrested the wrong person in Hubert Billups's murder. Won't you please hear me out?"

What he said next was preceded by a long, pained sigh. "Mrs. F," he said, "I know you're a smart lady and all, but you're wading in deep waters here, maybe water that's over your head."

"That may be," I replied, "but I'm willing to take that chance. Besides, I'm a pretty good swimmer."

Another sigh. "If I talk with you, do you promise what I say will stay between us?"

I hate making promises that I might not be able to keep. If I didn't get any satisfaction from Mort, would I push further and bring in another law enforcement officer or agency? It was a possibility. But I decided that Mort was the one I had to convince, and promised him our conversation would remain between us.

"All right," he said, "but I don't want to do it here at headquarters. I'll come to your house."

"Fine. Tonight?"

"I'll drop by at eight."

"Wonderful."

"Just remember, Mrs. F, that I have to go by some rules."

"I understand, Mort, and I don't expect you to violate those rules."

With a great weight lifted from my shoulders, I spent what was left of the day working on my book, with frequent trips to the window to see if Carson was on the road. He wasn't. I assumed Mort would have dinner before coming by my house, so I limited refreshments to cookies, his favorite ice cream—chocolate chip—and a fresh pot of coffee. He arrived precisely at eight, wearing jeans, a red-and-black plaid shirt, and boots.

He seemed uneasy from the moment he walked through the door, and I tried to make him comfortable.

"I appreciate this," I said after we'd settled at the kitchen table and I'd served us.

We made small talk for a few minutes, avoiding the reason for his visit until I said, "Mort, I'd like you to hear me out before responding."

"Okay, Mrs. F," he said. "Shoot."

I laid out for him the conclusions to which I'd come about Victor Carson and Hubert Billups's murder. I tried to gauge Mort's reactions from his facial expressions, but he was a blank. When I finished, I sat back and waited.

He made a few false starts before getting to his response. "Mrs. F, you never fail to amaze me," he said.

My mood brightened. "Are you saying that I'm right, Mort?"

"No. I'm not saying that."

"I understand how important it is for you as the sheriff to keep under wraps the fact that someone in the Witness Protection Program may be living in Cabot Cove. I respect that. But I also know that if that same person were to commit a serious crime, you have an obligation to come forward. Surely protecting the identity of a man who turned state's evidence isn't as important as solving a murder."

"*If* he killed anyone," was Mort's retort.

"Of course, "I said, "but isn't it incumbent upon you to at least question him about it?"

"Sure, and I'll do that. That doesn't mean I'm agreeing that he's who you say he is, or that he's here in Cabot Cove under the Witness Protection Program. You have to realize, Mrs. F, how many agencies are involved, all the red tape I have to go through. The U.S. Marshals Service is the one in charge, but the decision to put somebody in the program comes straight out of Washington, the Department of Justice. Any idea how much money is paid guys in the program?"

"No."

"Sixty grand a year."

"That's quite a reward for someone who's broken the law."

"I'll tell you something else. Only about seventeen percent of criminals in the program ever break the law again, compared to forty percent of cons coming out of prisons. Based on those statistics, I think it's doubtful that Carson did what you're accusing him of doing. But like I said, I'll clear it through channels and arrange an interview. That satisfy you?"

"I can't ask for more," I said. "I know you've arrested Wally Winstead, but—"

Mort waved to stop me. "The DA doesn't think we have a strong enough case to formally charge him, too circumstantial," he said. "I'm releasing him tomorrow, only he'll know we'll be watching him and doing more digging. I still think he's the perp."

Mort hadn't eaten his ice cream, which had melted into a cold chocolate-chip soup.

"I'll get you a fresh bowl," I said.

"Don't bother, Mrs. F. I'd better get on home. Remember, nothing said here leaves here."

"Like Las Vegas," I said.

"Huh?"

"A TV commercial. Thanks for letting me share my thoughts with you."

"Anytime, Mrs. F. I'll be in touch."

Chapter Twenty-four

I slept soundly after my conversation with Mort. I suppose having taken action, *any* action, had been therapeutic. To use a sports metaphor, the ball was in his court now, and all I could do was wait to hear from him again.

I awoke refreshed and eager to tackle my novel. After fixing myself a large breakfast, a rarity for me, I settled at my computer and got to work. The writing went smoothly. Despite my sizable morning meal, I was ravenous by one and took a break, sending George a brief e-mail update on my meeting with Mort. I returned to the book after a lunch of leftover turkey salad. At five o'clock I sat back and allowed a welcome feeling of satisfaction to wash over me. The book was back on track.

Aside from a few phone calls, my only serious disruptions that day were self-generated. At each break from the computer, my mind drifted to the scenario I'd conjured. I wondered when Mort would call Victor Carson to ask him about the Billups murder. I no longer had any doubts that Carson had been relocated to Cabot Cove under the Federal Witness Protection Program. Mort's responses, while not involving an outright acknowledgment, certainly supported that thesis. I was tempted to call him but sat on that urge. I'd already put our sheriff, and my friend, in an awkward position, and I knew he wouldn't appreciate being prodded. That old virtue, patience, had to be the byword at this juncture, and I was determined to practice it. But by seven that evening my curiosity was threatening my good intentions.

Seth had called to see if I wanted to go out for dinner, but I'd declined. I did the same with the Kosers, who invited me to their house for turducken stew that Richard had concocted from Thanksgiving leftovers. I'd had enough of my own leftovers and was happy to treat myself to a hamburger I'd taken from the freezer earlier.

The weather had turned nasty, with strong winds and heavy rains in the forecast. The thought of leaving my warm, dry house wasn't appealing. I contented myself with the burger and a salad, after which I changed into my robe and slippers, intending to spend the rest of the evening finishing a novel I'd started reading days earlier.

I was immersed in the story when I heard a thud at the rear of the house. The wind had picked up, bending trees in my backyard and sending the rain in horizontal sheets. I went to my rear kitchen window and peered into the darkness. I couldn't see anything and decided a loose piece of lawn furniture or tree limb had caused the noise. I returned to the living room and picked up the book again. A few minutes later I heard a similar sound that made me jump. This time I flipped on the outside light, opened the kitchen door, and squinted into the storm, seeing nothing but wind-whipped rain.

Back in my chair, the book opened to where I'd left off, a different sound reached my ears. I looked up to see Linda Carson, her face pressed against the glass of my front window. This apparition was followed by a pounding on my front door.

I wasn't sure what to do. There I was, in my pajamas and robe, hardly in the mood for an unexpected visitor. But a far greater concern gripped me. Why was she coming to my house on such a dismal night? Could it have been prompted by what I'd told Mort, and what he might have done as a result?

I went to the front door and heard her say, "For heaven's sakes, Jessica. Please, open the door." I looked out. She stood in the rain, water running down her face and matting her hair. The expression on her face was what I can only describe as desperation. Comforted that I didn't see Victor standing with her, I opened the door a crack and said, "I'm really not dressed for company, Linda. Couldn't you have called?"

"Please, Jessica," she said, placing a hand against the door and pushing it open farther. "This is really urgent."

I stepped back to allow her to enter. "I can't imagine what could be so urgent. Is your telephone out?"

"No," she said, shaking off the rain. A small smile appeared on her lips and I turned to see Victor looming in the doorway. He stepped over the threshold and forcefully closed the door.

I was suddenly stricken with fear.

"I really don't think that—"

Victor pushed by me and went to the living room.

I said to Linda, "Can't whatever brings you here on this dreadful night wait until tomorrow?"

"No, it can't," Victor barked from the other room.

I drew a deep breath and said to Linda, "Then go into the living room and wait with your husband. I need to change clothes."

"You're not going anywhere," he said, checking the windows, then pulling the curtains into place.

"All right," I said, tightening the belt of my robe. "Why are you here?"

They turned to face me.

"Smart lady like you, I think you can figure that out," Victor said, his tone menacing.

"Yes, I think I do know," I said, trying to keep my voice steady so as not to betray my nervousness. "Why don't you sit down and we can discuss it?"

Linda looked to my couch, and I knew what she was thinking. "It doesn't matter if you're wet," I said. "It'll dry."

She sat, and I joined her. Victor went into the kitchen, checked the back door and closed the blinds.

"Why did you have to do it?" Linda asked.

"Do what, Linda?"

"Go sticking your nose into our business."

"That was never my purpose," I said. "I found the body

of a murdered man across from this house; that was the *business* I wanted to know more about."

I glanced at Victor, who'd come back into the room and stood with his arms crossed over his sizable chest.

"You don't understand," Linda said. "You don't understand what we've been through."

"I'm sure I don't," I said, "but that doesn't seem to be the point. A man was killed. There's no possible excuse for that. I didn't know Mr. Billups, but—"

"That didn't stop you from inviting that . . . that bum to your Thanksgiving dinner," Linda said.

"No, it didn't. I enjoy including newcomers to Cabot Cove at my holiday table, which should be obvious. I didn't know you and Victor when I invited you to join us."

"I don't care about Thanksgiving," Victor said to his wife. "Get on with it."

"Sheriff Metzger said you went to Boston. How did you know we were from Boston?"

"I went to Boston to look into Hubert Billups's background," I said, dismissing any initial disappointment at Mort having involved me. I suppose he didn't have a choice. He had to explain to them why he'd called them in. "I guessed you were from Boston when I met you, Linda. You named your cat for a Boston College, and a Boston accent is hard to camouflage, especially from a fellow New Englander."

"I told you," Victor growled at her.

"And on the assumption we were from Boston, you poked your nose into our affairs."

"I knew nothing of your affairs. All I knew was that you had all the physical signs of a liar and I wondered why you would lie about such unimportant things. However, once I was in Boston, I learned about Vincent Canto." I shot a look at Victor, but his face was impassive. "I came back from Boston, Linda, with suspicions about your husband, suspicions you're now confirming."

She flared in anger. "Confirming what, Jessica? That Victor and I were sent here by the stinking feds, that they took our lives away and settled us in this hick town?"

I wasn't about to debate the merits of Cabot Cove. Instead, I said, "It's my understanding that you and Victor were sent here because your husband turned state's evidence about a murder and beating that took place in Boston some ten years back."

"Victor had nothing to do with that," she said, chin raised, lips pressed together to put an exclamation point on her denial.

"That may be true," I said, "but it isn't the issue. Evidently, Mr. Billups thought otherwise. He must have believed that your husband was responsible for his beating and the death of his brother. Isn't that right? That's what you thought he believed too, and you assumed that he came to Cabot Cove to seek vengeance. It seems to me that the real question is whether your husband confronted Billups and—"

"And killed him?"

"Yes, and killed him."

"Victor did not kill that man, Jessica," she said. "He's innocent."

I looked to Victor for confirmation from him. He said or did nothing, just glared at me.

"Don't you see what your snooping has done, Jessica?" she asked, her voice hard. "We've been living like Gypsies for years, first one town, then another. We're never allowed to return home to see family and friends, always living a lie with phony names, trying to keep to ourselves so the truth doesn't come out, attempting to fit into every new community without giving away too much. It's been hell, pure hell. I tried to make a normal life for us no matter where we lived, a rinky-dink town in the Midwest, some dreadful place in Texas. Always someplace remote because we were afraid that Victor's whereabouts had been leaked. Do you know what it's like to get up every morning, look out the window, and expect to see someone standing outside with a gun waiting to kill your husband?" Her eyes glistened with anger. "Always having to make nice with people you could care less about so that they'll think you're just a normal couple, stay on their good side, don't risk having them raise questions about you." A small, sardonic smile crossed her lips. "Always hoping you won't run into a self-righteous busybody like you who insists on satisfying her curiosity no matter who it hurts. I despise people like you!"

I listened to her rant. At the same time my mind went in different directions.

I didn't doubt that being in the Witness Protection Program was a difficult life. On the other hand, those who enter the program are often criminals who avoided jail time by cooperating with authorities. Being relocated to a new town with a set of restrictions attached seemed to me to be eminently preferable to a life behind bars. If what I'd learned about Carson, aka Canto, was correct, he'd ordered the beatings of Harry and Hubert Billups, resulting in the death of one and the permanent injury of the other. Who knew how many other innocent people he'd ordered be killed or maimed to achieve his dishonest goals.

While it was true that the spouses of such people were forced to suffer along with them, the decision to link their lives with criminals was their own. Didn't she know what he did for a living when she married him? Maybe, maybe not. Nevertheless, all her whining about their life in the Witness Protection Program didn't change the fact that Hubert Billups had been murdered, and that whoever killed him deserved to be punished.

I decided to be more direct. I stood, approached Victor, and asked, "Did you kill Hubert Billups?"

He hesitated a long time. "No," he said finally, his dark eyes meeting mine. "Do you really think I'd tell you if I did?"

I turned to Linda. "Do you have any idea who killed him, Linda?"

She looked down and squeezed the bridge of her nose. "No," she said in a soft voice.

I was tempted to accuse her of lying but said instead, "Are you sure about that, Linda?"

She glanced at me, then looked away again.

As silence engulfed the room, the initial fear I felt upon their arrival began to build again. Here I was directly confronting them about a capital crime, alone with them in my house, the wind howling outside, rain beating against the windows, and the curtains shut tight to prevent anyone from seeing in. What was their purpose? Were they here to threaten me, to force me to recant the questions I'd raised? I'd already given Mort my hypothesis regarding the case. Did they want to inflict punishment, and leave me with a daily reminder that my investigations could end in pain? If so, no one would be able to hear my cries for help.

I now knew who Victor Carson was. He was in reality Vincent Canto, a mobster from Boston for whom inflicting human suffering was not a foreign concept, a man who'd murdered before and would undoubtedly do so again if it served his purpose.

"I realize this is awkward for you, and I'm not looking to make your lives more difficult," I said. "You've already spoken with Sheriff Metzger, and I suggest we all sit down with him again tomorrow. If indeed you had nothing to do with Billups's death, you have my apologies." I stood and took a few steps toward the door to indicate that I wanted them to leave. For a moment, I thought Victor was about to follow me. But Linda remained on the couch, her eyes fixed on the floor, fingers of one hand drumming against the others. She looked up at Victor and said sharply, "We're not going anywhere."

The bluntness of her statement froze me.

The phone rang.

"Don't answer that, Jessica," Linda ordered, but I'd already reached the phone and lifted the receiver.

"Mrs. F, it's Mort."

"Mort!"

I tried not to let them see the expression on my face, but my relief faded away when I turned to see Linda standing in the kitchen doorway. She held a small handgun and lifted her arm.

"I just wanted you to know, Mrs. F, that I had the Carsons come in for an interview. Frankly, I don't think he had anything to do with Billups's murder. I really pressed and—"

"Thank you, Mort."

"Mrs. F, are you okay?"

The weapon Linda held was now pointed directly at me. I shuddered when I heard her release the safety and pull back on the hammer.

"Yes, I'm fine, Mortimer. I'm afraid I can't talk to you right now."

"Mortimer?" He laughed. "You've never called me that before. That's not my name."

"I appreciate the call Mortimer. I have to go. Thank you for calling."

I replaced the phone in its cradle and faced Linda Carson. "Set the gun down, Linda," I said gently. "You'll only make things worse."

She seemed momentarily unsure of herself, and I thought she might put the gun away. But her face mirrored a newfound resolve. She said, "If you think for one minute, Jessica, that I'm going to let someone like you make our lives even worse than they've already been, you're crazy." She stepped closer to me, the gun pointed at my chest.

"That was Mort, calling to say he didn't think Victor killed Hubert Billups."

"Too late now," she said.

"He's right," I said. "Victor wasn't the murderer."

"I already told you that."

Victor came up behind his wife, his cold eyes taking in the scene, revealing nothing. "Hurry up," he said. "I don't want to wait here all night."

I backed away until reaching the kitchen counter, next to the door leading to my patio. I leaned against the counter, drew a deep breath, and said to Linda, "It was you who killed Billups, wasn't it?"

"You're guessing. You have no proof whatsoever, against either of us."

"That's not true. One thing that always bothered me about the case was the angle of the knife, the way it had been jabbed into Billups's chest. Your husband is such a big man, and Billups was so small. The knife went straight in, parallel to the ground. Someone your husband's size would have brought a knife down from above or maybe up from below. Isn't that how you would have done it, Victor?"

"Don't listen to her," he said.

"But when you put your arm out," I continued, "it's at exactly the height of the fatal wound."

"Is that all you have, Jessica?" she said, her voice more sure.

"Billups's landlady knew you weren't the type to rent one of her rooms. You went there pretending to be interested in renting a room, didn't you, Linda? Did Victor know you'd done that?"

Linda paled.

"You're lying," Victor ground out.

"Tell him, Linda. You went there looking for anything that might link your husband to Billups. And there was nothing. The landlady had already cleaned his room."

She answered with a barely discernible nod.

"Stupid!" Victor spat out.

"You see, you're not a very good liar, Linda. All along you've exhibited the signs of someone who isn't telling the truth. When they put you on the stand, they'll see right away when you're lying. Your gestures give you away. You'll never be able to bluff your way through their questions. I knew right away when you didn't answer mine truthfully."

"You and your questions," she muttered.

"And if you think that killing me will solve your problems, you're not thinking clearly. I've never meant harm to either of you," I said, "but you won't get away with murder, mine or Hubert Billups's."

"Put the gun down, Linda," Victor said, surprising both of us.

She spun around and leveled the weapon at him. "And what, Vinnie, ruin what little we have left? I can't believe you didn't have the courage to get rid of that old man."

"I didn't need to. He didn't have enough of a brain left to hurt us. He thought he knew me, but he wasn't sure."

"He was stalking us. Everywhere I went, every time I turned around, he was there. He was driving me crazy. And you did nothing. You used to have guts, Vinnie. What happened to them?"

"C'mon, Linda," he said in a soothing voice I'd not heard from him before, "it'll work out. Believe me, it'll work out."

She guffawed. "Oh, sure, Vincent. 'It'll work out.' How? I go to prison for the rest of my life and you find another town to live in, maybe with another woman? I've suffered enough."

During this exchange, I'd slid my left hand behind me until it reached the inside lock of the door, which I turned slowly to avoid making noise. My hand then found the doorknob. I twisted it until the door was free and would open easily. I yanked on it. My fingers flipped up the hook and eye on the screen door and I pushed through it, out into the rain and wind. I raced across the patio, aware that one of them, maybe both, was in pursuit. I stumbled off the patio's edge and ran across the yard, my heart pounding, lungs gasping for air, the cold rain stinging my face, the wet lawn soaking through my slippers. The wind whipped the skirt of my robe, entangling my legs in the wet fabric. I lost my footing and stepped out of one slipper, my foot sinking into the icy mud. Was that a shot? I tried to run faster but tripped on a tree root and fell face-first, landing in a pile of leaves that had fallen from the trees. I rolled to the side as another shot rang out, pulled myself up to a sitting position, and braced for an attack. Instead, I heard the wail of sirens and saw flashing red lights from the road in front of the house, like a kaleidoscope through the curtain of drenching rain. I looked toward the open back door to see Linda and Victor Carson on the patio. There was no escape route as two of Mort's uniformed deputies came around each side of the house, and I heard, "Get your hands up. You're not going anywhere."

I rose slowly, sore, soaking wet and shivering from the

cold but otherwise uninjured. I limped toward the house, snagging my sopping slipper along the way. I'd just reached the patio when Mort came from around the front.

"You okay, Mrs. F?" he asked, taking note of my dishevelment.

"Yes, I'm fine, Mort, now that you're here."

"I figured something was wrong when you called me Mortimer."

"I was hoping you'd pick up on it, and I'm so glad that you did."

"What about these two?" he asked, indicating Victor and Linda, who were in custody of the deputies.

"I suggest you take them both down to headquarters while I get out of these wet clothes and dry my hair. I'll be there as soon as I can."

"Mortimer," Mort said, shaking his head as he escorted me into the house. "I can't believe you thought that was my name."

"I promise never to call you that again," I said.

Chapter Twenty-five

Victor and Linda Carson were remanded to jail under a variety of charges, including theft (Seth's knife), assault with a deadly weapon, kidnapping (I was considered to have been a kidnap victim since I'd been held against my will), possession of a deadly weapon (a clear violation of Victor's status under Witness Protection Program rules), and suspicion of murder in the Hubert Billups case. I spent a good part of that night and the following day giving a detailed report of what had occurred at my house, including Linda's quasi-confession to having killed Billups. Mort called later that afternoon to announce that she'd formally admitted that she'd stabbed Billups to death, claiming his stalking had put her in a constant state of panic, which precipitated a nervous breakdown. Mort was convinced she was planning to enter a plea of temporary insanity.

"I don't know how she's going to explain away the knife she took from the senior center," he said. "Sure looks like a case of premeditation to me."

The incident had drained me, and when I returned home from police headquarters, I tried to catch up on some sleep. The phone rang incessantly, prompting me eventually to ignore my well-wishers and let the answering machine pick up. It was a full day later before I felt up to e-mailing George to tell him of the resolution of the case. I ended my message by apologizing for murder having tainted what was to be a tranquil, joyful introduction for him to our treasured national holiday.

He e-mailed me back:

> I'm just sorry that murder once again injected itself into your life, Jessica, which seems to happen with startling regularity. I assure you of one thing. Should you decide to join me here in London over the Christmas holidays, I will labour intensely to issue a total ban on anything nefarious happening within a hundred miles of us. You have my word.

I spent the next few days writing my novel. It felt good to be back into it, and the pages piled up as I headed for the climactic scenes that would end the book. The only distraction was the pile of mail I'd received containing the letters clipped from magazines that eventually spelled GLOTCOYB. I was relieved that the letters had stopped coming, but that didn't satisfy my natural need to know why they'd been sent to me in the first place, and who had sent them. I intended to toss them out or burn them in my fireplace, but something kept me from doing that and I knew I would forever be haunted by those unanswered questions.

My writing momentum was more tangibly derailed one morning when Mort called and asked me to meet him at his office. When I arrived, he introduced me to an FBI agent who'd come to Cabot Cove from Portland, and a representative from the Department of Justice in Washington, D.C.

"I thought it only fair, Mrs. F, that you be alerted to a decision that's been made by these gentlemen. Since it was Mrs. Carson who killed Hubert Billups, and because you say in your statement that it wasn't Victor Carson who threatened you, he's going to be moved to another location under the Witness Protection Program. He claims that he didn't have any knowledge that his wife had a handgun, and has agreed to testify against her when she comes to trial."

"He has? Oh dear," I said. "While her actions cannot be condoned, his wife was only trying to preserve what life they had left. Granted, she went far beyond what was reasonable, but for him to testify against her is—well, it's insensitive at the least."

The two federal agents in the room said nothing, just stared at me with blank expressions.

"What will happen to *him* after he testifies?" I asked. "He'll simply go free, be given another pass?" I was bewildered by the decision.

"Yes, ma'am," the gentleman from DOJ said. "We're really not interested in his wife and the fact that she killed a homeless guy here in Cabot Cove. That's your sheriff's problem. But Vincent Canto—you know him as Victor Carson—has been a valuable witness for us in a number of mob-related matters, and will continue to be. We have more cases pending in which we need his testimony."

I shook my head in disgust. The FBI agent noticed my expression and changed the subject. "Sheriff Metzger here says that it was through your good investigation that the murder his wife committed has been solved. Nice work, Mrs. Fletcher. Looks like you know more about murder than just writing about it."

"I wish that weren't true," I said, "but I appreciate the compliment. It couldn't have happened without Mort's help. Our sheriff is a highly regarded professional with an astute sense of timing I'm particularly grateful for. I wouldn't be here if it weren't for him."

"Thanks, Mrs. F."

"You're more than welcome, Mort." I turned to the other men. "I appreciate being told about all this," I said. "Where will Victor Carson, er, Vincent Canto go?"

The FBI agent and DOJ representative looked at each other. The agent said, "We can't reveal that for obvious reasons, Mrs. Fletcher."

"Of course," I said. "I shouldn't even have asked. I do have another question, however. With all the secrecy surrounding the Witness Protection Program, how did Billups learn that Carson, or Canto, was here in Cabot Cove?"

The man from DOJ smiled. "Nothing's perfect, Mrs.

Fletcher. We've had to move Canto and his wife a few times after someone with a grudge tracked him down."

The FBI agent turned to Sheriff Metzger. "Speaking of tracking people down, Sheriff, we're looking for another recent Cabot Cove citizen. He's wanted on suspicion of fraud in Florida and other states."

"Who's that?" Mort asked.

"Are you talking about Archer Franklin?" I said.

The FBI agent's eyebrows went up. "You know about him, Mrs. Fletcher?"

"I'm afraid so."

"Do you know where he is?"

I mentioned that he'd been staying with the Copeland sisters, after having lived on a houseboat.

"We've checked all that out," the agent said. "He's skipped, something he's good at. But we'll find him. Looks like you're really on top of things, ma'am. Anytime you'd like to join the Bureau, we'd be honored to have you."

"Thank you, but I think one career is enough for now."

"Good luck, gentlemen," Mort said, escorting them out.

I returned home to find a message from Seth inviting me out for dinner. I hadn't seen him since the fracas at my house, and was finally ready to talk about it. "Let's make it early," he suggested when I called back.

It was good being together, and with the benefit of a few days' rest, I filled him in on every detail of my quest for Hubert Billups's murderer, and that Archer Franklin was a wanted man.

"Ayuh, I know all about that," Seth said. "Willie Copeland was in early this afternoon. She's got herself a spanking new cane."

"Oh?"

Seth laughed. "Seems she found out about Mr. Franklin's checkered past and broke her old one over his noggin. He tried to steal money from her before he left. I imagine he's got a nasty headache wherever he is."

The image of Wilimena going after Franklin with her cane made me wince—and smile.

"When will you get your knife back?" I asked.

"I won't," he replied. "I told Mort he can keep it as a memento. Somehow, using it to slice a ham or carve a turkey after it'd been used to kill a man wasn't appealing to me."

"I don't blame you," I said.

"Mort said he'd have a display case made and hang it in his office." He sat back and smiled. "Looks like my good friend Jessica Fletcher managed to solve another mystery in her life. Not that I'm surprised. You've been racking up a pretty impressive track record."

"George said the same thing to me in an e-mail. It's hardly the sort of reputation I aspire to."

"Doesn't matter what we aspire to, Jessica. It's what becomes our reality that counts."

"I still have another mystery to resolve," I said as the waiter poured coffee for us. I'd resisted a slice of key lime pie, but not Seth.

"What might that be?" he asked, taking a bite of the tart custard.

"Those strange letters that I received over a period of days. I still don't know who mailed them, or why."

"If I were you, I'd let it go," Seth suggested. "Not worth worrying about. You haven't received any more of them, have you?"

"No, I haven't, but I can't stand not knowing who and why."

"Probably just some prank."

"Prank!" I said. "I certainly hope not. I had Mort send the early letters to a crime lab to see if they could trace fingerprints. That would've been a terrible waste of public money if this was just someone's idea of a joke. No. I think this is something more serious and I plan to get to the bottom of it."

He grunted. "You must've been born with a terminal case of curiosity. Remember, madam, curiosity killed the cat."

"But, as I recall, sir, it was also said that satisfaction brought the cat back. I need to satisfy my curiosity."

"Well, wouldn't surprise me if you figure it out eventually. Good luck." Seth sighed deeply and finished his pie.

"That's the second time today I've heard that expression," I mused as we walked to his car.

"What expression is that?"

"Good luck."

"Not so unusual, is it?"

"No, but for some reason it's rattling around in my head."

"Well, while you're cogitating on that, mind if I stop at

the pharmacy before I drive you home? I need to check on a prescription."

"No, of course not. I'll wait in the car."

Seth pulled up in front of the drugstore and I watched him enter the shop. "Good luck," I whispered. "Good luck," I said aloud. "Oh my goodness! Those are the first two letters of GLOTCOYB. *GL*. Good luck!" *Was Seth right? Have I been looking for something nefarious when all along the message was not a threatening one? Good luck! Good luck on what? Oh, the* O. *Good Luck On. What could the rest of it be?*

"Seth! I think I'm getting it," I said, when he'd climbed back in the car.

"Getting what?"

"GLOTCOYB!"

"That again? Really, Jessica. You're worrying this thing like a worm on a hook. You're going to give yourself a headache."

"Maybe so, but solving it will bring immediate relief. Listen. The first three letters of GLOTCOYB are *GLO*. They could stand for 'Good luck on' . . ."

"Good luck on what?"

"That's what I haven't figured out yet."

"Well, let me know when you do."

As Seth drove me home, I noticed that he kept checking his watch as he proceeded slowly toward my house.

"Do you know something I don't?" I asked.

"Ayuh! I know a lot of things you don't," he said. "That's why you're always asking me questions."

"I do not!"

"Did you or did you not just ask me a question?"

"Something funny is going on here," I said, eyeing my old friend.

As we turned onto my road, I looked ahead and saw what appeared to be a flashing light in front of my house. At first I wondered why the police were there again, but as we got closer, the source of the light became more obvious. It was a rotating red signal, the kind people place on the roadway to alert oncoming cars of a vehicle broken down in the lane ahead.

Seth pulled to the side of the road opposite the house and turned off the ignition. There was a group of people gathered on my front lawn. I spotted Lee from the post office, the town's favorite baker, Charlene Sassi, the mayor's wife, Susan Shevlin, Kathy Copeland, the Kosers, Mort and Maureen Metzger, and a dozen other familiar faces. But what really captured my attention was a huge yellow sign strung between two trees. Printed on it in large red letters was GOOD LUCK ON THE COMPLETION OF YOUR BOOK.

I turned to Seth. "What is *this* all about?" I asked.

"I suggest you go see," he said, a wry smile on his broad face.

A cheer went up as I stepped out of the car and approached. Standing in front of the pack were Josh and Beth Wappinger.

"Hello, Jessica!" Josh shouted. The group broke into song: "For she's a jolly good writer, for she's a jolly good writer, for she's a jolly good writer that nobody can deny."

"I can't believe this," I said.

"Come on in," Beth said, grabbing my arm and pulling me toward the house. "There's plenty of dessert, and the coffee's made."

"No, wait a minute," I said, resisting her tug on my arm. "That sign. GLOTCOYB. That's what the letters mean, 'good luck on the completion of your book'? My book, the one I've been struggling with?"

"Sure," she replied happily. "We knew you were having writer's block and—"

Seth came to my side and placed a hand on my shoulder.

"I almost had it, didn't I?" I said to him.

"Almost."

I frowned at Beth. "Do you know what those letters did to me?"

"I know you're surprised, Jessica," she said, "even shocked. We wanted you to be. Come on. The party's starting."

I followed her inside, where a variety of sweets from Sassi's Bakery were laid out on my dining room table, along with carafes of coffee and open bottles of wine. A half-dozen smaller signs reading GLOTCOYB had been taped to the walls.

"But why. . . ?" I said.

"We thought we'd help get your artistic juices flowing," Josh said. "We all love having a bestselling writer living in our midst, especially this one. And we knew you needed inspiration."

I didn't intend for my expression to be glum, even annoyed, but it reflected what I was feeling. I'd spent so much time worrying about those letters, wasting time trying to decipher them. I turned to Josh. "You were in Ohio on your last business trip, weren't you? You sent those letters while you were traveling."

"Sure did," he proudly proclaimed. "Pretty clever of me, huh? Bet they had you guessing for a while."

"For too much time," I said. "Do you realize how much anxiety those letters caused me? I even took them to Sheriff Metzger, and he brought them to the state crime lab for fingerprint analysis. Getting those letters day after day has been extremely stressful."

Josh and Beth's faces fell. "Gee, Jessica, we just wanted to have fun and motivate you," she said. "We wanted to give you a mystery to solve."

"If we thought you'd take it this way, we never would have done it," Josh said.

Susan Shevlin, who'd witnessed the exchange and read the expression on my face, sidled up and said into my ear, "I told them it was a dumb idea, Jess, but they wanted to do it. They didn't mean any harm, but . . ."

I looked across the room at Richard Koser, who shrugged, threw up his hands, and grabbed a cream puff from the table.

Seth had stayed at my side. He placed a hand on my elbow and whispered, "They meant well, Jessica. They're good friends who care about you and who went a little overboard, that's all."

"Were *you* in on this?"

"Only as of yesterday. Beth came in for a physical and told me about it. She asked me to get you out of the house this evening."

I looked at the dozen people who stood around my table, waiting for me to say something that would lift the pall that had descended over the room. I pointed at Lee, our postmistress. "You!" I said. "You pooh-poohed those letters when I brought them into the post office, and even wished me luck in my writing."

"Actually, to be precise, I wished you 'good luck on the completion of your book,' " she said.

I laughed and that broke the tension. "All right," I said to those gathered, "I appreciate your good wishes. I admit I was upset when the letters started arriving, but I know you did it out of love."

"That's right," Josh said, raising his wineglass in a toast. "To Jessica Fletcher, one of the world's best mystery writers and our beloved neighbor."

Others joined in the toast.

"To Jessica!" they said in concert.

"To the completion of her latest murder mystery!"

"Here, here!"

There didn't seem to be much of a choice for me, so I, too, went to the table, where Kathy Copeland poured white wine into a glass. I picked it up, raised it, and said, "Speaking of murder, my initial reaction was to want to strangle all of you."

"I'd have to lock you up then, Mrs. F," Mort said.

"When did you find out about this, Mort?" I asked. "You seemed serious about trying to trace the letters."

"Only today, Mrs. F. I *was* serious. Glad it turned out to be only some good-natured fun."

"The only reason I'm stifling the urge to commit murder right here in my dining room is because I don't want to end up behind bars. Besides, maybe you did help me break through the difficulties I was having with the book. It's almost finished. And I was pretty close to figuring out what GLOTCOYB meant, too."

"Maybe we should have given you another day to work on it," Josh said.

"Oh, no. This has gone on long enough," I said. I held my glass high and looked at the smiling faces around the room. "To my friends in Cabot Cove!"

I finished my book *almost* on time, delivering it to my publisher three days late. Memories of that year's Thanksgiving stayed with me, the pleasant and the not so pleasant. With Christmas looming, I knew I had to make a decision about spending it with George in London. While I looked forward to spending the holidays with my friends in Cabot Cove, the contemplation of seeing George again, hopefully without a murder to gum things up, was powerful. I made my decision in mid-December, and e-mailed him:

> I'm hoping your invitation to spend Christmas with you in London still holds, George—because I'll be there!

LITTLE FALLS PUBLIC LIBRARY
3 6045 00077019 1